JEWELS FROM THE ASHES

Anita Post

Jewels From The Ashes
www.anitapost.com

Acknowledgements

This book is dedicated to anyone who has suffered in any way at the hands of an abuser. May the words on these pages be an inspiration for you to move on to a new and better life.

Thanks to my sister for putting up with my "pestering" during the editing process to "hurry up" while my "fans" follow suit. The term "patience is a virtue" certainly does *not* apply to me!

As always, Jamie, you are my heart and soulmate.

Introduction

In the aftermath of the terrorist attacks and losing their friends, Amanda and Jamie Grayson pick up the pieces of their lives and move on. Their small family of three suddenly turns into the house-full of the kids they've always wanted, including an unexpected pregnancy. Jamie is ecstatic over the new pending arrival of their natural son. Despite Amanda's doubts and a difficult delivery, the Grayson family begins the next chapter of their lives, only to stumble into yet another adventure that nearly rips their family apart.

Amanda/Celina Jackson-Grayson leaves her musical career on hold to enjoy family life for awhile…until the past comes back to haunt her. In this third installment of the Jewel series, the scope broadens as we learn more about much-loved surrounding characters in their lives. But, can they escape the dangers that lurk in the shadows and find a good life?

November 1, 2000

That was too easy! Some people are so gullible, much to my benefit! Aubrey got an extra bonus for getting me off on the insanity plea. That part was sweet! And so what if he wanted five million? It was worth it in the end.

January 4, 2002

Dr. Dorothy Collins is so easily manipulated. Just have to pretend to take my meds, until I can put my next plan into action. If I play my cards right, I can be out of here soon. Then I can call Aubrey to take care of things...and start my new life...with her...

PART 1

THE GRAYSON FAMILY

Chapter 1 • Jamie

It was three a.m. when my taxicab pulled up to the front gate and Rob, the overnight guard at the security gate smiled at me, as I rolled down the window in the backseat. He reached over the console in the glass hut, pushed the button to open the gate, and the driver drove on through towards the driveway that led to our house in Chelsea. I opened the door and unfolded myself from the back seat, while the driver retrieved my luggage from the trunk of the cab and handed them to me. I paid him and he left.

My flight back from Crystal Pines felt longer than normal, as I'd been restless to get home. The plane touched down at about 1:30am, but it ended up being over an hour of the usual security hassles that was now the norm in the wake of the terrorist attacks. It was nearing the end of November 2001, and the air was chilly, as I shuffled towards the front porch.

I was grateful for the security lights that flashed on as I approached the front door, so I didn't have to fumble around in the dark, trying to put my key in the lock. I pushed my way through the front door, lifted my bags, setting them just inside the hallway and closed the door behind me. The house was quiet, save for the high pitched hum of the alarm and the automated voice, instructing me to disarm the system. I punched in my code to silence the alarm, and locked the deadbolt. I then re-entered my code, to set the alarm to the 'Armed/Stay' function, pulled my cell phone out of my pocket and opened it to shine the light up over the key hooks on the wall in the hallway, hung my keys up in their proper place, without turning the lights on. The kids slept with their bedroom doors open and I didn't want to risk rousing them, in case the hallway door was ajar.

I carefully pulled the mirrored sliding closet door open, slipped off my boots and set them inside the closet. I shrugged out of my leather jacket and felt for an empty hanger to hang it on. I waited a few moments for my night vision to kick in further, before I lifted my bags, to carry them down the hall to our bedroom. I didn't want to chance rolling the bag on its wheels in case one of the kids left out a toy for it to catch on. I said a little prayer that I wouldn't step on anything or stub my toes.

When I reached the hallway carpet, I set the bags down as quietly as I could beside our bedroom door and gently turned the lever knob to open it. I hesitated, while I pulled the door back slowly and breathed a sigh of relief, when there was no creaking sound. *Good!* Matty remembered to grease the hinges after I left for Crystal Pines! He was always so good about taking care of my never-ending list of things to do around the place.

I hitched the strap of my carry-on bag over my shoulder and grabbed my laptop and rollaway bag's handles with my other hand, juggling them for a moment as I stepped inside the door while carefully closing the bedroom door behind me. I managed to pad my way up the steps without smashing the walls with my luggage, made it to the bedroom closet doors and set them down. I carefully placed the laptop case on the dresser and decided to leave the unpacking for the morning.

The moonlight shone through the terrace French Doors, illuminating Amanda's tiny figure on the bed. She was curled up with her arms and legs wrapped up around my pillow. Her raven hair was fanned all around her on *her* pillow. The only other light I saw in the room was the little night light that she often borrowed from the downstairs bathroom and plugged into the wall of our bedroom, while I was away. My heart tightened in my chest, as I thought about her being afraid during my absences, in the wake of all that had happened to us in the past few years. After Ian Fairbanks tried to kill us in London, her insomnia took hold of her and her mood swings almost ripped us apart. And since coming home from the tour, after the plane crashes, she told me the only thing that allowed her to sleep, when I was away, was the scent of my aftershave on the pillow.

I decided I needed a shower to rinse off the sweat and wash my hair, before joining her in bed. I always made sure that I was clean and fresh before touching her – even when we weren't going to make love. I peeled off my clothes, left them on the chair beside the closet, padded down the steps and slipped into the bathroom across the hall. I quickly showered and toweled myself dry from head to toe wrapping the towel around my waist, before making my way back up the steps to the bedroom.

I stood at my side of the bed, pondering how I was going to slide in beside her without stirring her, since she was still wrapped around my pillow and was basically taking up the entire middle of the bed. She was tiny, but she could stretch across that king sized bed from corner to corner, leaving little room for me to lie down. I watched her breathing in the moonlight in awe of this beautiful woman I was deeply in love with. I saw her lips twitch as the corners of her mouth curved up. I almost spoke to her, thinking she was awake, but her eyes were still closed. Then I heard my name escape her lips, ever so softly, and knew she was dreaming…about me. She started to giggle softly and I wondered what I was doing to her in the dream. I felt the familiar stiffening between my legs. *Dang!*

Now I was facing the dilemma of what to do about my predicament. Ignore my urges and somehow get myself curled up around her to sleep, or wake her, with the full intention of ravishing her and satisfying the slowly building aching need inside of me. *Oh, how I'd missed her!* She seemed to answer my thoughts, when she stirred and rolled towards her side of the bed slightly. Her left arm rose up and over onto her side of the bed, but her right arm was still wrapped around my pillow. Her left leg opened up and rested on the other side of her, exposing herself to me. She was wearing a silk teddy and panties, but the swell of her ever-growing breasts was enough to send me over the edge. The top sheet and blanket were pushed down to the foot of the bed, just covering her feet, but I could see every inch of her, every curve rising and falling, with each of her soft breaths. I let the towel fall to the floor.

I managed to sit on the edge of the bed without waking her, but my heart was pounding in my chest so hard, it sounded like a drum echoing in my ears. I gazed down at her beautiful, angelic face and scanned her body up and down. The small round bump of her belly had grown a bit since I last saw her, but it wasn't nearly as big as she was always making it out to be. When she looked at herself in the mirror, she saw a stuffed pig. But all I saw was the beautiful, curvy, amazing woman she'd always been.

I held my breath as I reached out my right hand and gently traced a line with my forefinger from her knee up her inner thigh. She stirred, but her eyes remained closed. I didn't want to startle her, but I knew I couldn't hold out much longer. My whole body ached for her touch and I finally let out my breath. My lungs felt like they were going to explode, *along with other things.*

I gasped for air as quietly as I could. I bent down and let my lips graze hers. Her eyes fluttered open. I froze for a few beats, praying that I didn't frighten her. The last thing I wanted was for her to think that she was being attacked by an intruder.

She blinked, breathed softly and then sucked in a deep breath through her nose. As she slowly exhaled, her lips parted. Just before I bent lower to cover her mouth with mine, she said, ever so softly, "Jamie, you're home!" I said, "Yes, darlin', I'm home." And our mouths ground together in a hard kiss with our tongues reaching for each other hungrily.

She started to squirm beneath me as she said, "Jamie, I missed you *soooo* much!"

Our reunion love-making was explosive. I was still inside of her, when I felt the baby stirring and we both reveled in the joy the pending arrival of our first natural child together.

This baby had been a surprise. After several attempts at trying to conceive before we were married, Amanda was told she would never be able to carry a child of her own. Chelsea was a blessing, a gift from God after our first failed attempt at adoption. And then Jenny and Bobby's twins, after losing our friends in the terrorist attacks, had come to live with us when their grandmother died of cancer.

I started to roll off of her, but her legs tightened around me and she said, "No, baby, not yet!" She laced her fingers through my hair and gave me wet kisses. I nuzzled her neck and we lingered there in that position for a few more moments before she released her grip. I rolled over onto my back and welcomed her into my arms. I felt her cheek sliding up and down on my chest as she settled in to get comfortable. I traced a line up and down from her shoulder to her elbow as I felt her breathing softly against me. The last thing I remembered was the soft touch of her fingers drawing little circles through my chest hairs as I drifted into sweet slumber.

****

I wasn't sure how long I'd been asleep before I felt Amanda stir and cry out in her sleep. Another nightmare had taken hold of her. She bolted upright in bed and started to scream my name. I sat up and slid my arms around her, soothing her. She'd tried to pretend that her episodes had subsided. But I knew better. She was holding back, because of the children. And the evidence was plain as day with her nightmares.

"I'm here, darlin', I'm here."

"I'm sorry, Jamie!"

"Why are you sorry?"

"I'm being such a baby!"

I shook my head as I dried her tears. "No, Raven. You're not. I understand. It's still too fresh. The plain crash...and your horrible ordeal the past few months. No one can blame you."

She swiped at her own tears and murmured, "I need to be strong for the kids and the baby," she chastised herself. I knew it would be some time before the aftereffects of what had happened would dwindle.

"You want to talk about it? Your dream, I mean."

She swallowed hard before she began telling me in elaborate detail the latest in a slew of nightmares that had plagued her since before my trip to Crystal Pines. I'd only been gone a few weeks, but I knew without me here, it was much worse for her.

"It's mostly the same each time. We're on the plane. The one the band was on. It's like I was there with them!" Her voice quivered as she continued. "It's like I can't get to you. I keep looking for you, but you're not there! And then I can hear screaming and shouting and then, there's nothing. Everything goes black all around me. I can smell the soot and rotting bodies all around me! But I can't see anything and it feels like I'm choking!"

It was another hour before I could get her calmed down enough to sleep. I held her tightly, at her request. Finally, she drifted off.

My eyes flew open. I thought I heard screaming. I rolled my head towards my alarm clock resting on the nightstand. It was four-o-two a.m. My heart started racing. With all the stuff that happened in the past couple of years, I slept much more lightly than I had in the past. I pulled back the sheets and blanket, reached for my robe, slipped my feet into my slippers, shrugged into the robe and tied the sash.

I made my way through my bedroom door and down the hall to the next two rooms and checked on the girls, before glancing in on Eric and found them all sleeping like little angels. The night lights were bright enough for me to see their sweet faces in dreamland. I padded down the hallway toward the front door and checked the lock to make sure I had secured it before going to bed. The alarm was still set to the "Armed/Stay" function. I then walked back down the hallway and made my way to the rear French doors, to make sure they were secure. Then I circled back to check on the front door again. I heard screaming coming from upstairs and I almost bolted towards the attic stairs when I stopped dead in my tracks.

I spun around and saw the front hall closet door was open. In the dark, the mirrored doors reflected the moonlight shining in through the front door window, but I could only see half of that reflection. I reached for the light switch and flicked it on. The smell of leather filled my nostrils as I spotted Jamie's leather jacket hanging there, then I glanced down at his cowboy boots at the bottom of the closet.

I smiled and breathed a sigh of relief, realizing he was home and the screams were the product of their lovemaking. I shook my head, flicked off the light and went back to bed.

Christmas was just around the corner. We set up the Christmas tree the way we always did, except this year we had the kids make some home-made decorations for it. We played all the popular kids Christmas carols and got them to sing along.

Jamie was flying back and forth to Crystal Pines regularly now. He'd been away from the club and his duties for over six weeks following the plane crashes. The Graysons stopped performing while he, Joey and Justin were at the crash site looking for me, but they managed to rent the space out to other performers and the place was still booming. I tried not to be sad when he was away, because I knew he needed this - to be with his family and have his musical career. I was extremely lonely for him, while he was away, so I spent many nights sleeping in the single bed in Chelsea's room. The crib had long since been taken down and put in storage. Chelsea now slept in the bed, but she didn't mind sharing it with Mommy when Daddy was away.

I knew it helped her not miss him too terribly, having me there with her at night and Jamie would always call just before bedtime so he could tell stories and we could sing them to sleep. The tradition of three stories and three songs continued, with Eric and Nina there. The twins loved it and always said, "Yay!" when Jamie called.

They would always fall asleep just before we finished the last song and Bridget would come in to help me carry the twins to their room. We decided to put them into the same room for the first couple of weeks as they became accustomed to being in their new home. But eventually, we redecorated the den to be Eric's bedroom. That left one more bedroom free to be transformed into the new nursery.

The large rear foyer in the house was remodeled into our new den. We retrieved Chelsea's old crib from storage and Matty and Jamie set it up once the nursery was ready.

Jamie knew how much I missed him, and often called me back to talk for awhile, before it was *my* bedtime, on the nights when he wasn't performing. He knew I might be feeling uncomfortable as my belly grew larger and that my insomnia would most likely return. He was such a great father and an even better husband than I believed I deserved. When he came home, the kids were overjoyed to see him and I felt the same way. Our lovemaking became quite difficult the bigger I got, but we tried our best to keep the magic alive. Christmas was going to be a crazy time with two new kids and another two babies on the way. My brother, Matty and his wife, Crystal were also expecting a baby in late spring.

Melissa came to visit on the first weekend in December and she threw Crystal and I a surprise baby shower. All the Grayson wives, my sisters and my niece, Molly, were there. Both Crystal and I got spoiled with new baby things. We laughed and had a great time. We hugged everyone as they left and thanked them for the gifts and the surprise.

There was a lot more Christmas shopping and even more packing to do for when we traveled to Crystal Pines, for the Grayson family's traditional Christmas Eve and Christmas Day celebrations.

The Graysons treated Nina and Eric like their own family. I was overjoyed that they accepted them this way. Jamie and I loved them to pieces and eventually they stopped calling us Auntie and Uncle and started calling us Mommy and Daddy. Jamie and I were over the moon the first time it happened! I never wanted them to forget their own parents, so we kept several pictures of Jenny and Bobby around the house, especially in their bedrooms. They would kiss their pictures good night every night and we included them in our prayers with them. The kids would automatically say, "And God bless Mommy, Daddy and Granny in Heaven," and then they would say, "And God bless our other Mommy and Daddy too!" This always brought tears to my eyes. They were so accepting of us. And all of their aunts, uncles, cousins and Grandma Sylvia, were included in all of their prayers as well.

Christmas morning was exhausting with all the little ones shrieking at the site of their new treasures.   But I was elated to be with this wonderful family that we made.

When the kids were finished opening presents and the cleanup began, Chelsea and the twins decided to surprise their Grandma Sylvia with a little song they'd prepared for her. The kids sang their song while the Graysons listened in awe. They sang in harmony and with perfect pitch. I'd been teaching them the song for the entire month of December. When they were finished, everyone cheered and I could see tears in Mom Sylvia's eyes.

Justin said, "Wow! How old are they now?" I proudly said, "The twins just turned six today and Chelsea is five and a half." Joey said, "You know, we might have some stiff competition if they ever go into the business!" I laughed and Jamie said, "Well that's another one of Sonia's predictions come true! I remember at our wedding, she said that our kids were going be even more talented than *we* are!"

I looked at him, surprised that he'd said that in front of his family. They all looked at each other and smiled. Reverend Sonia was a medium and an ordained minister with a Spiritualist church. She married us, on our property in Chelsea in June of 1995, and had christened Chelsea and the twins. She was also instrumental in helping to find me after the terrorist attacks. I didn't get on the plane that crashed on that fateful day, taking the lives of our manager, agent and band mates. I'd gotten sick and had to take a chartered flight, which also crashed, but both the pilot and I survived.

We celebrated the twins' birthday with cake and more presents. They were being spoiled rotten. Mom Sylvia was getting tired. She wasn't getting any younger and I suspected she wouldn't last much longer. I prayed that she'd be able to be around for the birth of our son.

The music, as always, was wonderful when the Grayson family got together. I loved listening to them sing Christmas carols and they always encouraged me to join in. Sometimes I would, but then sometimes I would just listen. Every now and then, one of the songs would hit home and I'd be moved to tears. I missed my musical family - The Bar Riders - deeply. Jamie made it a point to remind his family of my loss, and that occasionally I wouldn't feel up to singing with them.

We returned to Ohio, as always, for Boxing Day to celebrate Christmas with my family. They loved Nina and Eric as much as they loved Chelsea and had wonderful gifts for them. The kids repeated their performance from Christmas Day and my family all clapped and praised them for their talents. And then, we headed home to Chelsea to spend the rest of the season with Matty and Crystal. The kids sang their song, yet again for them, and received thunderous applause from their aunt and uncle as well.

New Years Eve was spent at Matty and Crystal's house, while the kids stayed with Bridget and the other new nanny, Maggie, so that we could have a break for one night. I was getting more and more tired each day and had to take little catnaps, with the extra weight I was carrying. I was six and a half months along, but it felt more like sixty months. We barely made it to midnight this time around. When the ball dropped on television's New York New Years Eve special, I kissed Jamie, Matty and Crystal and said, "I'm pooped. Jamie, can you take me home, please?" Crystal wasn't quite as far along as I was, so she wasn't feeling it yet, but they both said, "Good night and Happy New Year, you two!" and we left.

I gaze back at Dr. Collins, while I ramble on, telling her things she obviously wants to hear. I tell her about my troubles and heartbreak at the loss of my parents. She wears that usual unemotional mask, but I can see the flash in her eyes, revealing that she's delighted with my progress.

Little does she know that I killed my parents...well, my so-called parents. The Cravens had so charitably taken me in when my real parents died. My harlot mother over-dosed and my father was killed in prison.

She thinks I'm faithfully taking my meds. But they're safely tucked under the mattress of that cheap excuse for a lumpy bed in my room, wrapped in a tissue. They'll come in handy, when I make my escape...and head to the good old U.S. of A. – where my one true love lives.

And I wait for my chance to make her mine...

In the next few weeks, I made more frequent trips to Honeywood, to see my specialist. He said that the hormone supplements I'd been taking were working. It looked like my uterus was growing, even though I felt like a stuffed pig.

Dr. Stevens shook his head and said, "You're fine. You're not gaining too much weight and this is definitely all baby here. Keep it up. Take lots of naps and feel free to walk around. I understand you probably don't want to walk around in the snow but try to get a little bit of fresh air when you can. You can walk around the inside of your house for the exercise you need."

I asked him if I could still dance. He said, "Dancing is great exercise if you feel up to it but try not to do a lot of jumping. I understand that you're a professional dancer?" I told him, "Not as much as I'd originally planned on, but yes." He continued, "A little dancing is okay, but jumping might cause the umbilical cord to wrap itself around the baby's neck and we don't want that to happen. Or in some cases, it might cause you to go into premature labor." Dr. Stevens told me that he was going to keep the date of February 10th as the date of my cesarean section. He said that the hormone supplements were not doing anything for my twisted birth canal and that I still needed to have the C-section when the time came.

He said the baby was developing at a normal rate and that eight month's gestation would be acceptable for our son to be born. If he had any problems, he would be kept in an incubator until he was able to go home with me. I hoped and prayed that wouldn't happen. I couldn't imagine going home without my baby!

Jamie and I decided on the name for our son. We were going to call him Alexander James and call him A.J. for short. I spent an hour a day in the nursery just looking at all the baby things and the crib. Matty painted over the original pink with blue. There was a brand new mobile with little stuffed animals hanging over the crib, and Jamie and Matty had put up wallpaper with little blue teddy bears. There was a little night light plugged into the wall shaped like a moon with a little teddy bear on it.

One day, when Jamie was home, he noticed me standing in the nursery and he asked me, "What are you doing in here all by yourself?" My lips curved up as I said, "It feels like a dream that we're having our own baby after all this time of thinking it would never happen." He put his arms around me from behind and whispered in my ear, "Believe it or not, it's happening very soon!" I loved him more than anything and loved the family that we had made and all was right with the world...except for the nightmares.

February 10th was fast approaching. I found it harder and harder for me to get out of bed and when the baby kicked, it was like a stabbing pain. Every now and then he'd crawl up under my ribs and that was *very* uncomfortable. Jamie decided to stay home for the last couple of weeks before my C-section date, just in case. He and I had to stop making love when I discovered that I had traces of blood in my underwear one afternoon.

During my last appointment, the specialist told us we should refrain from having sex until after the six-week checkup, after the baby was born. I told him about the kicks hurting and that the baby loved to be under my ribs. Dr. Stevens said that was normal. "Babies like to do that for some reason. And the kicking pain is because your uterus is still quite small." He told me that he was going to be away for a couple of weeks, but that he'd definitely be back in time for the C-section date. I looked at him in horror, "What if he comes early?" Dr. Stevens shook his head and said, "I don't think that'll happen, but if it does, I have a colleague who will be on call for you, just in case. All you have to do is call my office and the twenty-four hour service will page him immediately."

Jamie and I returned home and enjoyed our time with the kids and Matty and Crystal. I hadn't been riding the horses at all – doctor's orders - and I missed it. Every now and then, I would go out to the stables just to talk to them. Silver was getting very old and we decided to put him down, as he was riddled with arthritis. We knew he was in too much pain to go any further. I grieved for him dearly, after the veterinarian gave him the needle. Jamie and Matty tried to cheer me up, but my hormones were all over the place and the tears kept flowing.

****

On February 1st I awoke with searing pain in my belly. Jamie helped me get out of bed and I said, "I think I need a bath." Jamie said, "I don't think *that's* a good idea. Remember, Dr. Stevens said you shouldn't have any baths during the last two weeks of your pregnancy." I relented, settling for a shower. Jamie helped me to get to our bathroom at the bottom of the stairs. The elevator had been built and we waited for it to take us down. He held my clothes and my toiletries while we waited. I closed my eyes and counted the seconds for the lift to take us down. I was still very claustrophobic from my childhood days spent in the Secret Room.

When we got into the bathroom, I pulled my nightgown up over my head. Jamie looked down at my stomach and took in a sharp breath. He said, "There are bruises all over you! What've you been doing?" I said, "I had a rough night. The baby was kicking a lot and it felt like a knife each time he did it." Jamie shook his head and said, "That doesn't look normal." He helped me to take my shower and then called Dr. Steven's office to page the on-call specialist. After he'd called us back, Jamie turned to me and said, "We need to go to the hospital. The on-call specialist is going to meet us there." I shook my head and said, "But it's not time yet!" Jamie said, "This is just a precaution, babe. He said it would be better to meet at the hospital just in case."

Thirty minutes later we walked into the St. Christopher's Family Birthing Center in Chelsea and announced ourselves at the front desk. They called an orderly, who showed up in a few minutes with a wheelchair and I was wheeled into a cubicle. One of the attendants came and brought me a hospital gown, instructing me to change into it. We sat and waited until the specialist came and introduced himself.

"I'm Dr. Cavanaugh. I'm filling in for Dr. Stevens." He looked at my chart, which had been faxed over to the hospital when Jamie called. He asked me to lift up my gown, while I lay down on the gurney. He examined my stomach for a moment and said, "I think we need to do a C-section right away. "But it's not time yet!' I protested. Dr. Cavanaugh said, "Don't worry, I've seen the results of your last sonogram and I believe that the baby is big enough to be born today. He'll likely have to stay in an incubator for a few weeks, but he'll be just fine and so will you. The bruising from the kicking is as a result of there not being much room in there, because your uterus is still quite small for someone at the gestation point that you are."

He told us he'd have me brought up to the delivery floor, where I would be given an anesthetic." Jamie and I looked at each other and I said, "Dr. Stevens said I could be awake for the baby's birth." Dr. Cavanaugh said, "I'll try to confine it to a local, but because you seem to be bleeding internally now, there may not be a choice here. Did Dr. Stevens discuss the possibility of you needing a hysterectomy after the baby's birth?"

I said, "Yes, he said there was a slight chance of that, but he didn't think that it would be necessary at that time." Jamie gazed at me with concern in his eyes, his thoughts seemingly mirroring my own. My mind was jumbled with thoughts of having to have a hysterectomy, our child's welfare and whether or not I could breast feed. This was something I'd given a lot of thought to during my pregnancy. Breast feeding. That was important to me. My heart fluttered in my chest while I was whisked off to the maternity ward.

Before leaving, the doctor informed us he would meet us in the delivery ward. A few minutes later, an orderly arrived with a wheelchair to transfer Amanda to her delivery room. I followed them into the elevator and held Amanda's hand, while we waited for our floor. I could tell that her claustrophobia was taking hold of her, as she squeezed my hand very hard and closed her eyes. Her breathing was pretty shallow, so I bent down and whispered in her ear, "You're okay, Raven. I'm here and everything's going to be fine." I started to stroke her hair with my free hand and she seemed to relax a bit. When we arrived on the delivery floor, the orderly wheeled her to the designated room and left us alone. I helped Amanda climb up onto the bed. A few moments later, a nurse came to check Amanda's vitals and said that the anesthetist would be there soon to set her up with an epidural I.V.

I could see that Amanda was in quite a lot of pain from the baby kicking so much, as she held her stomach after each time. It seemed like the baby was literally ripping his way through her. My heart was racing, but I pretended to keep my cool. I felt useless, since other than hold her hand, I knew I couldn't help her. I winced each time she gasped from the pain. She must have seen the concern in my eyes as she said, "I'm okay, Jamie, really!"

She was being so brave, and I felt powerless. For the first time since we'd met, I didn't have a clue of what I was doing. I bent down to kiss her and said a little prayer that God would look after my wife and son. It seemed as though it took the anesthetist forever to get there. Finally, we saw Dr. Cavanaugh and another doctor come into the room. Dr. Cavanaugh introduced us to Dr. Marshall. He asked Amanda if she could sit up and lean over the side of the bed. I helped her up and she tried her best to stay as still as possible.

Dr. Marshall brought out a needle that must have been at least six inches long and I really felt for her, as he inserted it into her lower back. She winced, but she didn't cry out. I could tell she was really trying to be brave for my benefit, but I saw how much pain she was in. I prayed that Amanda would not pick up on my own anxiety about the situation. *I need to be strong for her.* It took a while for the shot to take effect, but then she seemed to relax a bit and lay back on the bed. She couldn't get comfortable with the IV needle in her back, so I helped her to roll over onto her left side and she seemed to be okay.

I stood beside her and held her hand, while the doctors put up a tent–like sheet to block the view from her waist downwards. They said that she needed to be lying on her back for the surgery. She looked up at me and said, "Don't leave me Jamie!" I helped her to turn over onto her back. They inserted another IV into her arm and then they hooked her up to a baby heart monitor. We could hear the baby's heart beating strongly. They told me where I could stand, where I continued to hold her hand and stroke her hair.

They hooked her up to a machine, to monitor her heartbeat and I could hear that it was very erratic. A nurse came into the room to check on Amanda's and the baby's monitor readings, writing things down onto a chart.

The doctor and an intern entered, and they began. I couldn't see what they were doing past the sheet, but then Amanda cried out, "I can feel that!" Dr. Cavanaugh asked, "Isn't the anesthetic working?" He left the room and returned a few moments later with Dr. Marshall who went over to the IV tube that was hanging loosely down her one side and inserted more of the liquid. I held both of her hands and kept whispering into her ear, trying to get her to relax. But her heart rate kept getting more and more erratic. She was trembling and her breathing was labored.

Dr. Cavanaugh said, "Mrs. Grayson, you need to calm down, or I'm going to have to put you out!" She shook her head and said, "I'm sorry, I'll try to do better." I kept stroking her hair, whispering into her ear and then she seemed to relax for a bit. After only a few minutes, she seemed to fall asleep. Suddenly, I heard a loud beeping noise and the doctor said, "Get him out of here!" I looked at Dr. Cavanaugh and said, "What's going on?"

But his attention was focused on Amanda and he was using medical terms I didn't understand. The doctors looked concerned and the nurse pushed me out the door. I kept trying to get back into the delivery room, but the nurse was stronger than she looked. She nudged me down the hallway and said, "Mr. Grayson, you need to stay out now. Your wife is having complications and you need to let the doctors do their work, okay? She pointed to a room down the hall and said, "Have a seat in the expectant fathers' lounge and relax for a bit." My brows crunched together, as I said, "Please tell me what's going on!" She shook her head and said, "I have to get back to your wife. Please, just settle down and wait."

With that she turned around and went back to Amanda's delivery room. I heard a page on the intercom, "Code Blue, Delivery Room 5!" I looked at the room where I'd just been with Amanda. It had the number '5' marked beside it on the wall. I panicked. I tried going back into the room, but one of the nurses passing by grabbed my arm and said, "Mr. Grayson, you need to go and wait in the expectant fathers' lounge until we call you, okay?" I shook my head and said, "That's my wife in there!" She nodded and said, "I understand that you're worried about her, but you need to give the doctors room to work." She gently but firmly pulled me by the arm and led me to the lounge at the end of the hall. I felt like I wanted to scream, but I let her lead me into the room.

Inside the waiting room were a few simple office-type chairs and a couple of small love seats. On each end was a small table, a telephone on one and a box of tissues and magazines on the other. I couldn't just sit there, so I paced back and forth furiously for awhile. My heart was racing, and I felt that familiar feeling like I had back in September when I'd figured out that Amanda was supposed to be on one of the flights that had crashed on that day. I started to take deep breaths, because I knew that I wouldn't be doing Amanda any good if I freaked out. I was thankful that there were no other expectant fathers in the room.

My mind was racing and filled with thoughts of all the possibilities of what the outcome of this pregnancy could be. Amanda was just shy of forty-two years old and that in itself was a concern. But with her history, there certainly was the potential for disaster. My heart ached at the thought that I could lose both her and the baby. I decided I needed to calm down; I needed to pull myself together for Amanda's sake. I pulled my cell phone out of my pocket and dialed Joey's cell number. I figured if I could talk to him, I might be able to relax a bit. And I thought Joey would want to know what was going on.

He answered on the second ring with, "Yello!" I said, "Joey, it's me, Jamie. Amanda's in the hospital. They're doing a C-section now." Joey said, "Wasn't she scheduled for the tenth?" I said, "She woke up this morning with bruises all over her stomach. I didn't think that was normal, so I called

Dr. Stevens' answering service to page the on-call doctor."

I explained in detail what happened in the delivery room. "They pushed me out and then I heard a page of Code Blue to her room!" My throat thickened. Joey said, "I'm coming." I said, "No, you're too far away. I'll be okay." He said, "No way! I am going to call the family and we're coming in the jet, okay?"

I started to protest, but he said, "Jamie, I can tell this is serious! We're coming! I'll call you when we get there." And he hung up. I guessed it would be better for me to have some support. I called Matty and told him what was going on and he said he said he would call Crystal, that she had a shift today in the Birthing Center. He promised he'd ask her to check on me and that he'd call the rest of Amanda's family. I thanked him and hung up.

I started pacing back and forth again and thought I must be digging a big trench in the floor. My heart started racing and I couldn't breathe. A few moments later, the intern from Amanda's delivery room appeared. She said, "Mr. Grayson, I thought I'd give you an update." My heart skipped a beat. "Is my wife alright? What about the baby?" She gave me one of those 'mask-your-feelings' looks as she explained, "Your son was born twenty minutes ago. He's in the NICU." I remembered that term from before we'd adopted Chelsea. Amanda made a habit of visiting Neonatal Intensive Care Units in children's hospitals while she toured.

It was a form of therapy after having suffered numerous miscarriages – on the advice of Sonia.

I snapped back to the present as the intern continued, "They had to hook him up to oxygen and a feeding tube. He'll be in an incubator for awhile. His lungs aren't fully developed yet, so he can't breathe on his own or feed yet. But this is okay. Dr. Emily Barber is the best NICU doctor in the country and she's been assigned to your son's case."

I said, "And Amanda? What about my wife, is she okay?" The intern said, "Your wife was in quite a bit of trauma. She was hemorrhaging badly. They've taken her to an O.R., to perform a hysterectomy." I choked back the tears again and said, "How long will it be?" The intern said, "I would suggest you sit down and relax for awhile. These surgeries can take up to fourteen hours. I said, "Can I see my son?" She shook her head. I can't give you that authorization. I am not a NICU doc. But I'll try to contact Dr. Barber to come and see you when it's okay for you to visit your son. Now please, sit down and relax. It's going to be a while. Is there anyone we can call for you?" I told her I'd already called my family.

She said, "Okay, then just relax okay?" She put her hand on my arm and said, "This birthing center is one of the best in the country. You can trust that we'll take good care of your wife and son." She kept talking but I was in a fog at this point. My chest felt like it was going to explode. I couldn't breathe and my heart felt like it was jumping out of my chest. My knees buckled and then everything went black…

I was walking through a haze. I saw shadows all around me, voices talking to me, but they were incoherent. The most I could make out was that they were saying my name. "Mr. Grayson? Mr. Grayson!" I tried to blink my eyes to clear the fog, but it was useless. I tried waving my arms around to get the shadow people away from me. Then, I felt a sharp prick in my arm. It felt as though I was falling into an abyss.

****

My eyelids fluttered. I reached up to rub my eyes, to clear the fog. My head was spinning. I realized I was lying across one of the small love seats, my legs hanging over one end and there was a pillow propped under my head. I tried to get up, but the dizziness persisted, so I sunk back onto the pillow. When my eyes cleared, I saw Joey, Melissa, Mom and the rest of my brothers standing over me.

Joey said, "Welcome back, troublemaker!" I blinked a few times, letting the jab sink in before I said, "What's going on? Why do I feel so funny?" Joey said, "You had a panic attack. When we got here, there was an intern with red hair here taking your vital signs. She said her name was Sandy. She said she couldn't get you to calm down, that you kept calling out Amanda's name and you sounded like you were having trouble breathing. They had to give you some kind of shot with a powerful sedative.

I asked, "How long have I been out?" Joey said, "I don't know. You were lying here when we got here." I asked for the time and Joey said, "It's ten-thirty." I shook my head and said, "At night?" I couldn't believe it. I must have been out for over ten hours! We'd arrived at the hospital at about eleven-thirty a.m. I tried to get up again, but Mom put her hands to my chest, gently pushing me back down onto the pillow. She said, "Hush now! You need to stay put for awhile." She told me to do some deep breathing in order to relieve the effects of the sedative. Melissa was sitting in a chair adjacent to my legs and had her hand on my right knee.

The guys offered to get me something to eat, but I said I didn't think I could stomach anything yet. I asked if they'd seen Dr. Cavanaugh yet and they said they hadn't. Joey offered to go to the nurses' station to see what was going on with Amanda's surgery. He came back a few minutes later, saying there was no word as yet. I relaxed a bit, the effects of the sedative still weighing me down. My eyelids felt heavy and I drifted off.

I woke up with a stiff neck and sore muscles from lying on the uncomfortable couch. My family was still there, sitting in the chairs around me. Melissa was reading a magazine and Mom was knitting something. She looked up and said, "How do you feel, Jamie?" I felt one side of my mouth curve up, as I said, "Like I've been sleeping for days. Whatever they gave me, it was powerful." I stretched in my spot to work out the kinks in my back and neck and said, "Any word yet?"

Joey shook his head and said, "I'll go check with the nurse's station. I glanced at my watch and noticed it had stopped. "Anybody know what time it is?" Justin glanced at this watch and said, "It's two-thirty." I swung my legs over the side of the loveseat, sitting up and raked my fingers through my hair. I took a few deep breaths and rubbed my palms down my bearded cheeks. A few moments later, Joey returned with Dr. Cavanaugh, still in scrubs. He removed the cap from his bald head, clutching it in his right hand and smiled. That was a good sign.

I stood, balancing myself with my arms out to my sides slightly, making sure I had a good footing.

The doctor said, "I've just finished the hysterectomy and your wife is now in the recovery room." I started to move past him to go and see her, but the doctor put up his hand and said, "You might as well sit tight here with your family. You're not going to be allowed in the recovery room. You'll have to wait until your wife is in her room, before seeing her. I'll have a nurse come to get you when that happens."

"How did it go?" I asked, tentatively. Dr. Cavanaugh cleared his throat and said, "She's resting comfortably. I think they've already told you your son is in the NICU." He turned and left.

It took all of my strength not to bolt past him and demand that I see Amanda. Melissa got up from her chair and she and Joey helped me back to my uncomfortable couch. Mom fluffed the pillow, urging me to lie down again. Mom put one hand on my shoulder, started stroking my hair with the other and told me to try to sleep again. She bent down and kissed my forehead. "You rest now, son. You've had a rough night." I tried to protest, but the sedative was still in my system. I was still kind of foggy and soon, I drifted off.

When I woke up, my family was still there; and this time Matty and Crystal were standing there as well. My family went into the hall, so I could talk to Matty and Crystal for awhile. Crystal was in her nurse's uniform and said, "Amanda's in her room now, if you want to see her. I just checked on her and she's resting comfortably. They gave her some strong meds to keep her still, because when she was in the recovery room, she was trying to get out of bed to go and see your baby. She's going to be frozen for awhile, so they want her to rest. But you can go in and look in on her if you like." Crystal left the room to resume her duties.

My family filtered back into the room. Justin said that Amanda's sisters stopped by for awhile, but they left and said they'd be back the next day. "They said that Molly's in New York and she sends her love. And Daniel's away doing family business over-seas." I nodded, got up out of the makeshift bed and stood there for a moment to make sure I was okay to move. I then walked over to the nurses' station to get Amanda's room number.

The nurse behind the counter had blond hair and blue eyes. She kind of reminded me of Jenny. She wrote down the number on a piece of paper along with the extension number so family members could contact her when she was awake. She then said, "It can only be you for now. I know that your family's here, but for the time being Mrs. Grayson needs her rest. They can come back in the morning."

I looked at the clock on the wall and saw that it was four-thirty a.m. I located the room where Amanda was laying very still on her bed. There were two I.V. bags hooked up to her arm. One was full of something that looked like blood, so I figured she must've had a transfusion. The other I.V. was full of clear liquid, so I assumed that would be saline solution or pain meds or something. She looked very pale and thin. Her stomach was much smaller than it was when we arrived here during the day. I wanted to pick her up and hold her in my arms, but she looked so frail, I thought I might break her. I sat down on the chair at the side of her bed without the I.V.'s. I took her hand in mine and held it. I wanted her to know I was here.

After about twenty minutes, Crystal appeared and said, "Try not to wake her. She needs her rest. She's been through a lot today." I looked up at Crystal and said, "Tell me everything you know and don't hold back, okay?" Crystal hesitated, before she said, "If you weren't my brother-in-law, I wouldn't tell you anything, you know." She paused to check Amanda's vitals and then said, "Amanda was hemorrhaging badly. They had to do an emergency hysterectomy, but then you knew that might happen anyway, right?" I nodded. "They had to get a crash cart because she flat lined before they even had her in surgery." My heart started racing again. My throat thickened. I looked down at Amanda and put my head down beside her on the edge of the bed.

When I'd regained my composure, I lifted my head and said, "Go on." Crystal said, "The surgery was a tough one. The doctor wasn't even sure if she would survive. They had to get some blood transferred from another hospital because Amanda has AB negative blood, which is very rare, and she'd lost so much of it. Our supply was running low. We almost didn't get it here in time. But she's in good hands here, Jamie. This is one of the best birthing centers in the country. And our NICU is run by a great doctor. She *is* the best in the U.S.A."

She urged me to go and see my son, but I couldn't bring myself to leave Amanda's side. I said, "The doctor hasn't come to let me know I can even go in and see him yet." I asked Crystal to go and talk to my family and ask them to check on Alexander for me, as long as the doctor cleared it. Crystal nodded and said, "You know, Amanda probably won't even wake up tonight." I said, "I don't care. I need to be here. I need her to know that I won't leave her. Before this all happened, when we were in the delivery room, and the doctors were getting ready to do the C-section, she begged me not to leave her."

Crystal said she would go and give my family the message. She told me to try to get some rest, if possible, and then she left. I fell asleep in the chair, with my head on the bed, never letting go of her hand.

When I woke up, Joey was sitting in the chair on the other side of the room. He smiled at me and said, "Morning, sleepyhead! How're you doing?" I asked, "What time is it?" He said, "Time to get a watch!" and he laughed. I tried to force a smile, but I was too exhausted from everything that happened. He said, "It's nine fifteen. Hey, you want me to get you some breakfast?" I shook my head and said, "I'm not really hungry." He said, "Liar! I can hear your stomach growling from over here." I grimaced and said, "Okay, bring me something, I don't really care what." He rose from his chair and said he'd be right back.

A few minutes later, Melissa shuffled into the room and said, "Hey bro! How are you?" I said, "Okay, how's tricks?" She smiled and said, "Everyone's here. We went and checked into a hotel, but we came back to make sure you're not getting into trouble or anything." And she winked at me. I shook my head and said, "You know, you should let that go. I was a *kid*!" I remembered all the spankings I'd gotten when I was little, for always getting into stuff I wasn't supposed to, talking back to my parents, and having a lot of temper tantrums. My sister and brothers always teased me about it because, out of all of us, I seemed to be the worst.

Melissa glanced down at Amanda and said, "Any signs of her waking up yet?" I shook my head and reiterated what Crystal had told me. "They want to keep her drugged up to keep her still. She was trying to get out of bed in the recovery room, as she wanted to see our son." Melissa nodded. "She's stubborn that one! Speaking of your son, have you seen him yet?" I said no, that I had to wait until the NICU doctor gave me the okay. Melissa said Dr. Barber had already been by to tell me it was okay to see Alexander, but I'd been asleep.

"Even so, I don't want to leave Amanda just yet. I almost lost her last night." Melissa came to my side, put her hand on my shoulder and said, "You know we're all here for you." I nodded and said, "I know and thanks for that. You all leaving your families back home and coming all the way here to be with me - I really appreciate it." I asked her to ask the family to look in on Alexander now and then, until I was ready to leave Amanda alone. She nodded and said, "Well, I'm hungry. We came here without having had any breakfast. You want something from the cafeteria?" I shook my head and said, "Joey just went down there to pick me up something."

Melissa left. Joey showed up a few minutes later, with two herbal teas and a breakfast sandwich for each of us. We sat and ate and drank in silence for awhile. When I was finished eating, I crumpled the food wrapper, looked at Amanda and sighed. I thought to myself, *when will all this end?* I thought about all the things we'd endured since we met. I knew that life was supposed to be hard, but with everything that God had thrown at us over the years…it had almost crushed us several times over. I loved her more than anything in this world and would never leave her, but I was really starting to question my faith. What if I lost Amanda? What if I lost Alexander - or both of them?

I thought about that vision Sonia told me about, the one with me holding our baby and the three kids dancing and running around me in the garden. Where was Amanda in this vision? I couldn't imagine raising four kids without her. That was one thing that I'd been grateful for, when Melinda died – that we'd never had any kids together. In the years that followed my grief had totally consumed me. I couldn't imagine having to raise our kids alone.

Joey's eyes narrowed as he looked at me and said, "Are you okay?" He must have seen the color of my eyes change. They were hazel blue and changed color with my moods. When I was sad, they were usually grey. I said, "I just don't want to leave her. I promised her I wouldn't. I can't even let go of her hand. I want her to know I'm here for her. I'm afraid if I let go and leave the room, she'll be gone, when I get back, just like Melinda!" I'd lost my first wife in 1976, to cancer. My throat thickened and my eyes started to sting. It took all my strength not to lose control. Joey jumped up from his chair and rushed over to me. He put his hands on my shoulders and started to massage them. It felt good, because I had a kink in my neck, probably from lying crouched over Amanda's bed all night.

After a few minutes Joey said to me, "You know we're all here for you, Jamie. I know you and Amanda have been through a lot for the last several years, and you've had to be the strong one. You've been her rock. Sometimes life throws us some curve balls we think we can't handle. And Lord knows you two have had more than your fair share. It's okay for you to let go once in a while, and we'll be here to catch you when you fall, okay?"

I nodded and said, "Thanks. You guys are the best." I swiped at a stray tear and sighed. Joey was right. I was usually the strong one. But right now, I felt helpless. Seeing her, lying there in the bed, she looked like a child. So small, so frail. The love of my life. And I knew I needed to be stronger than ever. I was, after all, the father of four children. It was something we'd both wanted. And even though Amanda tried to hide her pain, over the past few months, I knew she needed me more than ever.

I stayed with her for the next forty-eight hours. I didn't let go of her hand once, short of visiting the bathroom in her room. She was in a small private room that was kind of a step down from the Maternity ICU. I noticed there was a red flag on the front of the door to her room, which the nurses explained to me, meant she was still being watched carefully.

My family kept bringing me food and drinks, and tried to encourage me to go out and take a break, but I never left her side. Matty brought changes of clothes and some toiletries so I could get myself cleaned up, but I never went further than the bathroom in her room.

The next day Dr. Barber came in to see me. She introduced herself as Emily.

She had shoulder length straight blonde hair and forest green eyes. She was around five foot four inches tall, in about her mid to late thirties, and she was pretty. She shook my hand and said, "Your son is going to be here for awhile, so we might as well be on a first name basis." I nodded and said, "I'm Jamie." She encouraged me to go visit Alexander as much as possible.

She said, "Since your wife can't be out of bed for the next while, your son is going to need a lot of stimulation - lots of human contact. He's going to be hooked up to oxygen until his lungs are fully developed, and he needs to be fed through a tube, until he can take a bottle. You won't be able to touch him just yet, but eventually, we can take him out of there, for short periods of time, to get used to being touched. This is probably going to be hard on both of you. From what I understand, your wife went through a lot and needs to rest up for now.

I said, "Amanda wanted to breast feed." The doctor shook her head and said, "That's impossible. Since your wife can't be moved yet and your son must stay in the NICU, they won't have any contact for now. I looked at my shoes. "This is going to break her heart." The doctor nodded, "I know. She's going to need a lot of support. I've seen mothers go through this and it's not easy for any of the family members. I'm sorry this has happened to you. But I promise you, I'll do everything in my power to get your little family together as soon as possible, okay?"

I cleared my throat and said, "Are older kids welcome in here? We have three more kids and they're probably wondering what's going on." Emily shook her head and said, "Not for the next few weeks. When your son is able to be taken out of the incubator for short periods of time, maybe then we can discuss it. But they can't be rough with him. He's still very fragile. How old are your kids?" I said, "We have two six year old fraternal twins – a boy and a girl, and a five-and-a-half year old girl."

She frowned, "How did you two manage that? Was there another special case like your son's?" I shook my head and told her they were adopted. "We thought there would be no kids of our own. Amanda had a lot of issues with miscarriages, because of abuse in her life." Emily nodded and said, "So this was a surprise pregnancy then?" I nodded. "She's forty-one years old. We never thought she was even able to conceive, and then *this* happened."

Emily nodded, "So this was always a high-risk pregnancy then?" I nodded. She said, "I wish I'd known. I wish they'd referred you guys to me in the first place. Dr. Cavanaugh is good, but he's not nearly as good as *I* am." and she winked at me. I laughed and said, "Dr. Cavanaugh is just covering for Dr. Stevens, who is on vacation till next week." Emily said, "Ahhh! Dr. *Stevens* is your wife's doctor. I've heard very good things about him. He's working with very special needs patients using a naturopathic, hormone supplement. I've heard his success rate is very high."

I looked at her and said, "So he's okay then?" She nodded and said, "I'm looking forward to meeting him next week. I'm surprised we've never run into each other here yet. I hear he does a lot of traveling though. He works with some Naturopath in Germany, where he found this new herbal stuff. I want to look into this. I deal with mostly emergency cases, when the moms come in at the last minute, so I don't usually see them until it's a dire situation. But I also deal with the babies. Most obstetricians only deal with the moms and then they hand them off to me when there's a preemie or special cases with the unborn fetuses. But I have a double master's degree so I can deal with both the moms *and* the kids. I perform experimental surgeries, in-utero, when the obstetricians can't handle the case, then they hand them off to me. I've also done surgeries on the babies, after they're born. It's a learning hospital here."

I said, "Wow! You *are* good then!" She shrugged and said, "I try to do my best. I have a high success rate, but there are times, when there are cases that can't be helped."

I nodded. "I don't drink, but there are times, like this, when I actually think about starting!" Her nose wrinkled up and she laughed. "You're a funny guy! You must keep your wife in stitches." I said, "You gotta laugh sometimes. Life is tough and humor is how my family gets through the big stuff. And of course there's our music, too."

Her eyes widened and she said, "I *thought* you looked familiar! So you're *that* Jamie Grayson?" I nodded. She said, "Well if I do a good job with your son, maybe you'd be willing to share some concert tickets with me and my friends?" And she winked at me. I nodded and said, "Absolutely! But you have to fly to Virginia to see us now. We don't tour anymore. We own a nightclub in Crystal Pines. Our fans come to see us there."

Then she said, "Wait, then your wife must be Celina Jackson then!" and she pointed at Amanda. I nodded. "That's her stage name." Emily put her hand on my shoulder and said, "I've read a lot of stuff about you two in the papers. That was really something, how she ended up nowhere near the actual crash site in New York, but her plane crashed somewhere else?" I nodded. Emily said, "I was very sorry to hear about The Bar Riders dying on that day." I said, "Thank you. My wife has been through a lot this past year." She nodded and said, "Apparently, and so have *you*. There was a lot of stuff in the papers about your shooting two years ago, too." I nodded and my lips formed a hard line, as I thought about all of it. Emily then said, "Well, enough chatter here. I'm sure you're sick of hearing people talk to you about all of this. I really should get back to work. It was nice to meet you; and go see your son, okay?"

I said I would and thanked her as she left. I stayed with Amanda for three more days. She hadn't woken up yet and I questioned the hospital staff about it. They said that Amanda was still being heavily sedated, so that she could heal. I missed her beautiful blue eyes, her smile and her laugh, while she played with the kids. I felt the corners of my mouth go up as I remembered the last time she pranked me. Between my family and my wife, I was always the victim of practical jokers.

The next morning, I decided it was time to visit with Alexander. I went to the bathroom in Amanda's room, to get myself cleaned up. I gave myself a sponge bath, washed my face, washed and conditioned my hair and beard in the sink. I then put a comb through my tangled mop, as best I could. My hair was getting long and unruly, and I knew I needed a haircut. Amanda liked it long, but I decided to pull it back into a ponytail, to look more presentable. I hadn't shaved or trimmed my beard since arriving at the hospital, so it was getting kind of straggly. I found my beard grooming kit in the bag that Matty had brought for me. I trimmed my beard and shaved my neck. Then I trimmed a couple of inches off of my ponytail so my hair would look a bit healthier.

I changed into some clean clothes and put the dirty ones in the bag, so Matty could take them home to be washed later.   I put on some antiperspirant but decided to skip the aftershave in case Alexander would turn out sensitive to the fragrance. When I was finished, I cleaned up the mess in the sink and left the bathroom. I went over to the bed, where Amanda was still sleeping. I gently squeezed her hand, bent over, kissed her on the cheek and whispered into her ear that I'd be back soon. I headed for the NICU to see my son. When I arrived, Dr. Emily was there. Melissa and Mom were also there looking through the glass at Alexander.   Dr. Emily looked up, smiled and walked towards me.

She said, "Hello, Mr. Grayson! Nice to see you've finally come to see your son!" I nodded and said, "I was too afraid to leave my wife alone - and it's Jamie, remember?" She nodded, put her hand on my arm and said, "Don't worry, she's in good hands, I promise!" and she gave me a reassuring look. "Jamie, would you like to hold your son? It's been a few days, so we're going to try to get him used to being touched now, for a little while each day." I smiled, nodded and said, "Yes I would! Absolutely!"

Emily walked over to the back of the incubator where Alexander was lying. I noticed a square white tag on the front of the incubator, which had some colored stickers with printed letters on it saying, "Grayson, 3 pounds, 4 ounces." I looked around the NICU and saw that the other incubators were marked in the same way, except each one had different combinations of colored stickers on them. I assumed that each color was a code, indicating their special needs. Emily slipped her right hand inside her white coat pocket, pulling out a set of small keys, which she used to unlock the glass sliding door on the back of the incubator. She slid the door downwards, reached inside the incubator and disconnected the feeding and breathing tubes. She then picked Alexander up gently, and brought him over to me, placing him in my arms.

She instructed me how to hold him, by supporting his head and holding him as close as I could, so he would feel safe. I carefully drew him close to my chest. She then showed me how to rock him back and forth. She said, "Babies like that." I did as she instructed, and I gazed down at him in wonder. He gazed up at me, with his beautiful blue eyes. I hoped they would stay that color. They were as bright as Amanda's eyes. Melissa and Mom stood beside me, looking very proud. Dr. Emily said, "Looks like you've done this before." I said, "Not with a baby *this* small!"

She smiled and left me alone, looking down and marveling at this tiny, fragile and beautiful little human being that Amanda and I had created together. I kept holding and rocking Alexander for quite awhile. When, Dr. Emily came back, she said, "I'm sorry, Jamie, but it's time to put Alexander back and hook him up to his tubes again. I got called away to an emergency and I didn't realize how long I was away. It's been almost forty-five minutes since you started holding him. Normally, we wouldn't do this for more than fifteen minute increments." I looked down at Alexander and realized he'd fallen asleep." Reluctantly, I gave him back to Dr. Emily, who put him back inside the incubator and hooked him back up to his tubes. She pulled her stethoscope off her shoulders and proceeded to take Alexander's vitals. She smiled and said, "Everything looks good here!" She pulled the glass door back up and locked it.

Melissa and Mom wanted to leave and take me for lunch, but I said, "I want to stay here for a few more minutes, but can you bring me something when you get back? Just take it to Amanda's room, okay?" They agreed, both rose up on their toes on each side to kiss me on the cheek and left. I stood there for a few more minutes with my hand on the glass, staring at my little son and then went back to Amanda's room.

When I got there, a nurse was taking her temperature and her blood pressure. Amanda was wide awake and sitting up. When she saw me, she pulled the thermometer out of her mouth and said, "Jamie! Where *were* you? I woke up and there was no one here!" She reached her arms out to me, with her eyes glistening with tears. I went over to her, put my arms around her and kissed her deeply. I said, "I'm sorry, Raven! I was visiting Alexander. When I left, you were still asleep." The nurse gave up, pulling the blood pressure cuff off Amanda's arm, took the thermometer out of her hand, leaving us alone.

Amanda's gaze was intense as she said, "You saw Alexander? Is he okay?" I said, "Yes! He's beautiful! I got to hold him for forty-five minutes!" Her eyes welled up with tears again and she looked down at her hands. I knew she was likely feeling separation anxiety and wanted to be with our son more than anything. I stroked her hair and said, "I'm sorry, honey! Maybe now that you're awake, they might let you go and see him!"

Her face lit up like a Christmas tree as she said, "Can you go ask them for me?" I nodded, strode over to the nurses' station and spoke to a middle-aged woman, who was concentrating on her work, writing notes on a chart. I asked about Amanda going to see our son. The nurse glanced up and then started typing something into the computer. A moment later, she said, "No. Mrs. Grayson's file says that she needs to stay in bed until she's been cleared to move around by her doctor. I said, "Can you call Dr. Cavanaugh and ask him?" She nodded, saying she would call him right away and let me know. When I returned to Amanda's room, there was an attendant putting her lunch tray on the rolling cart, which sat beside the bed. Just then Mom and Melissa returned with my lunch. Perfect timing!

I sat down in the chair beside her bed and we both started eating our lunches. Melissa and Mom started talking about Alexander and Melissa said, "You should have seen Jamie! He was holding Alexander for almost forty-five minutes, and he didn't cry once! He looked up at him with his big blue eyes, as if to say, "There you are, Daddy! And then he just fell asleep!" Amanda suddenly put her fork down on the tray and burst into tears. I sat on the bed and put my arms around her, stroking her hair.   I figured her hormones were probably working overtime, and my heart ached for her. How hard it must have been for her to be away from our baby.

Melissa scurried over to the other side of Amanda's bed and sat down, putting her hand on Amanda's arm as she said, "I'm sorry, sweetheart! That was *so* insensitive of me! I should have known better. I can't imagine what you're going through, not being able to see Alexander, or hold him yet!"

Amanda dried her own tears and said, "I'm just being a baby! But I just wish I could do something about this!" She pointed to the wet spots on her hospital gown. "My boobs feel like they're going to explode any second!" She tried to laugh, but the tears rolled down her cheeks again as she bit down on her lower lip. Melissa said, "Hey! I have an idea! I'll be back later!" and she left.

I dried Amanda's tears and kissed her forehead. She seemed to calm down enough for us to finish eating our lunch. Mom told us she was going for a walk and left us alone. About thirty minutes later, the attendant was just picking up Amanda's lunch tray, when Melissa returned, holding a plastic bag. She said, "I got you something." She pulled a box out of the bag, setting it down on the rolling table, in front of Amanda.

Amanda looked at the box and we both read the label that said, 'Mega Miracle Breast Pump.' Amanda picked up the box and started reading the back of it. Her eyes lit up and she said, "I can use this so Alexander can drink my milk from the bottles, until I can feed him myself!" Melissa said, "Yes! I used one of these with my first baby, when I had to go back to work. The one *I* had wasn't so far advanced as this one is. I got some advice from the sales clerk, who said she used one like it and loved it! It comes with four bottles with natural nipples, and she said it's really easy to use."

Amanda opened the box and I helped her put it together. Melissa asked me, "Do you want me to help you with it? I can show you how if you want." Amanda looked up at me and curled her lips around her teeth. I glanced at Melissa and said, "Maybe she'd like to be alone for this." Melissa smiled, nodded and said, "I'll be back later," and she left. I asked Amanda if she'd like some privacy and she said, "No, I need you to stay, in case I need help, okay?" I walked over to the curtain beside her bed, pulling it closed around us. Then I sat down on the bed beside her. She held the breast pump up to her right breast and started pumping. She switched sides and within about twenty minutes she'd filled all four bottles with it. I was amazed at how much milk she was producing, considering how long she'd been sleeping and not eating or drinking, until just now.

Amanda's eyes sparkled. She was happy to at least be able to help our son with the breast milk, even if she couldn't be there with him. She asked me to bring the milk to the NICU and ask if they could feed it to Alexander. I took the bottles and left.

When I got to the NICU, Dr. Emily was just leaving as her shift had ended. When I asked her about the milk, she smiled and said, "That's fantastic that your wife is awake and able to use a breast pump! We can use it to replace the formula we're giving him now. The formula doesn't have the same nutrients that breast milk does. And I can see that two of the bottles have colostrum. This is very good for the baby's immune system. This is excellent! And we don't have to water it down like we do with the formula." She took the bottles and handed them to the doctor taking over for her. She introduced me to Dr. Cheryl Bridges." I shook her hand as Emily instructed her to label the bottles as belonging to Alexander Grayson.

Dr. Bridges took one of the bottles, with the colostrum in it, and she began to swap out one of the feeding bags for it. Dr. Emily said goodbye and left. Dr. Bridges labeled the rest of the bottles and put them in a fridge that was in the NICU, by the desk. I visited with Alexander for a few minutes and then returned to Amanda's room.

I told Amanda that Dr. Emily had cleared the idea of giving Alexander her breast milk. "For now, he's just going to receive it through the feeding tube, but Dr. Emily told me that maybe in a few days, he'll be able to take it from a bottle, unless you're able to leave your room and come into the NICU; and then, you might be able to try to get him to suckle your breast." Amanda's face beamed with excitement about this. I spent a few more hours with her and then she asked me to check with the nurses' station, to see if they'd gotten in touch with Dr. Cavanaugh yet. I walked over to the station and saw the same woman I'd originally spoken with.

When she saw me, she said, "Oh, Mr. Grayson, I'm sorry, I forgot to come and talk to you earlier. I had an emergency case come in and had to deal with it first. I talked to Dr. Cavanaugh's receptionist and she said Dr. Cavanaugh is going to be away for a few days. By the time he gets back, Dr. Stevens should have returned from Germany, so he'll be taking over Mrs. Grayson's case."

I asked the nurse if Amanda could get out of bed to go and see Alexander. She shook her head and said, "Unfortunately, we're unable to give that authorization, without the doctor's orders. I'm sorry that's probably not the news you were hoping for, but I could get fired if I let your wife out of bed and something were to happen." I nodded, returned to Amanda and relayed the message. Amanda burst into tears, yet again. I sat on the bed and tried to comfort her. She seemed to calm down a bit and then we just spent some time together, until they brought in her dinner. I asked Amanda if she wouldn't mind if I left, to go home for the night. I said, "I haven't had a shower since we got here a week ago, and I haven't seen the kids since then either. I'm sure they're wondering what's going on."

Amanda's eyes widened. "You mean I've been out for a whole week?" I smiled and said, "They kept you heavily sedated, to help you heal. And it must be working, as you look so much better than you did a few days ago." Her cheeks were a rosy pink – a far cry from the pale and frail skeleton of herself when she'd first come to stay in this room.

I could tell Amanda was tempted to ask me to stay, but she bit down on her lower lip, and then said, "Okay. The kids need you more than I do, so go ahead." I kissed her and said, "I love you, Raven!" She said it back to me and I kissed her again, deeply. I told her to call me if she needed me and then left.

I pulled my cell phone out of my pocket and called Joey, asking him to give me a ride. He'd taken my car home a few days ago, so I wouldn't have a huge parking bill. The hotel my family was staying in was close by, so it only took him ten minutes to get there. When we made it to the house, Bridget was just clearing the supper dishes and asked me if I would like some of the food. Joey and I both hadn't had dinner yet, so Bridget heated up the leftovers and put it out on the dining room table for us. After we finished eating, the kids had just finished their nightly baths and were ready for their usual bedtime rituals.

The moment they spotted us, sitting in the dining room, I heard squeals of delight. "Daddy! You're home!" And they pounced on me, smothering me with hugs and kisses. "I missed you so much, my little monkeys!" Joey and I spent some time with the kids and then Joey left. My eye lids were heavy the moment I'd gotten in the door, but I knew I needed to spend some time with the Chelsea and the twins, before going to bed myself.

I sang them three songs, as was our tradition, but I asked Bridget if she could tell them their three stories. This was out of order from the norm, but I was so tired I couldn't see straight, and she agreed. The past week must have been challenging for her; even though she had Maggie's help now. I saw she looked as drawn and tired as I felt, but she smiled and said, "Go ahead, Jamie! Get some rest. I'll handle this!" I kissed the kids goodnight and promised them they could go and see Mommy and Alexander, in a few days.

I'd fully intended on having a shower that night, but I was too dog tired to climb up and down the stairs, or even use the elevator, so I tumbled onto the mattress, without removing my clothes and fell asleep, as soon as my head hit the pillow. I awoke to the sound of the alarm at six a.m. Thankful that I'd remembered to set it, I turned it off and dragged myself out of bed. I unplugged my cell from the charger – luckily, I remembered to charge it, or it would have been dead! I grabbed some fresh clothes from our closet and plunked down the steps to the bathroom, to have my shower and get ready to go back to the hospital.

The kids were just getting into the kitchen to eat their breakfast, when I was having a quick drink of juice. They attacked me with hugs and kisses and asked if they could come with me to the hospital, to see their Mommy and baby brother. I shook my head and said it was too soon, that Alexander wasn't ready for so many visitors and Mommy wasn't up to it either. I wasn't sure if the latter was true, but I thought about the two I.V.'s Amanda was still hooked up to and I wasn't sure if the kids would understand what that was about.

When I got back to the birthing center, I learned from the nurses that Amanda had developed a fever during the night. She'd had a fitful night, calling out my name and Alexander's in her sleep. They said they'd tried to call my cell, but I'd left it on vibrate and must have been in such a deep sleep, that I hadn't heard it. I rushed to her side and saw she was still sleeping. They gave her some extra meds, to help with the fever and had applied cold compresses to her forehead.

The nurses checked on her every half an hour, to make sure she was okay. She wasn't eating and slept quite a bit that day. They added extra vitamins to her one I.V., to help her keep up her strength. I noticed the sack with the blood was no longer there, so I assumed she didn't need that one anymore. I decided to spend the night there with her again. The next morning, her fever was down a bit, but still high, so she still wasn't able to get out of bed.

The doctor had been called, but neither one of them were back yet, so it was another fitful night that night again. Her fever rose to 105 degrees and I worried about her. I held her hand, while she cried out in her sleep. I called home and told Bridget I wouldn't be returning home, until I was sure Amanda was alright. Then, I called Joey and told him that the family might as well not come to see her until she was able to receive company again. Mom and Melissa visited Alexander, but they stayed away from Amanda's room, as I'd asked.

When Dr. Stevens finally returned from Germany, he popped in to see Amanda. He examined her and said, "I heard you two have had a pretty rough go of it the last several days. I'm sorry I wasn't here to look after her. I promise I'll be here every day now, until Mrs. Grayson is ready to go home." I told him how hard it had been on Amanda, not being able to get out of bed without his permission and go and see Alexander. He nodded and said, "That's terrible that she hasn't been able to bond with your son. I've seen other women go off the deep end when that happens." I told him about the breast pump and that it seemed to placate her for awhile, until the fever started.

Dr. Stevens said, "Well I hope the fever breaks soon, otherwise, her breast milk will likely dry up and she won't even be able to pump. She hasn't been doing that while she's had her fever, right? The baby shouldn't get that milk. It might hurt him." I shook my head and said, "No, she's been sleeping a lot." I told him about how fitful her sleeping had been and he said, "That's common when the fever is that high. I'm going to prescribe something that might work on it a bit better. The stuff she's been getting doesn't seem to be working."

I went to see Alexander while Dr. Stevens was examining Amanda, but I didn't dare hold him, in case there were some germs I might be transferring from Amanda.

Dr. Emily was back and asked me what was going on. She was surprised that Amanda hadn't been able to visit with Alexander yet, and she noticed there wasn't a new supply of the breast milk coming. I told her what was going on. Her eyes showed genuine concern as she said, "That's unfortunate. But the *good* news is that Alexander isn't going through too much of the breast milk. He's only been taking small amounts of it, so there's still enough to last until the end of the day today. Hopefully, she's better tomorrow, so she can both visit and try to feed him herself, or at the very least be able to pump her breast milk again. I would advise that if she *does* pump some today that you discard the milk in case she has a virus." I nodded and told her I had to get back to Amanda. She said, "Goodbye and good luck, Jamie!"

Amanda's fever finally broke that night allowing for a more restful sleep. I stayed the night again, waking up with another sore neck, just as they delivered her breakfast tray. Matty brought me some more changes of clothes and Mom and the rest of the family visited one more time before they had to get back to Crystal Pines. The club had been without Joey and Justin for too long already. Jeremy and Jordie both returned to Virginia a couple of days ago. I said my goodbyes and they left. That afternoon, Amanda's sisters visited. It seemed to cheer Amanda up a bit, but she was still quite despondent about not being able to see and bond with Alexander.

She tried to pump her breast milk again but was having a lot of difficulty with it. It seemed that her breast milk was in fact starting to dry up. The nurses came to help. They said that she shouldn't get discouraged. They explained that it's supply and demand. So the more she tried to pump, the more milk she would produce. It was very difficult in her situation because of her allergies to dairy products. They had to give her a calcium supplement, to help improve the production of her breast milk. The next day, she seemed to be getting a little bit more and managed to fill a bottle and a half. *Well at least that's a start!*

I brought the milk to the NICU and Dr. Emily was there to accept it. She asked me how Amanda was doing and I filled her in. "Dr. Stevens told us that if she's feeling better tomorrow, she can come to the NICU in a wheelchair."

The following day she was feeling strong enough to get out of bed and walk around the hallways a bit, so Dr. Stevens gave her the all clear to go and see Alexander. My heart tightened in my chest, while she cried the first time Dr. Emily placed Alexander in her waiting arms. She tried to feed him with her breast, but he seemed to be having trouble latching on. Dr. Emily had already switched the feeding tube out for the bottles she'd filled.

She said, "Don't worry. It sometimes takes a bit longer for babies to get used to the fact that they must suck a bit harder on the mother's breast. Keep on trying. You'll get the hang of it!" She put her hand on Amanda's shoulder and said, "You need to try to relax a bit. It's possible that your milk isn't coming down because you're upset. This will make the baby get frustrated. I know this is hard, but just try to relax. Baby's can sense when Mom is upset and they react in turn."

Amanda tried her best, but it wasn't until a few days later that her milk finally started to flow a bit faster. It was enough for Alexander to finally latch on to her and stay there, until he'd gotten his fill. He was still attached to the breathing tube, but he was feeding quite well. This seemed to placate Amanda for awhile, until Dr. Stevens told her she could go home. We asked Dr. Emily if Alexander could go home with us. She shook her head. "He's still not breathing on his own very well yet. I'm afraid it's going to be a bit longer until he can go home."

Amanda burst into tears, when she heard this. She didn't want to leave Alexander and go home without him. She cried herself to sleep in my arms each night. In the mornings, we would go back to the hospital to be with our son. The kids were very confused and wondered why their mother was so sad all the time. They kept asking about Alexander.

I tried my best to explain it to them. We took them along a couple of times so they could see him, but Dr. Emily didn't allow them to hold him just yet. She explained to them that he was just too small for them to be holding him. They seemed to understand and were content just to watch him through the glass.

May 18, 2002

I gritted my teeth as I finished the last of the hundred repetitions of lifts. I lowered myself, placing my feet on the ground and released my grip on the door casing. I wiped the sweat off my brow with the sleeve of my shirt, reaching towards the nightstand for my cup of water. I'd been gradually increasing my workout times, preparing myself for the time when I would be released. Dr. Collins had been hinting that it was almost time for me to go out into the world again...out into civilization.

As long as I promised to take my meds and come and see her for regular appointments, we were going to start a trial release very soon.

I sunk down into the uncomfortable mattress that had been my bed since just after the trial. I swung my legs up over the bed and lay down for the night. I ran my fingers over my arms. I could feel the change. My muscle tone was almost where I wanted it to be. I felt my mouth curve up as I thought about her. It was just her type. I'd read somewhere that Grayson worked out...a lot. I'd taken great pains to make sure I would be up for the job of replacing *him* in her life.

Soon, Celina, soon.

On April 5, 2002, my baby was strong enough to be able to breathe on his own and had gained enough weight to finally leave the hospital with us. We thanked Dr. Emily and I hugged her before we left. Jamie gave her his business card and told her to call, when she wanted to go to Crystal Pines to see the Graysons in concert at their night club. He promised he would include a ride in the family jet with the tickets. She laughed and said, "Wow! You really are gracious and too kind!" Jamie hired a limousine service to bring us back home with our new son. Chelsea, Eric, Nina, Bridget, Maggie, Matty and a very pregnant Crystal were all there to greet us, when we arrived. I was over the moon about being able to finally bring Alexander home, where he belonged.

They were all outside on the front porch waiting for us. I could tell the kids were very excited, but I was sure Matty, Crystal, Bridget and Maggie had explained to them that they couldn't get too rowdy with the baby there, as they seemed to be on their best behavior.

When we entered the front foyer, I could see streamers and a big banner that said, "Welcome Home Alexander!" hanging on the wood trim on the entrance to the living room. I'd fed Alexander before leaving the hospital, so he fell asleep on the trip home. It was also my birthday that day. When we walked into the living room, I saw another banner that said, "Happy Birthday, Mommy!" and there were streamers all over the living room as well. My eyes welled, because I just assumed my birthday would fall by the wayside, with Alexander's big home-coming celebration.

Sitting on the coffee table was a big double slab of gluten-free decorated cake with Happy Birthday Mommy on one half and Welcome Home Alexander on the other half. The side for Alexander was decorated on top with blue teddy bears, and the side for me had purple and pink roses.

And on the dining room table was an assortment of flower arrangements, sent by the Grayson family, my family and from Two Ocean Records. At the center of them all was a big vase of Sterling Silver roses from Jamie.

I smiled at all the fuss they'd gone to for this special day. There were lots of presents for both the baby and for me. Chelsea, Nina and Eric had prepared a special welcome home song for me and their gift to me and Alexander was a big piece of Bristol board, with pictures hand drawn on it with love. The drawings were of pink and purple flowers and stick men of our new family. They even included Matty and Crystal, with a big stomach, that had an arrow pointing at it indicating 'new baby' and more stick figures of Jamie and I holding Alexander and the other three kids dancing all around us in the garden. It was almost as if they were trying to draw Sonia's vision.

I was filled with joy to be home, with my suddenly very large family. We sat and ate cake and drank herbal tea, while the kids drank chocolate rice milk out of their plastic tea set cups. When the festivities were done and the clean-up started, it was time for me to feed Alexander again. I took deep breaths as I took Alexander up in the elevator to our bedroom. My claustrophobia was still very much a part of me. As soon as the doors opened, I spotted a rocking cradle next to my side of the bed. It was a dark cherry wood and there was new baby bedding including a little quilt with blue teddy bears on it. I knew the bedding had been made with love by Mom Sylvia.

I sat on the bed and got myself ready to feed Alexander. I could hear the kids running around downstairs and squealing with delight, probably all wired for sound after having all that sweet cake and chocolate milk. I could hear Jamie and the others shushing them to keep it down, but I loved it! I'd always wanted a house full of happy kids running around.

I sighed as Alexander suckled my breast for awhile, and then switched him to the other breast. I hummed an old familiar tune that I suddenly remembered, but I couldn't quite place it. I closed my eyes and saw a picture of my mother rocking a baby and humming the same tune. Could it be that I remembered my own mother singing to me as a baby? I would never know for sure, but it seemed right that I keep up the tradition.

The next few weeks flew by. I was exhausted from all the feedings and running after the other three kids, but I was happier than I'd ever been. *Finally, I have the family I've always dreamed of!*

****

On April 29th, we were celebrating Jamie's forty-ninth birthday. I was upstairs in the bedroom feeding Alexander his late afternoon meal.

After Alexander was fast asleep for the evening (or at least a few hours), I placed him gently into the cradle. Turning on the baby monitor, I grabbed the remote for it and padded down the steps to the main floor. Jamie was sitting in the living room watching television and Bridget was in the kitchen making dinner. I saw the corners of his mouth go up, as he watched me approach as he said, "Hello my little Mommy! How's the bambino doing?" I said, "He's fast asleep and full with my milk."

I sat down on the couch next to him and he kissed me deeply. I was tired, but I could see his eyes were bright blue. More than enough time had passed since Alexander was born, but Jamie never initiated anything. I wanted him big time, but I wasn't sure how we were going to fit that part of our lives in again just yet. It seemed like every time I thought things were heading in that direction, one of the kids needed us, so it hadn't happened yet. I knew there was more than enough staff to help, but Jamie seemed to keep his distance and never asked me for anything. Maybe he was waiting for me to let him know I was ready.

He put his arm around me and I put my head on his shoulder, while he channel surfed with his other hand. I put my hand on his leg and folded my legs up under me on the couch. I drifted off. Beastfeeding every three or four hours was really knocking the wind out of my sails!

I was having a really nice dream, when Jamie nudged me awake. He whispered in my ear, "It's time for dinner, sweetie!"

I blinked my eyes and looked at the LED on the satellite receiver. It said six-thirty. I'd been asleep for over two hours. He took my hand, pulled me up off the couch and led me to the dining room table, where there were six adult place settings, and three kids' place settings on the smaller table beside the bigger one. Dinner smelled and tasted delicious. Crystal and Matty joined us for our dinner. After we were finished eating, I got up to clear the dishes but Bridget said, "Leave that to me. You go and relax with Jamie." I asked Maggie to pack up the leftovers for the rest of the staff, who were still working out front and making their rounds of our property.

Jamie, Matty, Crystal and I sat and talked and joked around for awhile. The nannies brought out a big birthday cake for Jamie. We sang happy birthday and after eating cake, we gave Jamie his gifts. He opened them and thanked everyone. I gave him a mug that had a picture of all the kids printed on it on one side with, "World's Greatest Dad," in gold lettering on the opposite side. The kids had drawn him a big picture that said, "We love you, Daddy!" on it. At about eight-thirty, I heard Alexander's cries from the baby monitor remote. I rose and headed toward the stairs up to our attic bedroom.

Jamie followed me and said, "Don't you want to take the elevator?" I said, "No, it's time for me to get back into shape. My husband's been ignoring me, since I'm still a little puffy with all this baby fat." His brows furrowed, "Hey, I haven't really been ignoring you, have I?" I sighed and said, "Well I guess I can understand it, if you don't want to be with the Pillsbury Dough boy..." He pulled me into his arms on the bottom step of the stairwell to our bedroom and said, "I kind of like you all soft and cushy!" I looked up at him and said, "Liar!" He kissed me and said, "You're really not fat, you know. I was actually amazed at how skinny you looked in that hospital bed, after your surgery!"

I pulled myself away from his embrace and said, "We can discuss this later. Right now, duty calls," and I started up the steps. Jamie continued to follow me. I picked Alexander up from his cradle and laid him on the bed to change him. There was a supply of baby things on the nightstand. When I'd finished changing his diaper, Jamie grabbed the dirty one and ran down the stairs to dispose of it. He returned a few moments after I'd started feeding the baby. He looked down at me and asked if I needed anything. I shook my head and said, "Nothing I can have right now, anyway!"

He smiled and sat down on the bed next to me. He watched as Alexander suckled my breast and said, "You know I'm kind of jealous of all the attention our son is getting!" He kept staring at my breasts and I said, "See anything interesting?" He nodded and said, "They're really huge!" I laughed and said, "You like that, don't you?" His smile widened into a big dopey grin and he said, "Too bad he won't share!" And he rolled his eyes.

I laughed again and said, "Maybe later, you know, when he's full up." Jamie sighed and said, "We'll see," and he left. I frowned. Did he think I was kidding? I finished feeding Alexander and laid him back in his cradle. He was fast asleep. Good thing that he slept a lot, so I could try to catch some zees or at least relax a bit while he was napping. I realized I'd left the baby monitor remote downstairs, so carefully made my way downstairs to find where I'd left it. I spotted it on the kitchen counter, snatched it up and slipped it in my pocket. Jamie was in the kitchen making himself a snack and I said, "You hungry again? We had a big meal, just a couple of hours ago, and then all that cake!"

He shrugged and said, "Gotta make up for something *else* I've been missing these days." I gave him a once over and noticed he'd also gained a bit of

weight. Not enough for him to look fat, he just
didn't look his usual pumped up self. Middle age
was setting in.

I grabbed the sandwich from his hand and
tossed it on the counter. He frowned and said,
"Hey! What's that about?" I took his hand, pulled
him out of the kitchen and down the hall to the
dance studio. I closed and locked the door behind
us, grabbed his hand again and pulled him toward
the stereo beside the baby grand piano. I searched
for some music, popped a CD into the player and
pushed play. I turned back around to face Jamie
and I took his hand again. I said, "Dance with me!"
He shook his head and said, "You know what
always happens, when we do that!"

I said, "So?" He smiled and said, "You sure
you're ready?" I did a pirouette and said, "What do
you think?" He laced his arms around my waist,
and we started rocking to the music. I pulled away
and did another pirouette followed by a jété, tomber
and spun around towards him. Jamie took my hand
again and we started dancing together. When the
song was over, we were kissing and he was nudging
me toward the barre. We were breathless as he
lifted me up onto the barre and tore away my
clothes. His hands and mouth took me with
urgency. It had been far too long…

****

"That was…" *Intense*. He didn't finish the
sentence, but the look in his eyes told me exactly

how he was feeling. We put ourselves back together before leaving the studio, hand-in-hand, basking in the afterglow of our love making.

In the middle of the night, just before Alexander's feeding time, Jamie reached for me and we made love again. We'd both just reached climax when our son woke up and cried out for his feeding. I turned to reach for him, but Jamie touched my arm and said, "Let me…" I waited for him to pull on his pajama pants, circle around the bed to pick him up and he handed me the baby. I checked his diaper and said, "I have to change him first."

Jamie reached for the diaper pad, spreading it out on the bed, then snatched Alexander out of my arms and laid him on the pad, while I switched on the table lamp on my nightstand. Jamie carefully changed his diaper, used a wipe to clean his hands and then handed him to me to feed. Jamie plunked down the steps to dispose of the waste. When he got back up the steps, Alexander was fast asleep in my arms. Jamie lifted him up and placed him back in his cradle and gently placed the covers on him.

He circled round the bed again, pulled the covers back and joined me in bed. He reached for me and said, "Is there any left in there for me?" I chuckled softly, slapped him on the arm playfully and said, "Really?" He made a fake frown and pushed out his lower lip. I stifled another laugh, pulled him close and kissed him on his pouty lip. He put his finger down the top of my night gown and peeked inside. He said, "They really are humungous!"

He started fondling my nipples and I said, "You know if you do that, my milk will start to come down again." He said, "So?" I rolled my eyes and let him continue to play. He then pulled my nightgown down to expose my breasts and began sucking, gently. When he'd had his fill on both sides, he looked at me and said, "Wow! It's really sweet!"

I smiled at him and said, "You'd better not do that too often, or you might steal all of Alexander's food!" His eyes sparkled as he said, "Remember what the hospital staff said about supply and demand?" I felt the corners of my mouth go up and said, "Okay my big boy, it's time to get some zees." I flicked off the table lamp and he pulled me close. I laid my head on his chest and we fell into a deep sleep.

May 25, 2002

I retrieved the meds from where I'd hidden them under the mattress, stuffing them inside one of my socks and carefully placed it underneath my clothes as I packed my bag. All was well in that stupid little hospital. The doctors were so delighted with my progress, that they let me out, long before I expected them to. Dr. Collins was especially nice to me, as long as I did everything she told me to. *I think she might have a crush on me...but I need to focus on the new plan.*

During my stay, after the usual nightly bed checks, I'd do my workout...when the goons were out of earshot. I was in very good shape for what was going to happen next. I was supposed to meet with my attorney and Dr. Collins at the end of the month. *But I need to get out of here, so I can be in the United States before then.*

I'd been taking some online courses to learn more about how everything worked. The computers at the hospital weren't as advanced as I needed them to be, but there was more than enough in my bank account to buy updated items - once I reach my destination across the pond.

Just before I was released, Aubrey brought me my laptop, so I could transfer all my money to a new account, in a new name. I purchased the plane ticket, easy as – *what do the American's call it? 'Easy as pie.' This internet thing is such a fantastic tool! The wonders of social media…this stuff is brilliant! I can do anything online!* I could even work on my accent with this site I'd found, with clips of people talking in their southern drawl and other speech patterns, so I could work on talking…*like a bluddy Yank.*

I spotted the advertisement, in the online paper. Blimy! Two prime Malibu properties, at the same time! What a bonus! It's funny how things work out when you have lots of money. I got the old tenant to vacate Celina's beach house, without notice so they would have to re-lease it in a hurry. A few clicks with a new account on this 'My Friend World' thing, and a bunch of malarkey about my new alter ego, there, and other places on the net. *And there you have it!* Keeping informed about their activities was very easy. She hadn't toured since last September, and they always do something special for Chelsea's birthday.

Who knew they would decide to go to California? It's like destiny is finally going my way!

Off to my new life as a beach bum. New life and soon to be new wife.

She has no idea what's in store for her. Better hurry. My flight leaves in two hours. But first, I need to pick a shade, and pick up the new contac lenses.   Bleached-blond-bum look.   That should do it – and a home permanent. California, here I come…

Chapter 11 • Amanda

Two more weeks flew by and Crystal gave birth to a beautiful little girl, on May 12, 2002. They named her Matilda Katherine McDougall and were going to call her Matty for short. I decided I had to call my brother Big Matty, and my niece Little Matty. It seemed fitting since Big Matty was six foot four and had a massive frame. The little family was very happy, and they stayed in their house alone with Little Matty for a few weeks, to get used to the new feeding schedule.

I only saw Big Matty occasionally, when he was working in the stables or on the grounds. Jamie decided to hire an assistant for Matty, so he didn't have to tire himself out juggling his work with his new family. It was getting very crowded around here, so we decided to build another house on the property, to serve as a residence for the staff. The contractors began their work right away and told us it was going to be done, within about four months.

The Paparazzi were hanging out a lot these days, trying to get some shots of Alexander. There were a lot of questions about whether I was going to go back to work. I always just said, "No comment." I had no intention of going back to work – ever. It just didn't seem right now, without the Bar Riders.

On June 1, 2002, we celebrated our anniversary by having a nice quiet dinner out, while the kids stayed home with Bridget and Maggie. On June 10th, we decided to celebrate Chelsea's birthday by taking the kids to Animation Dreamland, in California. It had been a long time since we'd visited my beach house. I was renting it out since we weren't using it much. The newest tenant, who'd just moved in at the end of May, said he was going to be out of town for the duration of our vacation and agreed to let us use it, while he was away, so it was just perfect. We took Bridget with us, but sadly, we had to leave Big Matty, Little Matty and Crystal behind, as they were understandably too pooped to party with us. Maggie also stayed behind, as she'd been helping out Big Matty and Crystal with Little Matty and Paddy.

Alexander, or A.J. as we'd started calling him, was growing like a weed and his full head of hair was very thick and wavy like his Daddy's. It was a rich chocolate brown, also like Jamie's, but his eyes stayed bright blue, like mine. That was the only facial feature our son and I shared.

He was definitely his Daddy's son, in every way, including his temper tantrums! But we loved him to pieces and decided to do what Mom Sylvia and Pops had done with Jamie, when *he* was young - all except for the spanking part. I told Jamie in no uncertain terms were we ever going to hit our children, no matter what. He told me that what he experienced was nowhere near what I'd been through as a child, but I said there would never be any anger, or violence in our home or we would end up in divorce court. When I told him that, he raised his eyebrows, but I knew he knew I was serious.

Our family had a wonderful time at Animation Dreamland, and we spent a glorious three weeks at the beach house. We visited the Dreamland site on most days, spending the rest of the time on the beach. Chelsea recently learned how to swim. The twins were already experienced swimmers, as Jenny had been adamant about them being able to go swimming, when she and Bobby vacationed with them. We decided to enroll A.J. in swimming lessons, as soon as he was old enough to be in the water with us. The private swimming coach we'd hired to help with Chelsea's lessons told us she could start A.J.'s classes at six months old. I was surprised to hear that, but I guessed she knew what she was doing.

We had so much fun on the beach that we decided to spend a few weeks each year at the beach house, and at least one week visiting the Dreamland theme park as well. We hoped that the new tenant would be agreeable. It sounded like he traveled a lot, so we decided to book our future vacations around his schedule.

We'd just spent the day at the beach near the end of our vacation. We returned to the house close to dinner time and we all needed to get cleaned up, to wash off the sea water and sand. Bridget took her shower first, while I got the kids ready for their baths. Before renting out the beach house, we decided to add another full bath, since our family had grown so quickly.

Bridget, who finished sooner than I expected, came into the spare bedroom, (where the twins and Chelsea were crammed in for the duration of our holiday) and offered to give the kids their bath, while I took my own shower, in the ensuite. A.J. was still napping in our bedroom. Jamie was starting supper and would likely have his shower after I had mine. I could hear the kids squealing, as they shared the extra-large-sized bathtub in the new main bathroom. I peeled off my wet bathing suit and rolled it up in the beach towel, with the intention of putting all the wet swimming stuff in the washer, when everyone was finished getting cleaned up.

I listened to make sure Bridget was finished filling the kids' bath, before I turned on the shower in the ensuite and got in. I soaped myself down with the baby soap that I always used, because my skin was sensitive to most other soaps. I grabbed Jamie's razor to shave myself in all needed areas.

I finished the task at hand and was just washing my hair, when I felt Jamie's arms slip around my waist from behind. My breath quickened when his fingers touched my breasts. "I thought you were making supper?" Jamie nuzzled my neck and said, "Most of it's in the oven and the casserole dish, with the veggies, is in the microwave, with the timer set. The oven'll shut off automatically when the stuff in there is done." I said, "Oh, so *that's* your secret to never burning the house down, whenever you have to cook and get distracted!" Jamie chuckled and said, "I have a magic stove that does whatever I tell it to do!"

I smiled and finished rinsing the shampoo out of my hair with great difficulty, while Jamie's hands wandered all over me, causing a stirring between my legs. I felt his strong hands grasp my shoulders and he spun me around, to kiss me deeply. After a breathtaking kiss that made my toes curl, and my body shiver with desire, I said, "I have to condition my hair or it'll be very difficult to brush through later." Jamie reached up over me to snatch up the conditioner from the shower's wall shelf. He snapped open the top and squeezed out a dab that barely lined his palm and went to put the bottle back on the shelf. I said, "Babe, that might be enough for *your* hair, but I need a lot more than that!" Jamie's eyes scanned me from the top of my head down the length of my hair that ended at my waist and nodded.

He added more conditioner to his palm and looked at me for approval. I shook my head and said, "More..." He kept squeezing out more and more, until I nodded and said, "That's good!" He closed the cap on the bottle and put it back in its place then put his hands together so that both hands were quite lubed up with conditioner, before applying it to my hair from root to tips. He turned us around in the shower, so that my hair was away from the water jets and he began playing again. There was still residue from the conditioner on his hands and his touch felt exquisite! I expressed my appreciation with a gasp and a moan and, "Mmmnnn! That feels really nice!"

I asked him to be careful where he wandered with his hands, as I wasn't sure if I would have a reaction to the conditioner, where I had just shaved in an intimate place. "I'm not used to shaving there. I usually have it waxed." He said, "So, you've never used a blade before?" I said, "Not *there!*" and I pursed my lips. He said, "I was *wondering* why it took you so long! I thought I would explode right out there in the middle of the bathroom watching you!" I looked up at him in surprise. "So you've been watching me this whole time?" He said, "Uh-huh! Why do you think 'Mr. Happy' is so happy to *see* you?"

I glanced down at 'Mr. Happy' and said, *"Oh, my!"*

Sweat beaded on my brow as I finished the last of the repetitions with the bar bells. I'd added a weight room to my second rental house on the beach. My plan was coming together perfectly. The surveillance system had been set up just before the happy family was due to arrive for their vacation. The security team had no idea what I'd been up to during the first few days after I'd moved in.

With my new identity, Blake Williams, I'd assumed a role in IT, so it wasn't questioned when I started bringing in a lot of technical equipment to the house. I'd learned enough with my online courses to get a feel for using the equipment comfortably. My state of financial affairs was hidden from the courts, so I couldn't post bail. While they had me locked up, I was getting all the education I needed to carry out my plan, even then.

So now, with the cameras in place, I was able to watch all their activities. I'd been following closely, while they enjoyed their time in California. They were away from the house for the most part, but that was to be expected as the property agent had told me that their main reason for coming here was to spend most of their time at Animation Dreamland. But when they returned each night, I could see everything that went on in the house. The nanny might be a problem. She kept the kids busy, while the happy couple did their dirty deeds in the bedroom.

I felt the anger simmering up from deep within as I thought of all the naughty things that horrid man did to her. With the lights off, I couldn't see for the most part. But the sound of her cries told me he was good at making her feel good. No matter, she would soon find out that he was no match for *my* skills in the bedroom. I would make her forget him…and them.

But with the nanny present, it might be difficult for me to carry out my plans. I had to wait until all of them were far enough away from Celina, before I could make the extraction. This plan left no room for mistakes. I could not underestimate his strength. I needed to make sure I whisked her away without having any dealings with the likes of Jamie Grayson. An altercation with him might prove disastrous.

Celina often takes a run of the beach on her own, so maybe, the next time she comes round this way, I'll snatch her then. I finished my work out and headed for the shower. I let the spray of the hot water melt away my stress. *I need to keep my wits about me in order to make this work. Soon, my love…soon…*

I was watching the kids out of the corner of my eye, while trying to finish a chapter in the latest romance novel. They were splashing around, squealing happily and occasionally I had to scold them, for getting the colored soap past the edge of the tub. I didn't want Amanda or I to have to do any more cleaning and laundry than necessary, as we were leaving in a few days. That colored-squirt soap was deadly to get out of light colored towels and the soft, plush bath mat was snowy white; so if they got any of that soap on it, Amanda would probably need to buy a new one, before we left and the tenant returned.

I put my marker on the page, shut the book and set it on the back of the toilet, while I went out and got a darker towel from the hall closet. I decided to swap out the white bath mat, just in case. While in the hallway, I glanced over into the kitchen and noticed Jamie wasn't there anymore. I did a beeline for the stove in case he'd gotten distracted and forgotten about our dinner – which smelled heavenly! I saw that he'd set the timer, to shut the oven off at exactly 6 p.m. and the timer on the microwave was also set to start at 5:45, so I guessed he was more on the ball than I realized. Typical Jamie - always had a plan!

I hurried back towards the kids and thought I heard some screaming coming from the opposite direction to where the kids were. I glanced at the master bedroom door and saw it was slightly open. I did another beeline towards it, and, quietly closed and locked it. I didn't want the kids to accidentally walk in on their parents. They might *never* forgive me for letting *that* happen! I heard the sound of the shower running, and a lot more than I *should* have overheard, as I closed the door. I blinked my eyes shut for just a second, as a flash of memory streaked through my brain. Steve - in those amazing black leather pants of his, that he *never* wore while he was working - and of course, *me...* taking them off...

I gave myself a mental head slap. *You're supposed to be working, dummy!* I ran back to the main bath and breathed a sigh of relief when I glanced down at the white mat – no blue and pink spots from the soap. *Whew!* I quickly placed the darker towel down in front of the tub and hung the white mat on the towel rack, farthest away from the tub, on the other side of the bathroom.

I repositioned myself on the toilet seat and resumed my reading for another few chapters, until I glanced at my watch and saw that it was a quarter to six. Dinner would be done soon. I wasn't sure if Jamie and Amanda were done their shower yet, so I pulled the plug on the tub and got the kids dried and dressed, as quickly as I could. I thought maybe I could get to the kitchen before Jamie did. I figured I would give them a few extra moments

alone, while I dished out dinner.   No such luck.
Jamie was already there...

I pulled the pans out of the oven and glanced at the microwave, to see how much time was left on the timer. I'd set the table before I went to join Amanda in the shower, so all that was left to do was dole out the food. We had a surprisingly long, luxurious shower, and other things, together, before I had to get out and get dinner on the table. I left her to get dressed. She was brushing and blow-drying her extra long locks, when I reluctantly left the bedroom, wishing there was time for another round. *Not so easy when you have four kids, one of which needed his mother's breasts every four hours!* But at least we'd gotten our fill before I left the shower.

I was smiling to myself at the thought when I heard footsteps behind me. I glanced over my shoulder and saw Bridget's damp blonde mop, out of the corner of my eye. I said, "Kids all dried, dressed and ready for dinner?" She said, "Yup! I left them in front of the T.V., bouncing around on the bed in my bedroom, watching their *Purple Dinosaurs* DVD, for the millionth time!"

I chuckled and shook my head. "Thank Heaven for the digital world. I don't know how my parents did it, without all that stuff! But then again, I seem to remember a lot of *Uncle Tyler's*

Corner, Cammy Hamster and Naughty Nelson, in *my* day." Maybe it was *Naughty Nelson* that influenced me to be a rowdy kid, always in trouble."

Bridget said, "*Who?*" I laughed and said, 'Old-guys' version of *Banana Boulevard*." It was Bridget's turn to chuckle and she said, "Okay. I was hoping to be done with the kids, *before* you got done in the shower. Let me do that, okay?" There was kind of a funny tone in her voice, when she said, "...done in the shower," and I gave her a sideways glance. She was looking at me, when I turned my head and had a full-on blush on her cheeks.

I felt the heat rise to *my* cheeks, when I cleared my throat and said, "Were we too noisy?" Bridget shook her head and said, "I was just making sure the bedroom door was closed, when I went to get an extra towel so the kids wouldn't mess up the white bathmat with their crazy, colored soap." I made a mental note to myself to talk to Amanda about maybe sound-proofing the walls, both in the beach house and at our home in Chelsea.

I stared for a moment at Bridget, while she got out the utensils, to dole out our food. She was looking haggard and I realized that we might have been unwise to let Maggie take the full three weeks vacation away from us and stay with Little Matty instead. I said, "Remind me to schedule a vacation for you, when we get back. Just let me know when you need some time off, okay?" Bridget frowned, stifled a yawn and said, "I don't need a vacation. I love my job and I love your kids! You, Amanda and the kids are like my *own* family!" I shook my head and said, "Come on, Bridget! I'm flattered that you feel that way, but you need a personal life, too!" Bridget said, "What makes you think I don't have one?" I paused for a few beats, as I stared at her for a moment. I said, "Oh, I see." I was going to ask more, but I thought better of it. *None of my business.*

I nodded and Bridget seemed to want to discuss it further, but looked at the floor instead. Not that I didn't want to be friends with my employees, but it was kind of awkward. It might be better for Amanda to broach that subject with her. Instead, I said, "The only time you take off to see your *own* family, is between Christmas and New Years." I shrugged at her silence and continued with, "My family's in Crystal Pines and I see them a lot more often than you see *yours*." Bridget said, "*My* family's in Crystal Pines, too, remember?" I said, "*Exactly!* Maybe you could come with me next time I go there, so you can stop in and at least say hi to your parents?" Bridget shook her head and said, "Amanda, the kids and I visit Crystal Pines more often, now that she's not working; and she lets me slip away from time to time, for a visit. I'm okay with that. I don't need any more, okay?"

I thought she might be worried that I would replace her if she took too much time off, so I said, "You know, the kids love you, and I would never judge you, if you asked for more time off. And since losing Jenny last year, I think Amanda might be thinking of you as kind of a friend now, you know? She probably needs more female companionship, since I only really see her hanging out with my sister and sisters-in-law, when we're in Virginia, and with Crystal, when we're in Chelsea."

Bridget looked at me quizzically and asked, "What's with the interest in what I do with my free time all of a sudden?" I winced. Maybe I was taking this too far. I swallowed hard and said, "I'm sorry. Your personal life is none of my business." Bridget took a step back and said, "No...I'm sorry. You were just making conversation and I know that you care about all your employees - a lot. I wasn't taking offense or anything. I just want to make sure that I'm doing a good job for you. I *love* being around your kids and I want to be their nanny forever – er – at least for as long as they *need* me to be."

Oh, boy! She *was* worried about her job. "Bridget, you know your job is safe here. Amanda and I...and the kids, love you as much you love us. We know how close you are to them. There's nothing for you to worry about. I just want to make sure that we're not keeping you from having a life."

Bridget smiled and said, "I promise, you don't have to worry about that, okay?" Maybe it was my imagination, but her smile seemed to carry more weight that she meant it to, and it almost seemed as though she had a bit more of a sparkle in her eyes. Since she spent most of her time with the kids and us, I couldn't imagine how she could actually *have* a personal life, *unless...*

The kids interrupted my thoughts, when they came running into the kitchen, with their mother in tow. Chelsea asked, "Daddy, what's for dinner?" I sighed and tore my attention away from Bridget, to look at my beautiful daughter and urged her and the rest of the family to sit at the table. Bridget managed to dole everything out, during our conversation, so all I needed to do was sit down next to Amanda. Chelsea already had a fork in hand, which sparked kind of a flash back to my own childhood, when my own father had to scold me, for being too anxious to scarf down dinner. I used a low and gruff voice as I said, "Chelsea..." I looked as sternly as I could manage at my daughter, who was going to put a forkful of the food into her mouth, but stopped with it midair, as she saw my gaze.

I was thankful that she was too young to recognize my eye color changes being linked to my moods, because Amanda saw *right* through me. I gave her a sideways glance, but kept my face turned towards Chelsea. Amanda's lips curled over her teeth, in an attempt to stifle a smile, because she knew I could never be angry with *any* of my kids...no matter what. She'd accused me, more than once, of being an old softy. I turned my gaze back towards Chelsea and said, "Honey, what do we do before we eat?" Chelsea put her fork back down on her plate obediently, and as quietly as she could, before she reached both of her hands out to her sides, to grasp her brother and sister's hands. We then bowed our heads, to give thanks to our Lord and Savior.

After a noisy but satisfying dinner, we chatted a bit before Bridget herded the kids back to her room, to watch yet *another* round of *Purple Dinosaurs,* while Amanda and I cleared the dishes and filled the dishwasher, with the plates and other easily cleaned items, and I filled the sink with soapy water to scrub the pots and pans. Amanda grabbed a tea towel and waited patiently for me to finish the first pot. She saw that I was pensive and asked, "You okay, babe?" I smiled and said, "Bridget and I were talking earlier, and it occurred to me that she doesn't really have a life, outside of the kids and us."

I turned my head and saw there was a Cheshire cat grin on her beautiful face. I took a breath and she said, "And how do you know *that*?" I said, "Seriously? She never takes a break, except during Christmas week, to visit her parents." Amanda finished drying the first pot and put it away. She dropped the towel on the counter, as I was working away at the next pot. She laced her arms around my waist and kissed my back, sending electrical impulses from her point of contact, down towards 'Mr. Happy.' *Dang!* She was so good at doing that!

She said, "Babe, you don't have to worry about that, okay?" I said, "But I do! I don't want our staff to think I'm some slave driver and don't care if they're happy."   Amanda sighed and continued to stroke my belly and kiss my back, which was driving 'Mr. Happy' insane! Then she rested her cheek on my back and said, "I love the way you care so much about everyone around you. Your parents did a good job of raising you, you know that?"

I stopped what I was doing and turned around to pull her close with wet, soapy hands. She didn't seem to mind as she moved her arms up, lacing them around my neck. I looked down at her as she gazed up at me. I saw how much love was in her eyes. I knew she agreed with me on the subject of Bridget's happiness. She then said, "So what do you think we should do about Bridget's happiness?" And without missing a beat, she added, "You thinking about having a tryst with her?" I had to blink a few times, to see if she was serious or not. I saw her caulk her jaw as I said, "Babe, blondes are *not* my type! And do you actually think I would do that to you? I'm *not* Terry Jackson!"

Amanda threw her head back and laughed out loud. "I know, you silly man! That was a *joke!*" And she giggled. I breathed a sigh of relief. I figured she was kidding but had to be sure that she wasn't feeling insecure about us, about our marriage. Her hands went up to dry her eyes, as she was breathless, from still laughing, when she said, "You should have seen your face!" I pulled her arms away from my neck and turned back around to finish washing the pan and casserole dish. I glanced over to the hallway, to make sure Bridget was still occupied with the kids, and not overhearing us discussing her possible loneliness.

Amanda picked up the tea towel and dried the casserole dish I'd just placed in the drain tray. She said, "It's a good idea you came up with, to build another house on our property in Chelsea, for the staff." *Man,* she was good at changing the subject! *Maybe I should just leave it alone.* But then, without missing another beat, she said, "It would give Bridget and the rest of the staff a chance to explore new horizons." I stopped scrubbing and turned my head to look at her. "New horizons?" She smiled and said, "You know that most of the staff isn't married, right?" I shrugged and said, "Yeah, so?" She bit down on her lower lip and then said, "Come, on, Jamie, really?" Suddenly, it dawned on me that maybe she knew more than *I* did, about the staff's personal lives. She had, after all been home with them a lot more, since last year…since The Bar Riders had been killed in the plane crash.

I paused for a few moments and then said, "Okay, what do you know?" She smiled that Cheshire cat smile again, and I knew she was holding back. I resumed my scrubbing and said, "Come on, Raven, *spill* it!" I looked at her again and she tilted her head to one side, as she continued drying the dish.

She said, "You really want to know?" I drew a hard breath and said, "I don't know, *do* I?" Amanda started giggling again. I could feel a hot blush rising, from my neck to my cheeks, as she said, "Well, do you?" I turned my head and said, "Yes and no. If you think there's too much information, then no." She giggled again and said, "Well, I don't really know for sure myself, but there was one night, before we left for our vacation, when I couldn't sleep. I went down to the kitchen around two a.m. and Maggie was there having a cup of tea."

Maggie had been sleeping at Big Matty and Crystal's house, because there wasn't enough room for her to sleep in our house, with our ever-growing family. And that was working out fine because of Little Matty. There was a small trailer set up near the front gates of our house in Chelsea, where the male staff took turns napping between shifts. Most of them stayed close by, unless of course, they had families to go home to between shifts.

I said, "What was Maggie doing *there?* She could have made tea in Matty and Crystal's kitchen." Amanda nodded and said, "Exactly!" I said, "Okay, so go on. What did Maggie say?" Amanda said, "Well, she really didn't say much of anything personal. She just made an excuse that Big Matty and Crystal didn't have any of her favorite tea left. She just made small talk, but she kept looking down the hall, towards Bridget's room, like something was going on. But you know, she kept steering the conversation, to distract me from looking that way."

I slowed my scrubbing down as realization kicked in. "Okay, so do you know who?" Amanda smiled and said, "I don't know for sure, but I think it's Steve." I blinked a few times, pondering the thought. "How do you know?" Amanda said, "Well, I *have* spotted them talking together, near the house, while we were out riding a few times, while the kids were napping. And, whenever Steve comes up in conversation between you and me, Bridget just seems overly interested; or when Steve comes into the house, for whatever reason, to talk to you, I could swear I've seen Bridget looking at him, you know, in that way; but, whenever I look towards her, she looks away quickly. When they're in the same room with us, it's like they're trying not to even *look* at each other. Like, on purpose, they're avoiding looking at each other when we're there."

I thought back to the last time I was giving Steve and Adam some instructions, when my cell phone trilled in my pocket. When I pulled it out to answer it, it was Bridget telling me something about the kids, while Amanda was busy feeding A.J. I could have sworn there was a flash in Steve's eyes, when I said Bridget's name, but I dismissed it. I looked at Amanda and said, "You're right. I think it *might* be Steve. And when Bridget and I were having a conversation, while you were drying your hair, Bridget seemed to deny my statements, my concerns, about her not having a personal life, a little *too* strongly." Amanda nodded and said, "I guess maybe Maggie was, you know, kind of standing guard that night, in case one of the kids woke up, to make sure they didn't wander into Bridget's room...or something." I smiled and said,

"Maybe she doesn't need a vacation after *all!*" I winked at Amanda and she giggled.

I paused a few beats and then I asked her, "So why didn't you tell me about this before? I mean, you usually love to talk about who is seeing who – at least, where our families are concerned. And you know Bridget is just like family to us." Amanda sighed and said, "You're away a lot and well, I really wasn't sure how you would feel about it. I mean, they work for us, and I didn't know if you would approve of the staff fraternizing, with each other."

I nodded and said, "I *did* kind of include that as a rule in their contracts. Maybe I should amend that part when it's time to renew them." Amanda smiled, kissed me on the shoulder and said, "You really *are* an old softy!" I looked at her and asked, "Should I be worried? I mean, we don't want them to get too distracted, with each other, so that it affects their work." Amanda smiled and said, "You need to do what's best for everyone. I mean, you *are* their boss, and it's your decision after all. But you know what they say about employee satisfaction. 'A happy worker is a productive worker'."

I smiled at Amanda. She was right. And who knew how long this thing, if there *was* one, had been going on between Steve and Bridget? It could have been years, for all we knew. And it certainly didn't seem to affect their work habits in any way. They were both fantastic at their jobs. I made a mental note to myself to have a general meeting with all the staff, when we got back. I decided to amend all their contracts, to remove the no fraternization clause. It really wasn't fair of me to expect that, since they spent ninety-nine percent of their time working for us.

We finished the dishes and I dried my hands. Amanda dried and put away the last pan, hung up the tea towel and grabbed the washcloth and wiped up the table. When the kitchen was clean, she hung the washcloth up on the faucet to dry.

She then went to the sliding doors and asked me if I wanted to take a walk on the beach to wear off dinner. I guessed she didn't have something *else* on her mind and I mentally told 'Mr. Happy' how sorry I was…

Chapter 15 • Amanda

June 30, 4:35p.m.

Our holiday was over. It was the last day of our vacation and we had to get back. Jamie said he needed to get back to work soon, so we were going to go home to Chelsea, for a few days, to spend Memorial Day together, and then fly to Crystal Pines, so we could be closer to Jamie, while he worked. I was cleaning everything up, getting it ready for when the tenant, whose name was Blake Williams, would arrive back from his trip.

I told Jamie to put the kids in the limo while I did the last of the cleaning. I hadn't met my new tenant yet, but his references seemed in order, when the renting agent did the background check. I wasn't expecting him back till the evening. It was late afternoon and I was just finishing up. Jamie and Bridget were piling the kids into the limo and putting our luggage in the trunk, with the driver's help.

I was giving the sliding doors a wipe, when I saw a tall and muscular man, with curly blond hair approach the back door. Something struck me as familiar about him, but I couldn't place it. He smiled when he saw me. I opened the sliding door and said, "Can I help you?" He said, "Hello, I'm

Blake!" I said, "Oh, hi! I'm Amanda Grayson. Sorry, I thought you said you weren't going to be back till this evening."

He shook his head and said, "I got back early and thought I would go for a swim before it got dark." I thought I detected a slight accent in his speech, but I couldn't tell from where. He was wearing a bathing suit, and was drenched, from his swimming. He asked me if I would mind getting him a towel, from the closet. I nodded and said, "Of course! I hope we left the place tidy enough for you."

I hurried down the hallway, to get his towel and I heard him step into the doorway. Just as I reached the closet door, I felt a hand come over my mouth. It felt like there was a cloth wrapped around the hand, and I smelled something funny. I suddenly had a sweet taste in my mouth. I struggled to get free, but a strong arm wrapped around my waist, gripping me hard and lifting me off my feet. And then I got dizzy and everything went black...

June 30, 4:37p.m.

I put the last of the luggage into the limo and went back into the house to check on Amanda. When I opened the front door, I called out to her, "Babe, you almost ready?" No answer. I glanced to my right, inside the small powder room and saw that it was clean and empty. I walked down the hallway and spotted a roll of paper towel and some window cleaner, on the kitchen table. I looked around the living room and didn't see her, so I thought she might have been cleaning the ensuite bath. I walked into the master bedroom and saw the door to the bath was open, and it smelled clean, so I assumed she was done in there. I scanned the bedroom and saw that it was in perfect condition, so I slipped into the hallway. I checked the other bedrooms and saw they were also spotless, so I figured Amanda must be straightening the patio chairs or something, as I'd noticed when I entered through the front door, the patio door was open.

I walked out to the patio, but I didn't see her, so I went back inside and I called out again, "Raven, are you here?" My brows furrowed. My eyes flitted around the room and saw there were little puddles on the floor, just inside the sliders and there was a trail of water all the way down the hallway, with wet footprints on the hall carpet. I followed the footprints to the linen closet, in the hallway, which was open and a beach towel was just sort of hanging there, like Amanda had intended to grab it – maybe to mop up the water on the floor. I checked the laundry room and noticed the basket of wet towels and swimsuits, sitting on top of the washer. *I thought she already* did *the laundry?* I loaded the washer, put some soap in and started it.

"Amanda? Angel, where *are* you?" My brows crunched together. *Where is she?*

I looked around everywhere...still no sign of Amanda. There was a strange odor filling my nostrils and I noticed a white cloth on the floor, just outside the main bathroom. I checked that bathroom to see if Amanda was there, but still nothing. I picked up the cloth, thinking that this was so unlike her. She normally was pretty tidy, especially with the kids around. I called out again, "Amanda! Amanda, where *are* you?" I kept running back and forth around the house and thought to myself, '*What's going on?*' I put the window cleaner and the roll of paper towels in their rightful place, under the kitchen sink and was just about to add the cloth in with the laundry. But then I lifted it up to my face and sniffed it. *That* was the source of the funny smell.

I retrieved the window cleaner again from under the kitchen sink, unscrewed the cap and sniffed it. It smelled kind of flowery, so this was definitely *not* what was on the white cloth. I replaced the cap on the cleaner, set it and the cloth on the counter and spun around and stared at the open sliding door, scanning the carpet in the hallway again. The footsteps were far too large to have been Amanda's. I originally assumed that she'd spilled something and walked through it, causing the wet footprints.

My heart started hammering wildly. I ran toward the front door, hoping she might be out there. When I reached the driveway, I looked around and then headed towards the limo. Bridget rolled down the window of the passenger side of the back seat and said, "What's the holdup?" I asked, "Have you seen Amanda?" She frowned and said, "I thought she was inside cleaning?" I shook my head and said, "I can't find her!" Bridget must have heard the panic in my voice, so she got out of the limo. She unbuckled A.J. from his car seat, snatched him up and said to the kids, "Stay here, okay?" She closed the rear passenger door, to secure the kids inside. The limo driver rolled down his window and Bridget asked him to watch the kids and lock the doors to the limo. His brows furrowed, but he nodded and did as she instructed.

Bridget followed me back into the house and I pointed towards the wet footprints. My heart was now drumming hard, and I knew if we didn't find her soon...

Bridget ran through the sliders to the patio and, putting her hand up to shield it from the late afternoon sun, peered down the beach. I was close at her heels and saw that there was no one there on each side, for quite a distance. But this didn't surprise me as Amanda owned quite a long stretch of property. Bridget said, "Did you see her at all? Did she say she was going somewhere?" I shook my head and tried to calm myself down, but my breathing was labored. I said, "I called out to her several times and she didn't answer."

We both turned and headed back into the house. I picked up the white cloth I'd left on the kitchen counter and said, "I found this on the floor, just outside the main bathroom, and there was a beach towel hanging from the linen closet, as if she started to pick it up, maybe to wipe the floors? At first I thought she might have spilled something and walked through it by accident, but the footprints in the hallway are *way* too big to be hers!"

Bridget could see that I was starting to lose it. She put her hand on my arm and said, "Jamie, I think we need to call the police. We don't have much time, before it gets dark out and we have to find her before that happens." She took the cloth with her free hand and sniffed it. A.J. was wriggling in her arms reaching for the cloth, so I took him from her. She then put her finger on the cloth and brought it to her mouth and licked it. She said, "Oh my God! This is *chloroform!*" Bridget must have known this because she was not just a nanny but also a registered nurse. *"Chloroform!"* My mind was reeling with thoughts of all the possible scenarios as I stared down at the cloth, dumbfounded.

****

I sat on the couch in the living room, giving my statement to the police officers that had shown up ten minutes after we'd called them. They put the cloth with the chloroform on it into an evidence bag and were taking pictures of the water puddles and foot prints on the carpet. I kept trying to breathe deeply, because I didn't want to have another panic attack, the way that I did back in September 2001 on the day of the plane crashes. Then again, when I was in the expectant fathers' waiting room in the hospital, after they'd pushed me out of Amanda's delivery room and called "Code Blue", just before Alexander was born.

The kids had been brought back into the house and were crying. Bridget was trying to console them. They must have been frightened out of their wits! We were going to send the limo driver away, but the police said he needed to stay, until he'd been thoroughly questioned. I leaned over, resting my elbows on my knees, and put my hands up the sides of my face. I started to rub my temples, as I was getting a headache.

The officer, whose name was Constable Morgan, was asking me stupid questions like, "Did you quarrel?" and "Does your wife often disappear like this?" What was that all about? I tried to keep my anger in check, as I knew he was just trying to do his job, but the very insinuation that Amanda and I weren't happy together was ludicrous! My response was, "No! We're happy and were just finishing up our vacation and going home!" The officer then asked, "So this is not your *permanent* residence then?" I said, "No this is my wife's beach house. She's had it since before we were married. She rents it out to some guy; I think she said his name is Blake something. Williams, I think."

The officer asked, "And where is the tenant now?" I said, "He was out of town for awhile, so we decided to come and stay here, when we took the kids to Animation Dreamland." The cop then said, "Okay, you said, he was out of town. When is he coming back?"

I blew out a sigh and said, "He's due back here tonight. We were just leaving to go back to Ohio, where we live most of the time." The officer then asked, "Do you have this Mr. William's cell number?" I shook my head and said, "I don't know, maybe it's on my wife's cell phone." The second officer was just returning to the room as he said, "Is *this* her cell phone?" and he held up the new phone I'd gotten her for her birthday, using a rubber gloved hand. I nodded and said, "She usually has it in her pocket at all times. Where did you find that?" The second officer, whose name was Constable Briggs said, "It was on the floor, just inside the linen closet." Bridget said, "So *that* must be where it happened. Because that's where Jamie found the cloth with the chloroform on it."

The cell phone trilled as Briggs was about to put it into another evidence bag. Briggs looked at the display and he said, "It says it's Daniel Landers." I said, "That's my wife's brother." I reached for the phone. The officer took another glove from his pocket, wrapped it around the cell phone. He said, "Try not to touch the phone with your bare skin, while you answer - and put it on speaker." I flipped the phone open, doing as he instructed and placed it down on the coffee table, pressing the speaker button with the glove.

I said, "Hello?" Daniel's voice rang out of the phone, "Hey, Jamie! I thought this was *Amanda's* phone." I said, "It is." Daniel said, "Well, I'm glad you're there. I wanted to talk to you both about something." I swallowed hard and was about to tell Daniel what happened, but he kept talking. He said, "I just got a call from London. It's about Ian Fairbanks." I looked at Bridget, who gave me a distressed look, when she heard Daniel say his name.

I cleared my throat and said, "What *about* him?" Daniel said, "Don't be alarmed, but I just got a call from the prosecuting attorney, from the case. He told me Fairbanks was released from the institution, several weeks ago."

My breathing started to become labored again. "Several *weeks* ago? And you're just telling me this, *now*?" Daniel said, "I just heard from the D.A. in London, ten minutes ago. I tried calling your cell, but it went to voice mail. Jamie, there's no reason to believe that he'll come after…"

"Son of a...!" I cut myself off from the curse that I continued in my head. "That must be who *has* her!" Bridget came to sit beside me and put her hand on my arm, but I waved it away. Daniel asked, me "What are you talking about?" I couldn't answer him. I felt an explosion inside my chest, and suddenly couldn't breathe.

Constable Morgan spoke up. "Mr. Landers, this is Constable Morgan of the Malibu division of L.A.P.D. We were called here today because your sister has gone missing. Apparently, she and her family have been here on vacation. They were just packing up to go back to Ohio, when an intruder may have slipped into the beach house and abducted her."

Daniel said, "Oh, my God! This just happened, with everyone there?" Morgan said, "Well it seems as though the family was just getting into the limousine outside, while your sister was still inside the house, cleaning up for a tenant's return. Daniel was silent and Morgan asked, "May I ask who this Ian Fairbanks is?" Daniel hesitated; I think because he wasn't sure who the question was directed at. He finally spoke, "He's the man that was charged with attempted murder, after he fired a gun at my sister and brother-in-law, while they were in London, England, in the spring of 2000."

Morgan cleared his throat and said, "And he was released just over two years later?" Daniel continued with, "Fairbanks was never convicted.

He was pronounced not guilty by reason of insanity and was institutionalized for Schizophrenia. When I got the call from the prosecutor, I was surprised that they'd let him out so soon." Morgan asked, "And how were *you* involved in all of this?" Daniel said, "I was there for the trial, basically on an advisory level only for Jamie and Amanda. I'm a corporate attorney here in Honeywood, Ohio, but I took criminal law, when I went to school."

Morgan said, "Okay, this is a whole other ball game now. I thought this might have just been a marital spat gone bad, but if this Fairbanks guy is here in Los Angeles, and is as dangerous as he sounds, we might have to call in Homicide or even the Feds, if this is an international case." Briggs was already on his cell calling in the big guns. I managed to catch my breath and say, "If Fairbanks is involved, it…it may already be too late! This guy is a *real* nutcase. The London police found all kinds of photographs and newspaper articles of us and our families, plastered all over his apartment walls. He'd been following our careers for years. They found pictures of my daughter that *no one* should have had!" My throat tightened and my heart raced at the thought of Fairbanks being here, and possibly trying to hurt us, again.

Daniel spoke up, "Jamie, I'm going to call you back. I want to call the prosecutor in London. He should know if there's any chance that Fairbanks fled the country. I mean how would he even have gotten away? Surely he would have been denied a passport…that is…unless he was travelling under an assumed name." I told him to call me back on *my* cell phone, as Amanda's phone was going to be taken in as evidence. He hung up.

There was a knock on the front door, which was still open, and I heard a male voice say, "Hello?" It was Carl, one of the security guards. He and Paul, the guy from the front gate, were our L.A. security team. Carl said he'd just finished doing a walk about on the beach. They didn't think anything was wrong, until the police showed up. They'd already been questioned about having seen anything out of the ordinary, or anyone suspicious walking around the property. Carl said that Blake Williams had shown up earlier, and because they recognized him as the new tenant, they let him through. When I learned that the tenant had already been there, I knew this was more than what it seemed, especially since Daniel called to inform me of Fairbanks' release.

The police had asked for the security cam footage, and Carl was just bringing it in. Morgan popped the disk into Amanda's computer, which was already booted up on the desk, in the living room. We started to watch the time in question. Morgan asked, "Can you zoom into the guy's face?" Carl did so, and there was no doubt in my mind that this was Fairbanks. His hair was dyed blonde and permed, and he'd lost quite a bit of weight, but this was the same man who'd nearly ripped our family apart in 2000. My throat thickened, and I choked on my words, "That's him! That's Fairbanks! But how did he get past us? I mean, wouldn't we have seen him?" Carl said, "Williams uses the side road and parks behind the house, so you wouldn't have noticed him arriving. I didn't think it was a big deal. I knew you guys were leaving and Williams was due back today anyway."

****

It was about thirty minutes later, when the homicide detectives showed up. They asked us a bunch of questions, many of them the same as the ones the constables had, and I was losing patience. "It's going to get dark out soon! You guys need to stop wasting time and find my wife!" The lead detective, whose name was Alan Carver, said to me, "We're just trying to get a feel for what happened here. There's no reason to believe that your wife is in any immediate danger..."

I spoke through gritted teeth, "He tried to kill us in London!" Carver held up his left hand and said, "Okay, Mr. Grayson, but if he wanted to kill any of you, or all of you, why wouldn't he just have gotten a gun and shot everybody in the place? It's obvious he wants more than to just kill your wife. He used chloroform to abduct her, which means, he may want something. It's obvious you have money, right? We may be just waiting for a ransom call here. My team is setting up a wire tap on the phones just in case."

I asked, "But what if he just wanted to kill *her?!* What if he doesn't want any money? I mean why wouldn't he have just tried to kidnap her in

London? Why try to kill us first?" The detective cleared his throat and said, "From what I've heard here, this guy's been tracking you for years. And if I understand what happened in London correctly, *you* were the one that suffered the brunt of it. Your wife just had a bullet graze her arm, right?" I'd showed him my scars when I told him about what happened. I nodded.

Carver looked around the house again. He picked up the bags of evidence, examined them further and I could tell he was thinking. When he finally spoke, he said, "I think this guy is obsessed with your wife. I think he meant to kill only you and she got in the way, because there was so much commotion. You said that there were screaming fans all around you, right?" I nodded and grunted, "Ah...yeah."

He said, "Since you've identified this guy in the video as Fairbanks, we need to call in the Feds."

I said, "So you're not even going to *try* to find her? You're just going to pass it off to someone *else*?" I was getting frantic and I knew I just sounded like a hysterical husband, but what about Amanda? We were wasting precious time! Carver said, "Whoa, wait a minute. We're not passing anything off here. This happened here in Malibu. I'm not going to drop this. But we need the Feds. They have profilers that can help in cases like this. This isn't just your run of the mill street criminal here. This guy is obviously a nut case, who has it in for your family. I'm not a shrink, but you know, as a homicide detective, we have to get into these guys heads. And if this is an international case, we have to get help on a federal level, do you understand? They have resources that we don't have. I'm here, right now, and I'll do whatever needs to be done to find your wife, but realistically, we need their help, okay?"

I looked at the floor. I felt powerless. I said, "It's always been *me* looking after Amanda. I guess I'm not the hero she thinks I am. I mean, how could I have let this happen? I was just outside, with the *kids*!"

Carver said, "Don't beat yourself up about this. No one saw this coming." I shook my head and said, "I should have *done* more. I should have hired more security. I let my guard down because I thought Fairbanks would be in that institution for good. I mean, things are not as crazy as they were when we were touring before what happened in London. But I shouldn't have let this happen! *I* should have been the one to rent out this beach house. Amanda is so trusting and she didn't even meet the guy. She let an agent take care of it."

Carver lifted his hand, palm towards me, "Mr. Grayson, this is *not* your fault. And you say she didn't even meet this guy face to face? I mean if this was Fairbanks, wouldn't she have called out when she saw him?"

I sighed and said, "When we were in court in London, she was so scared, she didn't even want to look at him. All she did the whole time was cling to me, and when she was on the stand, she had a panic attack. I don't think she would remember him, because he's lost a bunch of weight and looks like he's in much better shape than he was two years ago. And he's dyed his hair blond, and it wasn't curly before." Carver nodded. Okay, so if the patio door was open when you came back inside to look for Mrs. Grayson, he may have entered, without her even seeing him."

I said, "But then why was she reaching for a beach towel from the linen closet? He must have come and knocked on the sliding door or something, introduced himself as the tenant. If she didn't recognize him, she might have actually *let* him in." Carver nodded and said, "That's a possible scenario here."

June 30, 5:47p.m.

A team of federal agents arrived forty-five minutes later. Since there were so many strange people in the house now, the kids were scared. They were getting hungry, and Alexander needed to get fed soon as well. Amanda was still breast feeding him. He was only five months old and I had no idea how to figure out what I could feed him. He needed his mother. I felt so helpless and was starting to panic. I told Bridget to order some take-out for the older kids as I racked my brain to figure something out for Alexander.

Carver was still there; the other two constables left the house but were searching the beach for any evidence. There was a woman profiler called in to the case. Her name was Special Agent Sharon Albert. Her team was looking around the house and talking gibberish to each other - a lot of psycho babble I didn't understand. Then, one of the team noticed something that none of the other police had. He was tall and slender, not quite as athletic looking as the rest of them, and they called him Dr. Simpson.

He was the one talking the most gibberish, but I understood one thing. There were hidden cameras all over the house, including in our bedroom. Our surveillance system cameras were all *outside* the house, at the front and back doors, all down the road to the gate and along the driveway and one inside the garage. But these had been set up years ago, to protect us from intruders. There had never been anything set up *inside* the house. This was supposed to be our private space. The team searched everywhere, when the first camera was discovered. They took apart outlets, light fixtures and even the shower heads, both in the main bath and the ensuite. They found several listening devices and hidden cameras. This crazy son-of-a-bitch had been *watching* us! It was like he planned it all by renting the beach house, set all this up and was just waiting for us to come here.

My brain was starting to hurt from all the things they were saying. Schizophrenic, narcissist, delusional tendencies, psychotic behavior, possible hallucinations and disorder. How in Heaven's name were they figuring all this out just by looking at what little evidence they had? Some of the federal agents said they were from an elite squad known as The Profiler Special Crimes Task Force. They were the ones talking all this psycho babble.

I finally spoke up and said, "You guys, my son needs his mother. She's still breast feeding. I have nothing here to feed him. My poor kid is going to starve to death if we don't find my wife soon!" Bridget came to my side and said, "We can go out and get formula. We have some bottles we can use for now, okay?" I shook my head and said, "But

Amanda wanted to keep breast feeding. You know how important this is to her!" Bridget nodded and said, "I know, Jamie, but she's not here and we need to get Alexander fed, okay?" My breathing was so labored; I wondered if I wasn't having a heart attack. Bridget could tell I was having a difficult time, so she tried to get me to calm down. I said, "I don't *want* to calm down, I want to find my wife!"

Special Agent Albert walked over to me and said, "Mr. Grayson, I realize this must be difficult for you. But you need to keep it together, for your children, okay? Let *us* worry about finding your wife. Right now, you just need to talk to your kids calmly, because they will pick up on your anxiety and also have a negative reaction. Do you understand?" I could feel my throat working and realized she was right. My freaking out wasn't going to do Chelsea, A.J. or the twins any good. I said, "Okay, but I need to go out and get formula for my son."

Special Agent Albert shook her head and said, "I'm sorry, Mr. Grayson, it's not a good idea for you to leave here right now. There's camera surveillance here, and there are enough agents around the house and on the grounds to keep you and your family safe. But we can't protect you out there on your own. We'll send someone out to get formula for your son, as well as food for your older kids. Is there any particular brand of formula you would like us to look for?"

I shook my head and said, "I don't know anything about it. Amanda has been breast feeding this whole time, so I don't even know if he'll even *take* a bottle with formula in it, but he needs to be fed!" She nodded and said, "I have a couple of kids, so I think I might know what you need. I used a brand which they seemed to take well to the first time I started to wean each of them off the breast milk." I said, "Is there some sort of brand that is lactose free or something? My wife is allergic to a lot of stuff, and regular cow's milk is something she can't have. Chances are, Alexander might be sensitive as well." Ms. Albert nodded again and said, "I hear you. There are in fact different kinds of lactose free formulas out there. I'll make sure that the agent we send will get one of these kinds, okay?"

I asked her, "So you think this guy might be still watching us? Are we in danger?" Special Agent Albert replied, "We can't be certain what's going on yet, but we have a technical analyst, who's working very hard to find out the source of the camera feed. For all we know, Fairbanks could still be close by. It's possible this isn't the only beach house he's rented in the area. Your wife could be very close to us right now. Our friend in the office is a technical guru, so if anyone can do this it's her. My team and the local precinct are working very hard to search the area. There're agents knocking on doors all down the beach to see if anyone saw anything when your wife went missing."

I said, "But what if you're wrong? What if they're not here anymore? What if this guy took her, God knows where?"

Special Agent Albert replied, "That's being covered as well. We have agents and local PD searching all over Los Angeles and the surrounding areas. We've got agents showing Fairbanks' picture at all nearby airports, train stations and bus stations - both versions of himself - in case he tries to disguise himself again. It's good that you have a surveillance system here. That in itself is a tremendous help to this case. And there are roadblocks being set up on all major intersections. The police are checking everyone's ID, before letting anyone through. I promise you, Mr. Grayson, we're doing everything we can to find your wife."

"But for now, talk to your kids. Reassure them that everything is going to be okay. They're scared and need your support as their father."

I nodded and said, "Okay. Thank you for all your help. I just feel so helpless. My kids' Daddy is supposed to be their hero and I really don't feel like one right now." Agent Albert nodded and said, "You can still be their hero. It's okay to be human too, though. Let them see you're vulnerable. Just try not to freak out so much in front of them. Tell them it's okay for them to be scared; tell them you're scared too. They'll understand."

I nodded, turned away from the agent and walked into kids' bedroom, where Bridget had taken all of them to sit. When I got there, Chelsea ran to me and asked, "Daddy, where's Mommy?" My heart shattered as I gazed at their tear-stained faces. I sat down on the bed and said, "I don't know. There's a bad man who wants to hurt us, but the police are here to help us. They're going to find Mommy and bring her home to us. I'm sorry this has happened, and I wish I could tell you that Mommy's going to be okay. But I just don't know. I know you kids are scared. Daddy's scared too," and the flood gates opened. I was kicking myself for letting that happen, but the kids moved closer to me and all gave me a hug.

Chelsea climbed into my lap and gave me butterfly kisses all over my face as she said, "I love you, Daddy! Mommy's going to be okay. I promise!" I looked at my sweet little girl and wondered how she'd gotten so grown up all of a sudden. I pulled them all close, giving them a big bear hug and said, "Someone's going out to get us some food, okay?" They all said, "Yay!" And I laughed through my tears. Chelsea said, "But what about A.J.? He can't eat pizza or other stuff like that!" My heart squeezed at her thoughtfulness. "The person who's going to get our food will get some stuff for A.J. too. And thank you, my little Chelsea girl for thinking of your little brother. You're being so brave!"

****

About thirty minutes later a ton of food arrived, not just for us, but for the rest of the team of agents and police as well. The kids all piled into the kitchen to sit at the table while Bridget and I doled it out. Bridget got a bottle ready for Alexander. He was a bit fussy at first, but eventually, he settled down enough to drink some of the formula. My poor little munchkin was probably wondering what was going on and confused as to why his Mommy wasn't here.

After we finished our dinner, we were just cleaning up, when another agent arrived and walked through the front door. I could see Agent Albert talking to her in the doorway and she introduced her to Detective Sergeant Carver, who shook her hand. This new agent seemed to be someone important, as all the other agents seemed to look to her for advice. She was maybe in her mid to late thirties, had shoulder length light brown hair, standing about five foot seven inches. Special Agent Albert and the new arrival glanced over at me and started walking towards the kitchen. Agent Albert introduced the woman to me. "Mr. Grayson, this is Special Agent Eleanor Rhodes. She's our team leader. She used to work for ICSTF. That's the International Crimes Special Task Force, so she'll be able to help with this case immensely, because of her international connections."

I looked at them both and said, "Well it looks like we're going to be in close quarters for awhile, so why don't you all just call me Jamie." Agent Rhodes shook my hand and said, "Well okay, but only if you call me Ellie," and she smiled at me with bright emerald green eyes. I nodded and said, "Okay, Ellie." Ellie said, "Jamie, I want you to know you have the best team in the country working very hard here to find your wife. Just leave it in our hands and we'll get your wife back home to you as soon as we can."

The agents continued their work. They kept talking to this technical woman through their radios and numerous conversations on their cell phones. I wasn't sure what was being said, but it seemed like they were getting somewhere. I still didn't understand all the technical and psychological babble, but the agents seemed happy with their accomplishments.

I hoped for Amanda's sake they were going to find her soon. I kept looking at them while they worked. It was amazing how they figured out so much from so little - the beach towel, the chloroformed cloth, and fingerprints, which were being 'lifted' from all over the house. They apparently got a good one from the handle on the sliding door confirming that the visitor was in fact Fairbanks, but we already knew that from watching the surveillance video earlier. Ellie got a call from ICSTF, who gave them information, including the doctors' files at the institution, where Fairbanks had been treated and released.

They figured out that Fairbanks must have been obsessed with Amanda since the mid to late seventies when her career began. Apparently, he was trying to replace me in her life! I guessed that was why he tried to kill me in London.

They said that Amanda was most likely not in any imminent danger, because Fairbanks might have been delusional enough to think that she would set up house with him. The only thing that concerned them was the possibility that he might try to become intimate with her. This frightened me to my very core. After all was said and done, she might come back, but in what emotional condition would she return to us?

All that hard work on my part, from when we first met, until she could finally give herself to me completely, might be *undone*. What then? She was never comfortable talking to a shrink. And what would happen to us, to our marriage, if Fairbanks got his way before they found her?! I prayed that they would bring her home before any of that happened. All I could think about was getting her back safely away from that evil monster!

And then there were those cameras. Exactly what was he getting out of watching us like that? There were cameras in our *bedroom*, for Heaven sake! Had he been watching us making love? Had he been watching us - or the kids in the bathtub or the shower? The whole idea of it was just unbelievable and sickening.

June 30, 7:59p.m.

I dreamed about that dark and foggy tunnel again. This hadn't happened for several months now. I kept trying to get to Jamie and the kids. I could hear Alexander's cries in the distance. And I could hear Chelsea and the twins calling for Mommy. I tried to scream, but my screams were silent. All I wanted was to get to them - get back home to our house and to my family...

As I finally came back to consciousness, my head was spinning. I blinked several times to clear the fog of my dazed state. I was surrounded by darkness and there was an incessant ringing in my ears. It felt like I was back *there*...in the Secret Room...again. I tried to wrap my arms around myself, to ward off the chill that was seeping into my bones. But my hands and feet were bound, making that impossible.

I curled myself up, bringing my knees to my chest, sliding my arms up over my legs...and I shivered. My bare heels scraped across a floor of what felt like concrete. I heard scratching noises, somewhere in the distance. *Gasp!* I remembered hearing that very sound...in the Secret Room. *Rats!* Fear began crawling its way up inside me, from the pit of my stomach.

What is this place? I searched through the recesses of my brain, trying to remember what happened. The last thing I could remember was cleaning up at the beach house, getting ready to go back home. And there was a man...with blond, curly hair...

I tried to roll over to the side, in an effort to get myself on my feet, but the plastic zip ties, cutting deeper into my wrists and ankles, made that impossible. I gave up and leaned back on my behind again.

"Help! Somebody help"! The sound of my cries was muffled, as I realized I was gagged with some sort of cloth and there was tape over my mouth. Since my hands were tied together in front, I was able to reach up and remove the tape and pull the cloth from my mouth. I started to cry out, "Somebody please help me!" I heard footsteps above me. It was as though I was in the basement, only there wasn't a basement in my beach house. And as far as knew, there weren't any houses with subterranean floors in the area. That was what attracted me to the house years ago. No basement meant, no panic attacks.

This was very confusing to me. I blinked a few more times, as the haze in my brain started to clear. There was that tall, blond-haired man who'd come to the back sliding doors and introduced himself as Blake Williams, my tenant. I remembered him asking me for a towel, which I went to get from the linen closet. And then, I felt like I was being suffocated.

I wondered how long I'd been down here - *and why did that blond man look so familiar to me?* It was as if I knew him in another life...or something. I kept calling out, "Hello! Can someone hear me?" Suddenly, I found myself start to hyperventilate. Panic was setting in. *Breathe, Amanda, breathe! I need to get out of here and back to my family; somehow, some way, I have to get home!*

There was a building tightness in my chest. *Oh, yeah.* I could feel my breasts were really engorged, so it must have been past A.J.'s feeding time. *Where am I? Are the kids and Jamie okay?* What if something also happened to them? *Should I cry out?* If I was still near the beach house, no one would likely be able to hear me because of the surf. The waves from the ocean would be deafening and my cries would most certainly go unheard. But I still could hear footsteps above me. Maybe my captor would come down and I could somehow talk him into letting me go. Jamie and I had lots of money. *That would be good leverage, right?* If I'd been kidnapped, then Jamie would be negotiating my release. I knew he'd offer them everything we had to get me back.

All I had to do was be patient, right? I tamped back the tears and hoped my captor - or captors, could be bought. I hoped against hope that they were not after something else. Money could buy anything, right? Money would buy my freedom. But what would they do to me first? Or maybe they'd just take the money and run and God forbid, do something to hurt me - or worse. Maybe they had no intention of giving me back to my family. Hot tears stung my cheeks now. *Stop it! Don't let them win!* I had to keep it together if I was going to figure out how to get out of here. Maybe, if I felt my way around, I could find something sharp to cut through my bonds. I rolled myself onto my knees again and, leaning on my elbows, tried to drag myself across the cold, damp floor. I was still wearing my skirt and tank top, and no shoes. My knees and elbows stung, but I dragged myself around the room...hopefully the rats would leave me be...

If I somehow managed to get free, it would be very difficult for me to run without shoes, even if I was anywhere near the beach, it would be tough. What if it was dark out? Would I even be able to find my way home? And where were Jamie and the kids? Were they still at the beach house? My heart was thumping, hard. I knew I had to calm myself down, or I'd end up in a panic. I found myself against a wall. Okay, maybe I was getting somewhere. I kept moving along the wall in hopes of finding something sharp enough to cut my bonds.

****

It seemed like it had been hours. I was just moving in circles around the room. I kept hitting another wall. I'd still found nothing, no tools, or even fodder for the rats. Luckily, I hadn't come across any of the critters that lurked in the distance...somewhere. Maybe they were in the walls, outside this damp, dark, cold room. Eventually, I came across the cloth and tape that had been my gag. I tried calling out again. "Help! Somebody, please? Just let me out! I can pay you! Please, I'll give you whatever you want! I have lots of money! Please just let me go! I won't tell anyone, I promise, just please let me go home!"

My throat burned from crying out. *I need to conserve my energy.* I stopped screaming, as I knew it wasn't doing any good. *Defeat!* Hot tears stung my cheeks again. *Damn it! I need to stop this!* I needed to stop crying. "Just get a hold of yourself, Amanda. There has to be a way out of this, somehow," I said out loud.

My knees and elbows were raw now, from dragging myself around on the cold, hard cement floor. I gave up and rolled back on my behind. I pulled my knees towards me, lifted my hands to feel the broken skin on my knees and winced. I sighed and said, "So much for that!" Another hour maybe went by. Who knew how long I had been here? I found myself thinking about the secret room - all the time I'd spent down there, as a child. But at least back then, there'd been a cot and blanket. It was uncomfortable, but at least it kept me from catching my death of a cold. What if they kept me down here and left when they got their money? I would surely starve, or die of pneumonia, or some other affliction. *Stop it! You need to get hold of yourself. Think! What can I do?*

All at once, I heard a lock being unlatched. There was someone coming. I heard footsteps descending on what sounded like a wooden staircase. And then, I saw a light flicker on. It was dim, but it sounded like there was a pull string on the ceiling down here. I saw a man coming towards me. It was him. Blake Williams - the man to whom I'd trusted to rent out my beach house. The man I'd never met before today – *or was it yesterday already?* Who knew how long I'd been down here? As he moved closer, he looked at me with such love in his eyes. Why did he look so familiar to me? I saw there was a tray in his hands. He was bringing me food. My stomach was growling, *but should I even eat the food he was offering?* Maybe he'd poisoned it! Maybe he'd already gotten his ransom money and was just getting rid of me now.

I said, "Please, please, just let me go! My baby needs to be fed. He's never had anything but breast milk! Please!" The man set the tray down in front of me. I said, "I can't eat if I have my hands bound like this." He reached his hand up to my face and, wiping my tears away, he said, "There, there, Celina! It's going to be alright." I said, "No it's not! My baby boy needs me!" Williams continued to stroke my cheeks and hair but didn't acknowledge anything I was saying to him about Alexander. It was as though he wasn't hearing me. He reached for the glass with the straw and put it to my lips. I shook my head and said, "Is there any wheat or dairy in that? I can't have milk or juice that's been made from anything but berries, but not strawberries, or I'll get sick.

He said, "It's just water." Finally, he was hearing me. I took a sip, carefully. He said, "Keep drinking. You need to keep up your strength!" When I noticed that I wasn't passing out or feeling funny from the sip I'd taken, I took some more, but just enough to wet my mouth. He put the glass down. I was hoping that it would be made of glass, so I could break it, to somehow get myself free, but the beverage container was just cardboard - a fast food type of glass with a plastic straw.

He picked up the food that was on the plate, also made of cardboard – a flimsy paper plate. He tried to pop something into my mouth but I jerked my head away. He put his left hand on my chin, turned it towards him, and, using his thumb, he opened my jaw, forcing the berry into my mouth with his right hand. I was so hungry that I relented and ate it. It was a blueberry. He kept feeding me the blueberries until the pile on the plate was gone. He then picked up the glass again and put the straw in my mouth. I took a few gulps of the water.

I looked at him and said, "I have money. My husband can give you anything you want! We have lots and lots of money. Please, I promise, I won't tell anyone about you. I just want to go home!" And the flood gates opened. Williams put his hand up to my face and dried my tears again. He said, "This is going to be your new life, Celina! And, when I can trust you enough to remove your restraints, you can come upstairs and we will live happily ever after!"

Wait, what? Suddenly, it hit me like a ton of bricks! I recognized the voice. Oh my God! This was Ian Fairbanks! Oh no! No, no, no, NOOO! I thought he was in an institution? How did he get away? *Gasp!* Had this been his plan all along? Was that why he tried to kill Jamie?

I thought back to that fateful day in London. The bullet just grazed my arm. He must have been aiming for Jamie all along. Did he want Jamie out of the way, so he could have me for himself? I saw a flicker of realization in his eyes, as though he'd read my mind, for he said, "He wasn't right for you, anyway. I'm going to take good care of you, I promise!" I shook my head and my eyes stung again. I said, "Please, please let me go! Please! I just need to go home!" Fairbanks replied, "You *are* home." And he kissed me on the lips. I was stunned at this bold move. I felt my stomach roll at the thought of someone other than Jamie kissing me. Fairbanks then got up, picked up the tray and started walking back towards the steps. I called out to him, "Please tell me what happened to my family! Are they alright?"

Fairbanks turned on his heel to face me and said, "Don't you worry about a thing. I'll take good care of you. We can make our *own* family now." And with that, he turned back around, pulled the string to turn out the light, and walked back up the steps, leaving me there alone again – in the dark…

Chapter 19 • Jamie

June 30, 9:51p.m.

Daylight was gone and Amanda was still not home with me, with us. The team of federal agents was still in our beach house and as yet hadn't figured out where she was. The kids had long since eaten their dinners and gone to bed. It was difficult to get them to settle down for the night, but I managed to work up enough emotional strength to read them their three stories and sing three songs, without Amanda. Something that seemed so simple in the past was suddenly one of the hardest things I'd ever had to do. My eyes burned at the thought of having to do this...alone...without her. I knew I had to hold it together, for the kids' sakes. Alexander had been quite fussy without being able to suckle his mother's breast. But between Bridget and I, we managed to get him to take half of the bottle of lactose free formula, brought home with the dinner by one of the agents.

The kids managed to fall asleep peacefully an hour after they had their dinner. I left Bridget in their bedroom to watch over them, despite the officer that was placed just outside in the hallway and another posted outside their bedroom window. I paced the hallway, furiously throughout the rest of the evening. While the team of agents continued their work of trying to figure out where Fairbanks may have taken Amanda, a thousand images raced through my mind of what that monster could be doing to her. My heart was beatng frantically in my chest, while I continued to fret over her welfare.

There was no word from the outside, at least none that they would share with me of the roadblocks and constant searching of the beach and surrounding area. I overheard the team talking about CCTV footage and this invisible person named Tina, who was continuing to maintain contact with phone calls to Agent Ellie and the rest of her team. Most of their conversations were centered around the psychology of it all, Fairbanks' profile and more chatter I didn't understand. I knew they were doing their jobs, but I felt helpless while I listened to it all.

All I knew was that my wife was gone and I couldn't fathom having to spend the rest of my life and raising our kids, without her. I felt a hand on my shoulder and spun around, ready to take a swing at the agent, who put up his hands, palms out in front of me. "Whoa! Easy, Mr. Grayson! I think you need to calm down. Why don't you sit down and watch some television or something?" I blinked a few times. Was he serious? At a time like this? I shook my head and said, "Are you crazy? My wife is out there with that lunatic, who is doing Lord knows *what* to her and you think I should watch TV?"

The agent tilted his head to one side and caulked his jaw as he said, "Mr. Grayson, please. I understand that you're worried. But you're starting to wear a trench in your carpet here," and he pointed towards the floor beneath my feet. I glanced down and saw that he was right. I'd left my running shoes on, and the carpet was starting to look worn and flattened. Amanda had recently remodeled the beach house before renting to the new tenant, and the carpet was looking much too used to be brand new. I swallowed, hard and said, "I just…feel so helpless! I feel like I should be doing something!"

The agent, an African American, tall and slim with genuine concern in his eyes licked his lips and said, "I know it seems hard, but we're doing everything we can to find your wife. Let us do our job. Find something to keep your mind occupied. There's no sense in getting all worked up. Your kids need you to be strong for them. When we find Mrs. Grayson, she'll probably need you to be well-rested and calm when she comes home. Maybe read a book?"

I closed my eyes and took a few deep breaths to ebb the anger that was boiling deep inside of me. It would do absolutely no good for me to lose my temper. He was right. *I need to let these agents do their jobs.* And the last thing *they* needed was to worry about me. "I'm sorry, sir. You're right. And thank you for…being here and…" I couldn't finish. My emotions were starting to surface. I rubbed my palms over my bearded face. The agent nodded and our eyes locked in a silent message. It seemed as though he really cared about the people he helped in his every day work. I nodded and turned towards my own bedroom. I turned back to face him and said, "I'll leave you to your work." The agent's lips curved up into a smile that didn't touch his eyes. It was encouraging, nonetheless. I sat down on the bed and buried my face in my hands. I leaned backward and tried to relax on the mattress that Amanda and I had shared and made love on, countless times. The memories we'd made, here in this very room…all over the house, flitted through my brain. And some time afterward, I fell asleep.

****

July 1, 12:21a.m.

I awoke with a start. I turned my head and stared at the alarm clock on the bedside table. It was after midnight. I must've been asleep for at least two hours. I sat up and swung my legs over the side of the bed and headed towards the ensuite bath. I turned the tap on in the sink, splashed water on my face and gazed at my reflection in the mirror. I leaned down, gripping the edge of the sink. I glanced down at my hands and realized that I was grasping the sink so hard, my knuckles were turning white. Releasing my grip, I reached for the towel to dry my face.

I ventured out into the kitchen and found the team of agents and police detectives was still hard at it. Agent Ellie had her cell phone in her hand, and she had it on speaker. But something was different. Something in the case must have broken wide open because they suddenly sounded very excited. I could hear Special Agent Ellie saying, "Thank you so much, Tina! You're a legend in your own time!" She ended the call and I stood there with baited breath, waiting for them to tell me something. I assumed that Tina was the technical wizard Special Agent Albert had been raving about earlier. And then, Agents Ellie, Albert, Simpson and some of the rest of the team started heading for the sliding doors to the beach.

My brows slammed together and I said, "What's going on?" But they were already out the door.   There was a dark SUV parked just outside and the agents were all reaching into the back. They started donning bullet proof vests and checking their weapons. Detective Sergeant Alan Carver, who was following close behind the agents, turned to me on his way out and said, "Wait here!" I said, "No way! I'm coming with you!" Carver put up his free hand, holding his palm outward and said in a very assertive tone, "STAY...HERE!" And with that, he grabbed his gun with both hands and disappeared into the night...

****

July 1, 1:42a.m.

It was almost two a.m. and I hadn't heard anything yet. There were two agents left in the house and I said to them, "Please, tell me what's going on!" Agent Andrew Taylor responded, "They think they've located the place, where your wife is being held - or at least where the video feed source is located. There's a beach house about a mile down the coast, where Tina locked onto a signal. She's really good at what she does. She had to hack into his system.

My heart was thudding, wildly. I asked him, "Is she alright? Is my wife okay?" Agent Taylor said, "They haven't found her as yet. They're just discussing how they're going to get into the place. They noticed some surveillance cameras around the house, so they need to try to avoid being spotted by Fairbanks. He's probably watching the video feed constantly. Tina's working with the local power company, asking them to cut the power in the house. This way they can enter the premises, without being detected. We're counting on Fairbanks not catching on that we're onto him. She disabled the actual live feed from your beach house hours ago and has been running a loop of tape showing all of us agents here, still talking. And she managed cut the sound, so Fairbanks can't hear us."

The agent cleared his throat and continued, "Tina wants them to cut the power to a few houses down the beach, so it looks like a normal power outage happening. So be prepared for this house to lose power. Tina's trying her best to exclude your house just in case Fairbanks isn't in the other house. If he's out there somewhere, on your property, watching us, then he may come after you and the kids. Cutting the electricity *here* would leave us blind, even though there are several agents surrounding this place, including two with your security team. Tina's hoping that this house isn't on a direct line to the other houses around Fairbanks' other place."

I made a mental note to myself to invest in some generators for both this house and our house in Chelsea, for the future. *I need to step up to the plate and be a better protector for my family, from now on - if Amanda gets out of this alive. I need to upgrade everything...and get more security staff. Yeah...that's what I'll do...*

My heart stuttered. I must have been having an adrenaline spike because I was suddenly shaking uncontrollably. Agent Taylor put his hand on my shoulder and said, "My team is very good at what they do. Hopefully this'll be over soon, without anyone getting hurt." I nodded and said, "I hope s-so." Agent Taylor said, "Why don't you check on your kids, okay?" I knew he was just trying to distract me – to keep me busy, but I did as he instructed.

I shuffled over to the kids' bedroom where all my little angels were. The night light was on in there, so I could see their faces and they were still fast asleep. Bridget was sitting in a rocking chair next to Alexander's cradle. A.J. was also sleeping soundly and Bridget was reading her latest book of interest.

She looked up and said, "Anything?" I said, "No news, but they're outside another beach house and they think he's there. I sighed and thought, "Well at least *most* of my family is safe!" I heard my cell phone ding and slipped it from my pocket. It was another text from Joey, asking me if there'd been any news. I'd called Daniel back earlier and told him that it was in fact Fairbanks who'd taken Amanda. I then dialed Joey's cell to tell him what had happened. Between answering his, Daniel's and Matty's texts, I'd been kept busy for a while before I'd fallen asleep. I answered the latest messages, before going back into the hallway and beginning, yet again, to wear more marks into the carpet.

I was still feeling very powerless. I wanted to run outside and down the beach to find Amanda myself, but I knew the agents would likely stop me before I got too far. It probably wasn't a good idea anyway, as I'd be distracting them from doing their jobs of finding and saving Amanda. But I couldn't help feeling that I was doing nothing to help. I needed to know that she was safe from harm.

What if when, or even *if* they found her, it was too late? What if he'd already killed her? I couldn't imagine trying to raise our beautiful children without her. I thought about everything that had happened to us over the years and prayed my heart out.

I found myself making deals with God, asking for Amanda's safe return. After everything we'd been through, and after Melinda died, I didn't think I could survive another loss – especially not in *that* way. I found myself on my knees in front of the kids' rooms begging God for another chance with my wife. I couldn't live without her! There were hot tears streaming down my face and all I could think of was getting her home, safe and sound. I took several deep breaths, to prevent another panic attack. I thought of all of these years, what Amanda had endured with her own panic attacks. I knew now, exactly what that felt like.

I dried my cheeks with the back of my hand and then, I got up and made my way to the kitchen. I snuck past the two agents, who were distracted, talking on their phones. I made it to the sliding doors, opening them quietly. *I need to get to her!* I started running in the direction the other agents had been going when they left, almost two hours ago. All I could think about was getting to Amanda, come hell or high water…

I'd been running for God knew how long when I stopped to catch my breath. I looked back and didn't see anyone coming after me. My lungs were bursting. I peered through the darkness and spotted some outdoor lighting illuminating the shoreline, guiding me toward her. Just before I got off my knees in the hallway, something clicked in my brain. If she was captive in some dark place, how would she react? I realized I'd forgotten to mention to the agents that Amanda was severely claustrophobic, and what her reaction to being in a small enclosed space could be like. I was kicking myself for not telling them that she was prone to panic attacks.

What if they went in there and started shooting up the place and Amanda accidently got caught in the crossfire?! *I need to be there!* I started running down the beach again. I had to be close. I stopped again to look around and catch my bearings. I'd never been this far down the coast before. Everything in the dark seemed ominous and threatening. What if Fairbanks was counting on the fact that I would come and find her? I had to give myself a mental head slap for doubting myself and my abilities.

I *was* after all the man of Amanda's dreams, *literally*. After having read those pages in her diary just over seven years ago, I made it my mission in life to be that man that she'd always dreamed about. I knew I probably wasn't even half of that man, but in her eyes, I was. I had to get to her! Suddenly, I felt a hand on my shoulder and I almost jumped out of my skin! I spun around, ready for a fight, in case it was Fairbanks; but I saw that it was in fact Agent Simpson, the one that found the first hidden camera at the beach house. He shone the flashlight into my face and said, "*Whoa!* Are you trying to get yourself killed? I thought you might be Fairbanks!"

I squinted, protecting my eyes from the bright beam of light as I said, "I'm sorry, I had to come. There's something you don't know about my wife. She was terribly abused as a child and during her first marriage. Her father used to lock her in some sort of secret room, behind the wine cellar of her home, after being severely beaten. She suffers from extreme claustrophobia and is prone to horrible panic attacks. If your team goes in there with guns blazing, she might react terrily and get hurt!"

Agent Simpson nodded and said, "I'm glad you told me, now go back to your beach house!" I shook my head and said, "I have to be there when you find her! I'm one of the only two people in this world who can calm her down, when she has one of those episodes." Simpson shook his head and said, "We're highly trained profilers, who've dealt with hundreds of situations like this. We can handle it, trust me!"

I shook my head and held my ground. I said, "She doesn't talk to shrinks. It doesn't matter *how* well trained you are, I'm telling you it won't work! I'm not going anywhere. I need to be there for her!" Simpson lifted his free hand to his ear, seeming to push a button just below his earlobe. I heard him explain the situation to whomever was on the other end and he ended the conversation with, "Tread lightly. This woman has suffered severe trauma in her life and her husband says he needs to be there, when we go in."

I didn't hear anything but his side of the conversation. But he eventually turned to me and started to remove his vest. He handed it to me and said, "Here, put this on." He explained how to fasten the Kevlar vest. It was tight, since Simpson was a smaller build than I was. But I managed to get it secured. He looked as though he was receiving another message. Then he said, "Okay, Tina's going to turn the power off in about thirty seconds. When that happens, we need to move fast. Follow me and don't get distracted. Stay right behind me. You're unarmed and we need to protect you as well as your wife, should we find her. I know you know what it feels like to get shot, and I'm sure Mrs. Grayson would never forgive herself, or us, if we let that happen again. Do you understand?" I nodded. I heard him counting down from ten, so I assumed that Tina was ready to turn the power off. I braced myself to follow Agent Simpson into the second beach house...

Chapter 20 • Amanda

July 1, 2:29a.m.

I was still in that dark, cold and damp place. I felt a chill in my bones to the point where my teeth were chattering. Or was this fear? I called out to my captor. "Can I please have a blanket? It's cold down here! Hello! Please?" I heard the footsteps above me again. I'd long since given up on the idea of finding anything sharp to undo my bindings. This basement, or whatever it was, was empty short of me being down here. I prayed very hard to God, asking him to protect my family and to let me please be with them again. I kept taking deep breaths, so I wouldn't have a panic attack.

I started to cry out again, as I was worried I'd get sick from being so cold. It was the end of June in Malibu, but the night winds could be chilly here. And there was obviously no heat in this room. "Hello! Please, can I have a blanket! I'm very cold!" There were more footsteps and finally, I heard the lock to the door at the top of the stairs being unlatched. Maybe I could distract Fairbanks and somehow get out. But my feet were tightly bound, so I knew running was impossible. Maybe I could convince him to remove my restraints if I promised to be good.

Fairbanks came down the steps and pulled the light chain at the bottom of the staircase. He was holding a thick quilted comforter. It looked like one of mine. He stopped short, about six feet from me, tossing the blanket towards me. I said, "Thank you! Can you please cut me loose? I promise I'll be good. I won't try to run. My wrists and ankles are very sore!" Fairbanks laughed and said, "Nice try, my love - maybe another time, when you're convinced that I'm the man for you." And with that, he spun around and walked back to the light, pulled the chain, climbed the stairs and closed and latched the door, putting me yet again in the darkness. I let the flood gates open. What was the point in trying to remain calm? I was *never* going home now! This guy was so crazy - he actually thought I was going to fall in love with him! I kept thinking about Jamie and the kids.

I pulled the comforter over me as best as I could, but I still couldn't get comfortable. The floor was ice cold and the blanket would not co-operate with me. I tried to somehow wrap the blanket around me, but it wasn't working. I had to be content with it just covering my arms and legs. Well, at least he was kind enough to give me the blanket. I wondered how much time I'd spent down here. Who knew how long I'd been passed out?

I started to hum softly to myself. I was singing myself to sleep, just like I had when I was locked in the 'Secret Room', when I was a child. Who knew I would come full circle in my life, to end up yet again in a cold, damp and dark basement? I kept up my singing, but I couldn't lull myself to sleep. I kept thinking how long it would be before he figured out that I would never love him. Jamie was my heart, my forever love and my life. I would never forgive this man for taking me away from him and my children.

I thought of a song that I remembered my mother singing to me when I was a child. It went:

Hush little baby, don't say a word
Mama's gonna buy you a mockingbird
If that mockingbird won't sing
Mama's gonna buy you a diamond ring
If that diamond ring won't shine
Mama's gonna...

Wait! What's that sound? I heard more footsteps upstairs. This time it wasn't just Fairbanks. There were more footsteps, more people. It was quiet, but I heard it! *Does Fairbanks have accomplices?* Then, I heard shuffling noises. And there was shouting going on. It was muffled, but there were most certainly several voices involved. Okay, maybe it wasn't any accomplices; maybe it was Jamie or the police! I started crying out, "Hello! Somebody please help me!" I heard more shouting and then I heard more shuffling noises and then, I heard it.

The same crack that I'd heard in London. There were at least three of them. It was gun shots! All I could think about was the possibility of Jamie getting hurt again. *No...no....Nooo!* I started to panic. What if Jamie was trying to find me and he got hurt by that monster again! I started to hyperventilate, and I started to scream, "Jamie! Jamie! Oh, God! Please, not my sweet Jamie!" Hot tears stung my cheeks as I imagined the worst. My head was spinning and I knew I was heading into a full blown panic attack. My heart was hammering in my chest and I couldn't breathe. All I could do was scream, "Jamie! Jamie!" I was sobbing. *Jamie, please, God don't let him be dead!*

There were all kinds of noises now but my heart was racing so fast, and my vision was blurred. It was still dark and then, I thought I saw flashes of light everywhere - maybe flashlights? Maybe Fairbanks was back to kill me! My chest felt like it was going to explode. There were still flashing lights everywhere, but all I could see were shapes all around me. I felt a hand on my shoulder and I almost jumped out of my skin! There were several people in the room – *or am I imagining this?*

Maybe I was hallucinating. I was gasping for air and my heart felt like it was going to jump out of my chest. I was still sobbing and screaming for Jamie. Suddenly, I saw what looked like a knife coming out of nowhere. I started screaming again and again, "Jamie, Jamie!" Then, I was suddenly free. Someone had cut my restraints. And I felt some familiar arms around me. I thought I heard Jamie talking to me in a soothing voice.

But this *had* to be a dream! Jamie was dead! I heard the shots! Was I in Heaven with him now?

The arms around me were warm and strong and, rocking me back and forth. Was this Fairbanks? I tried to pull free and started screaming again. But the arms held fast around me. I still heard a soothing male voice and his warm breath on my neck. "Shhh! Raven, it's okay now! You're safe! I'm here! I'm here!"

I heard the pull string from earlier and the light flickered on. I blinked several times, to try to shake the effects of the panic attack. My breathing finally slowed down and I looked up and saw Jamie's beautiful eyes looking at me. Was I dreaming? Tears were still streaming down my cheeks, but my vision was clearing. It *was* Jamie! It was Jamie, and he was okay! "Jamie?" He answered back, "Yes, darlin', it's me and you're safe now. Fairbanks is dead. He can't hurt you anymore." I felt his lips, those beautiful, soft lips on mine, and I knew it was him. He was here with me and I was safe. I held on, tightly, drinking in his beautiful scent, praying he wouldn't let go.

I could see people all around me, but they let Jamie work his magic with his soothing voice and his strong hands, stroking my back and hair and wiping my tears away. After what seemed like an eternity, he gently lifted me up in his arms and carried me up those steps and out of the house that had been my prison, for God knew how long. I could see flashing lights all around me. There were several black SUV's parked in front of wherever we were. There were all these people with black vests on that said, 'FBI' and 'Police', standing around us, while he held me. Jamie, the man whom I thought I would never see again - my handsome Jamie. He was here and we were both safe.

I said, "Where are the kids? Are they okay? Did he hurt them?" Jamie shook his head and said, "They're snug in their beds at the beach house, sleeping. They're with Bridget and there're a bunch of cops there too. They're safe, I promise you, they're safe and so are you!"

I looked into Jamie's beautiful eyes. They were changing back and forth between turquoise and green – which meant he was happy, but concerned.   I leaned into him and said, "Let's go home, okay?" Jamie smiled at me, glancing out sideways and said, "Well, if *these* guys *let* us!" There was an ambulance in front of us, where two E.M.T.s were urging Jamie to set me down, In the back of the vehicle. Jamie walked toward the ambulance and put me down, gently. When I pulled away from him, I noticed he was wearing one of the police vests. My brows knitted together as I saw him pull at the Velcro straps, unfastening the vest.

The medical rescue team started examining me, checking my vitals and swabbing at the scrapes on my elbows, knees and shins. My heart was still racing, but my breathing slowed down. After they were sure that I was relatively unharmed, they let me go, but there were some agents that wanted to question me. I said, "I just want to go home now, *please!*" Jamie introduced me to a bunch of people by their first names. It was as though he was friends with them. He said, "This is Alan, he's a homicide detective." He handed another cop the vest he was wearing and said, "And this is Special Agent Gerard Simpson." The tall and thin man took the vest and said, "Thanks." Jamie then gestured towards another two women and said, "And these ladies are Ellie and Sharon. They're special agents from the PSCTF. That's short for Profiler Special Crimes Task Force. And, oh yeah, there's this computer wizard named Tina that I hope to meet in person some day. She saved our lives. She's the one who *really* found you."

My jaw nearly dropped on the ground. I gaped at all the people around us. They were smiling and all took turns hugging me. Sharon said, "Your husband is a really great guy. I think if he hadn't insisted on coming with us, you might still be downstairs in that basement, screaming your head off." And she smiled. I blushed and said, "Yeah, I have these really bad panic attacks..." Sharon nodded and said, "Yeah, we know. Jamie here slipped past the agents that were trying to protect him, at your beach house, and ran all the way here, till Gerry here almost shot him!" I heard chuckles all around me.

The woman named Sharon was pointing to Agent Simpson. I frowned and gasped all at the same time. The agent must have seen horror in my eyes as he stepped forward, putting his hand on my shoulder and said, "I promise, I wouldn't really have shot him! He was just so stubborn about going in with us. I thought he might have been Fairbanks when I spotted him running down the beach towards us. He ran right past me, so I put my hand on his shoulder and he spun around like he was going to hit me or something! You should have seen him! There was *fire* in his eyes!”

Jamie cleared his throat and said, “Well, nobody messes with my wife!” They all laughed, then Ellie said, “Well, if you ever want to retire as a singer/musician, maybe you should come and work for our team! If you can outrun us, then maybe you’re in pretty good shape for the job!” Everyone laughed again. After a few more minutes, they said we could go home, but they needed to come back in the morning to question us thoroughly, so they could finish their reports.

Sharon offered us a ride back to the beach house. When we got there, I ran to the kids’ room and kissed them all good night. Bridget was standing there in her nightgown and started crying. I stepped closer, hugged her and said, “I’m okay, really!” She smiled through her tears, as Jamie put his arms around me, kissed me on the cheek and said, “You gave us the scare of our lives! This can’t ever happen again!” I smiled at him, grateful to be home and said, “No - never again! What time is it and…er…what *day* is it?”

Jamie laughed softly and said, “It’s about four-thirty in the morning.” He looked at Bridget and said, “She went missing, what - about twelve hours ago?” Bridget nodded. Jamie said, “I think we should go to bed. The kids are going to be up soon and I don't think you got any sleep where you were either." I said, "You got any food? I'm starving!" Jamie smiled and said, "There might be some Chinese food left in the fridge. We ordered take-out, since they wouldn't let us leave." We walked back into the kitchen and Jamie got out the food, put it on a plate and popped it into the microwave for me. I ate my fill and then we went to bed. I'd never been so happy to do something as normal as fall asleep, with my head on Jamie's chest, his arms wrapped around me…

Chapter 21 • Amanda

I felt the bed bouncing all around me and I woke to the sound of the kids giggling and shouting, "Mommy! Mommy! Wake up!" I glanced at the digital alarm clock on my nightstand and saw it was already eleven fifteen. Jamie was standing beside the bed, smiling down at us as he said, "I tried, but I couldn't hold them off any longer." I felt my lips curve up as I said, "Best way to get woken up, ever!" I gave all three of them butterfly kisses all over their faces and murmured, "I missed you soooooo much, my little angels!"

Jamie sat on the bed beside me, amongst the kids, and we started a tickling match. We were all laughing so much, our sides hurt. Above all the ruckus, I heard the doorbell ring. Jamie said, "I guess they're here." I frowned and asked, "Who's here?" Jamie said, "The Federal agents and probably Sgt. Carver. They're here to get our statements. You know, duty calls and they need to get their reports all straight." I groaned and said, "I wish we could just forget that yesterday ever happened!" Jamie looked excited as he started talking animatedly, "You know, they were incredible. I mean, I never thought it would be like that. These people are fantastic. And although it felt like it was taking an eternity while it was happening, they found you in less than twelve hours. Who knows what could have happened to you if it wasn't for them?"

I asked Jamie to stall them for a bit. I wanted to jump in the shower and make myself presentable. I figured I looked hideous from all the crying and screaming night before, and my throat was very sore and scratchy. Jamie said, "Do what you need to do. I'll talk to them until you're ready." He kissed me on the cheek. I grabbed some clothes from the suitcase beside the bed and hurried into the bathroom. When I was presentable enough for our company, I went out into the kitchen, where I found Gerry, Sharon, Ellie, Alan and a couple of other people I hadn't seen the night before.

Jamie introduced me to a tall, African American man, Andrew Taylor, and there was another young woman with blond hair and blue eyes, sitting there at the table. Jamie motioned towards her and said, "And this is Agent Tina! She's the technical wizard all the rest of the agents were raving about last night." I smiled and gave her a big hug and said, "Thank you!" I heard her say, "Oh!" as I must have surprised her for hugging her so hard. I moved around the room, saying a big thank you to each one and hugged them all for saving my life. Ellie said, "Well, Jamie here did a lot too!" I shrugged and said, "I know. What can I say? He's my hero!" Jamie rolled his eyes as his face turned a rosy-pink.

Bridget came into the kitchen with Alexander in her arms. She said, "Sorry to interrupt, but I've changed him and that's all *I* can do..." I looked at Bridget and knew what she meant. My boobs felt like they were going to explode! She put A.J. in my lap and handed me a receiving blanket. I said, "Sorry guys, A.J. really needs his breakfast or whatever this is now." I frowned and said, "Hey, I haven't fed him since yesterday afternoon. Why isn't he screaming *bloody murder?* Er...excuse the pun." Jamie said, "One of the agents got us some formula for A.J. last night. It was enough to cover three feedings. I fed him earlier this morning, so you could sleep in." My eyes stung, as I said, "So he might not even *want* me anymore?" Jamie shook his head and said, "I doubt it. It was like pulling teeth to get him to take it! But between Bridget and I, we managed to get him to take some of it each time."

I blew out a sigh of relief, put the blanket over my shoulder and started feeding him, while we continued our conversation. Alexander cooed and wiggled in appreciation at being able to suckle at my breast again. My shoulders slumped in relief at the way he gripped my breast possessively with his little fingers. It felt as though it was much longer than just a day since we'd last been together.

The agents all smiled and I asked them what was happening, while I was down in that 'dungeon.' I said, "It appears I missed all the excitement! I mean exactly how did you guys find me?" They started to explain about how Agent Simpson found the first hidden camera and – "Wait, what? *Hidden camera!*" I must have had a look of horror in my eyes, as Jamie kind of gave them all a look like, 'Do we have to tell her?' I slapped Jamie in the arm playfully with my free hand and said, "Come on, spill it!" Jamie looked at Agent Simpson, who began to explain where the first camera was and then the rest of the team found several of them throughout the house.

I said, "Even in our bedroom?" They all looked at each other grimly and nodded. I buried my face in my free hand as I felt rage bubbling up inside me. I said, "What kind of sicko was he?" And I felt the tears welling up in my eyes again. Jamie sat down next to me at the kitchen table, put his arm around me, glanced at Ellie and said, "We can destroy the tapes, right?" She tilted her head to one side and said, "Its evidence, so I'm afraid we *can't* destroy it."

My jaw dropped and I said, "Nooo! I mean, we're in the newspaper all the time! What if the wrong person gets hold of them and posts them on the internet or something?" Sharon said, "I promise, that won't happen. This doesn't need to go to trial, since Fairbanks died last night; so the case is basically closed. We just need to dot all our 'i's' and cross all our 't's' in our reports." They then explained about how Tina hacked into the camera feeds to find out where Fairbanks was, how she' d gotten the electric company to turn off the power so that the agents, and Jamie, could get into his house. I asked, "So how did this happen? I mean, did you *have* to kill him?"

Gerry said, "When the power was cut, the team went in and tried to use a diplomatic approach, but Fairbanks came at Jamie with a knife. You should be proud of your husband. He really held his own. Fairbanks looked like he had the upper hand at first; and we tried to talk him down, but to no avail. Then, Jamie managed to turn things around when he grabbed the knife right out of Fairbanks's hand! You should have seen him! I couldn't believe it! It was just like we've been taught during training at Quantico!"

Jamie blushed again and said, "Well, my brothers and I got some martial arts training through Daryl Adams once, when we put a choreographed routine in our act. I never thought I'd have to use it other than for show, but I guess the classes came in handy." I looked at Jamie like I'd never looked at him before. *He really* is *my hero!* I then asked, "So how did Fairbanks get shot, then?"

Sharon continued the story with, "Well, Jamie slid the knife across the floor to the other side of the room, but Fairbanks tried to get the upper hand back. Jamie got in a few good punches before Sgt. Carver here, pulled him off, you know, so Jamie wouldn't go too far. We try to keep the violence to a minimum when we can. But then, Fairbanks managed to grab my service revolver and he pointed it right at Jamie's face. He disengaged the safety and had his finger on the trigger, so both Sgt. Carver and Gerry had to shoot him. The first bullet hit him in the shoulder, but he kept waving the gun at Jamie and moving closer towards him. Unfortunately, the next two shots were kill shots." I thought back to the night before when I heard the gun shots, and it took all my strength not to cry. I took a few deep breaths to avoid having another panic attack.

I looked at Jamie and said, "When I heard the shots all I could think about was London! I panicked and thought that you were dead!" My throat thickened, choking my words. Jamie put his arms around me, stroked my hair and said, "Well it's over now and we're okay, babe." He swiped a stray tear from my cheek and I said, "Okay, let's get this over with now." I finished feeding A.J. and Bridget took him and the kids outside to play on the beach, while the agents and Sgt. Carver started their questioning.

About an hour later after answering a bazillion questions about what happened to me, they said that they had enough to make a good report. Then, I thought of something I wanted to know. I said, "Okay, so how did this even start? I mean, how did Fairbanks even have the money to get here? I thought it came out in court that he was diagnosed with Schizophrenia, quite early in life, and he didn't have any family." Jamie nodded and said, "That's right, I remember them saying he was on disability benefits, only working odd jobs, here and there. I mean, how would he have had the money to finance such an elaborate plan? Just his air fare I could see, maybe, but he rented not one, but *two* prime beach front properties here. And had all the brains and equipment to put us under expensive surveillance like that."

Ellie said, "Well that's where Tina's technical talents and my contacts at ICSTF came in handy." She paused when I frowned at the letters and then she said, "That's short for International Crimes Special Task Force." She turned to Tina to finish the story. Tina opened her lap top on the kitchen table and typed something into it. She said, "I just need to open my file here, so I can get all the information right. Fairbanks has a really long and colorful history. His medical and personal files from his childhood were sealed up tight and that's why none of this came up in court. He was not actually Ian Fairbanks. I mean he *was*, but this is where the story gets really interesting. He was born Ian Fairbanks. His mother was a heroin addict named Charlotte Fairbanks, living in East London, who funded her habit by turning tricks on the street."

"Fairbanks's father was Charlotte's pimp and her supplier, drug dealer, Timothy Siebert, AKA T-Man, also from the same area. Charlotte died from an overdose September 30th, 1964, and Seibert was arrested for drug trafficking and running a prostitution ring on July 11th, 1966. He was later killed in prison, leaving Fairbanks an orphan at age six. Enter Mr. Gordon Craven and Mrs. Stephanie Craven, who adopted him two months later."

"The Cravens were quite a well–to–do couple. Gordon was a multi-million dollar heir to his family fortune. They owned several rental properties throughout England and Scotland, as well as a large business conglomerate, and, when they adopted Ian, they changed his name to Arthur Craven. When they died suddenly, under mysterious circumstances in April of 1981, the family fortune was left to their only son, Arthur, slash Ian. It says in the police file here, that they suspected him of murdering his adoptive parents, but they couldn't find enough evidence to convict him, or even arrest him."

"*And*, since he'd already reached the age of twenty–one when this happened, he had full access to his parents' money. The Cravens had already set up a huge trust fund in his name. They had lots of power to cover up all of Ian slash Arthur's misdeeds, resulting from his diagnosis, which included vandalism, drug misdemeanors and a whole other slew of petty theft and assault charges - which were all dropped, probably because the Cravens likely paid the victims off for their silence. Arthur went on to take over his father's conglomerate and ran the business successfully for decades, after his parents' deaths. But for some reason, he started selling everything off during the last eighteen months, before he was arrested for your shooting in London."

"When the police and ICSTF found all the photographs in his apartment, they figured that he'd been following your career since the mid to late seventies, Mrs. Grayson. So maybe it was his obsession with *you* that triggered him to start putting his plan into action." She pointed her finger towards me.

Then, she continued with, "Fairbanks's defense attorney, Leonard Aubrey, kept quiet about his link to the Craven family and the huge business conglomerate, likely because he was getting a big paycheck to get him off, when Fairbanks was charged with attempted murder in London, back in March of 2000. I managed to get a digital copy of Leonard Aubrey's bank statements. It looks like there were two large deposits of two and a half million dollars each, transferred to his personal account, one just before the trial and one just after he got Fairbanks off, on the insanity defense. Fairbanks's family history with the Cravens and his criminal record had been sealed up tight, so none of this came out in court."

"The connection to the Craven family wasn't discovered by the ICSTF, until after Agent Rhodes contacted them for their help in this case, yesterday. Fairbanks never showed up for a scheduled meeting with his psychiatrist and his lawyer, after his release from the Charlton Hospital for the Criminally Insane in Darcey, England near the end of May of this year. And it looks like he assumed his original identity, before going after you and your family two years ago."

"The ICSTF did some more detailed searches of his most recent residence in London and found a bunch of different passports, with his face and several identities, hidden underneath the floorboards of his bedroom at his apartment. It's amazing we managed to find you, because this guy had the means to take you anywhere in the world that he wanted to. I'm actually surprised he didn't get you on a private jet out of here, as soon as he *took* you. The ICSTF also managed to find a big paper trail linked to all of his different identities and a bunch of people he paid off, to do his dirty work for him. There are several offshore accounts, under all his aliases. Most of his people weren't giving up the information that easily, so their loyalty to Fairbanks/Craven was strong. But they managed to find one that sang like a canary, when he was caught, in exchange for a deal."

I heard a cell phone buzz. Carver and all the agents looked at their phones and Ellie sighed, "Looks like The ICSTF found some..." she paused for a moment, looking past us towards the kids and Bridget playing outside. The sliders were open, letting a breeze in through the screen door. She glanced at Jamie and I. Jamie said, "What?" Ellie responded in a lower voice, "Several unmarked graves were just discovered, behind the hospital in Darcey. They've found several bodies, which may be linked to Ian Fairbanks. Two of the bodies were identified as employees of Fairbanks...er...Craven."

Jamie and I looked at each other and shuddered. He tightened his grasp around me and we both sighed with relief that Fairbanks was no longer able to hurt us.

Ellie said, "Okay, if you two don't have any more questions, we can let you and your family members get back to your lives now." That was the team's cue to get up and leave. They scraped their chairs back and headed towards the front door.

Gerry turned to us at the door and made a joke, "You know Jamie, like Agent Rhodes said last night, if you think you might want to become an agent, let us know! You'd certainly be a force to be reckoned with!" Sgt. Carver cut in with, "Or maybe, you might want to join the L.A.P.D." And everyone laughed. Jamie sighed and said, "I don't think my wife would approve. Playing guitar and singing is much safer than using a gun, right?" and he winked at me. I smiled and thanked them all again as they left.

After having some lunch, we spent the rest of the day swimming and playing on the beach with the kids, and then, we decided it was time to go back home. We had enough excitement for a lifetime in just the past twenty–four hours. The Grayson family sent Skip to pick us up in the family jet, so we didn't have to book a flight. Jamie called ahead, on my insistence, to alert the security team, and Matty, to have the houses on our property as well as the stables, in Chelsea, swept for any hidden listening devices and cameras, just in case Fairbanks slash Craven was watching us, prior to our vacation. Jamie thought it was unnecessary, because there was always so much commotion going on at the house, even when we weren't there, that the chances were pretty slim anyone could go through our place, without being detected by the security team. He was right, of course, there was nothing found. But I needed the reassurance.

The news of our recent 'adventure' hit the media in a flash, because the task force that helped us had to make a formal statement, about the case and Fairbanks' fatal shooting, as to whether or not it was justified. So of course, when we got to the airport, the Paparazzi were all over us. I just wanted to go home, so we answered most of the questions with, "No comment," except for the obvious ones like, "Are you okay?" and "Did Fairbanks hurt you?" When we arrived at the Honeywood Airport, we got mobbed by the press yet again, but luckily, Steve and Adam met us there, to control things and kept them all at a safe distance.

I looked at Jamie, but he just continued walking, holding my hand and herding Bridget and the kids away from them, as fast as he could. We managed to keep them at bay, until one of the reporters actually had the audacity to ask questions, directly to the kids. I almost lost it! I said, "Stay away from my children!" Jamie and I got to the limo, piled Bridget and the kids into it, and finally left the airport. Of course, when we got to our front gate in Chelsea, there were more Paparazzi waiting there for us. Trevor opened the gate, while Adam and Steve kept the reporters away, to give us room to get through.

Three days later, Jamie called a press conference, after reading a lot of junk in the paper, because we hadn't made a formal statement yet. It got all twisted into reading that Jamie had been the one who killed Fairbanks! I wanted to just hide in the house forever, but Jamie said that we had to come clean and tell the truth, before the press had made minced meat out of our reputations. I held Jamie's hand just outside the front gates of our home, while he did all the talking.

Jamie said, "We had quite a scare after spending a wonderful vacation, at our house in California and Animation Dreamland. This was supposed to be a birthday celebration for our daughter, Chelsea, but on the last day, it turned into a nightmare for us. My wife was abducted by the man who tried to kill us in London. He was never convicted for the shooting and attempted murder charges in 2000, because the judge ruled that Ian Fairbanks was not guilty, by reason of insanity. He was treated at Charlton Hospital for the Criminally Insane in Darcey, England and released, after less than two years. He somehow made it into the United States, using an assumed name, with forged documents."

"He answered an ad in the newspaper when Celina's beach house was advertised for rent. Celina let an agent handle the rental, so she had no idea to whom she was renting it. Fairbanks, who called himself Blake Williams, pretended to be away for three weeks, while we vacationed there, so we could spend it at the beach house. On the last day, while we were getting into the limo to come home, Celina was doing some last minute cleaning in the house, when Fairbanks, posing as Williams, came through the back door and managed to abduct her using a cloth doused with chloroform. With the help of the local police department, and the heroic actions of a special task force of federal agents, they managed to find and rescue Celina before she was harmed."

Jamie cleared his throat and continued with, "That's not to say, this hasn't been a traumatic experience for all of us. I did *not* shoot and kill Fairbanks. Yes, we had an altercation, when the task force entered a second beach house that Fairbanks had also rented. It was the agents and local police who chose to take this unfortunate action, when Fairbanks managed to get hold of a service revolver, aiming it at me. He had every intention of killing me, so they had no choice but to do what they did."

"I hope you all can understand that this has been a very difficult time for us. We would appreciate your patience. We need time to heal. Our children need their mother and father. I'm sure that many of you have families and will understand, we need our privacy at this time. Thank you." He led me away from the reporters, who, of course, continued asking a bunch of questions. But we turned and went back to the house.

It was several days, before Jamie and I started making love again. He could tell I was hesitant, and he said, "Babe, they didn't find anything. We're okay." When I was still uneasy, Jamie looked at me with concern in his eyes, "I know you told the agents you weren't harmed, but this is just you and me now. You can tell me if something happened." He waited for my response, but I didn't know what to say to him. No, Fairbanks hadn't gotten as far as he might have, if the police and Jamie hadn't found me when they did.

The table lamp on Jamie's nightstand was still lit, so I could see his eyes. They were suddenly a color I hadn't seen before. They were almost purple. I put my hands up to his cheeks and felt him trembling. I realized that this meant he was filled with dread! I decided it was *my* turn to comfort *him*. I said, "No, No! Jamie, it didn't get that far. You and the agents got there in time. He didn't hurt me, at least not like *that!*" I kept thinking about the kiss, and though I really didn't want to tell him about it, I knew I had to be honest with him. "Sandman, you know, it wasn't like that but...there was a kiss..."

Jamie's eyes turned immediately from that dark purple color to grey and they welled up with tears, which fell like rain drops all over my face. He lowered his face to my chest and I held him and stroked his hair, until his breathing slowed and his sobbing stopped. I thought about everything we'd been through in all the years we were married. We'd weathered some terrible storms and still, we came out safe and sound, despite all the danger and emotional upheaval we'd both suffered.   It was finally taking its toll on both of us. Jamie was the one to be strong for both of us, when I went off the deep end. When I thought about all the times, I'd been in my darkest hours, with my depression and anxiety. I was amazed Jamie hadn't washed his hands of it all and walked away. He really *was* my hero, in every way.

When he lifted his head and looked at me again, I dried his remaining tears and said, "Jamie, please make me forget!" I put my hands on his cheeks and stroked his beard. That night, it was almost like the first night we'd spent together. He paid special attention to every inch of my body, and our love making was passionate and sweet. When we were finished, waiting for our breathing to calm down, I laid my head on his chest, his arms around me. I pulled away slightly and looked up at his face, which was bathed in the moonlight coming through the French doors.

I noticed a few silver hairs, peeking out from under his chocolate brown mane, both at his temples and just a few in his cropped beard. His face was still chiseled, and the grey hairs seemed to make him even more handsome, if that was even *possible!* He was still fit as could be and I marveled at how he was managing to age so gracefully. He was now forty-nine years old. But, although he looked more mature than that seventeen–year–old boy whose picture I'd fallen in love with, while looking at a teen magazine, when I was just ten, he was more handsome to me than ever. And he kept himself clean and quite lean with regular exercise.

I, on the other hand, was not quite so graceful at aging. When I noticed I was getting a few silver hairs at my roots and crow's feet around my eyes in the last couple of years, since turning forty, I made sure that my hairdresser kept up the pretense of my youth, with her skillful hands and magic dyes. I invested in some pretty expensive face creams, to make sure the crows feet were kept at bay. I made regular appointments for full body waxing, herbal masks and other spa rituals.

I once broached the subject with Jamie of the possibility of getting Botox injections and maybe a boob lift, but he shook his head and said, "Raven, you're more beautiful than ever, and I'd rather be with a real, live woman, than some sort of fake Barbie doll." He still looked at me the same way he had that first day we met, and I knew he was sincere. It was dangerous for me to bend over to pick up something up off the floor, without having his arms suddenly around me and groping me, and our love making was still better than ever. I knew he still saw me as young and pretty. We grew closer and fell more in love with each other, with each passing day.

****

In the middle of the night, I awoke to the sound of Jamie thrashing around in the sheets. He was calling my name out in his sleep. This was unusual for him. It was *me* who always had the nightmares and fitful sleeping habits. I reached for him and gently touched his arm, hoping I would wake him up, without startling him. The moment my hand made contact, he bolted upright in the bed.

I said in a soft voice, "Hey! Jamie, it's okay! It's just a dream." I encouraged him to lie back down again. His breathing was still labored, but he started to relax as he lay back and pulled me into his embrace. I said, "Do you want to talk about it?" Jamie hesitated a moment before he spoke.

"It…it was about what happened in London." I could see he was still struggling with it and he swallowed hard. I said, "Baby, we're okay! We're all safe. Fairbanks can't hurt us anymore." Jamie shook his head and said, "I dreamed that he was successful." His Adam's apple was bouncing up and down, while his eyes blinked. I could tell he was fighting back tears. He continued with, "I was trying to talk to you and the kids, but you couldn't hear me – like I was a *ghost* or something!" I put my hands up to his face, stroked his beard and said, "Shhh! It's okay, I'm here and we're okay!"

After several moments, his breathing slowed and I thought he was going to fall asleep again. But then he said, "You know, I'm not who you think I am."

I made a joke, "Okay, then who are you, a cartoon character?" Jamie's lips twitched and the corners of his mouth went up slightly, but it was not his usual reaction to my jokes. Suddenly, my heart started racing as I began to wonder what he meant. He cleared his throat and said, "I'm not the man you *think* I am!" I rolled over on top of him. We were both still naked from our earlier love-making session. I propped my head on my fists which were on his chest, as I said, "What are you talking about?" He didn't answer me.

Instead, he wrapped his left arm around my waste, tightly and brought his right hand to my face. His chin touched his chest as he gazed into my eyes. I saw the moonlight dancing off his bright blue eyes. I could feel his hardness growing under me. He used his forefinger to trace a line across my lips. I took the tip of his finger into my mouth and gave him a gentle love bite, which made his hardness grow even bigger. His gaze held mine. When I let his finger go, he pulled me close and we kissed, deeply.

He then traced a line down the side of my face and tucked my hair behind my ear. I was expecting him to release his grip so I could roll off of him, to allow him to do the usual pleasing me with his mouth, but he held fast with his left arm still around my waste. He instead used the fingers of his right hand to stroke my back and down my bottom. He reached down to gently pull my left leg off him so that my knee was bent. I lost my balance for a moment and had to place my palms down on the bed on either side of him, to hold myself steady. I lifted myself off him slightly so that he could stimulate me with his fingers. His left hand was still around my waste, while his right hand wandered up and down my spine and back down my bottom. He traced a line up my left side and up towards my breast.

I closed my eyes and moaned softly as he teased my nipple until it went hard. He whispered softly, Raven, please look at me. I complied. His eyes were intense, as he continued to caress and tease both nipples, until I started to writhe and shudder. I ached for him to be inside of me. After several moments of this, his right hand made its way down between my legs. He'd never stimulated me that way before. His gaze was fixed on mine as he worked his magic and I exploded into a sharp orgasm.

I bent down and kissed him deeply and expected him to release me, but his eyes were still intensely fierce, as he braced himself on his right hand, forcing us both into a sitting position. I wrapped my legs around his waist and he slid himself deep inside of me. We rocked and moved in circular motions. My insides clenched, as I neared my second orgasm and I felt his body go rigid as the pressure built, until we both climaxed loudly.

After we were finished making love for the second time and our breathing had slowed, he finally released his grip and I rolled over onto my side of the bed and we did the usual cuddling. I was almost ready to fall asleep again when Jamie spoke. He resumed our earlier conversation, "You know, Raven, I'm not the guy you think I am."

I felt my heart skip a beat because he sounded so serious. I thought he might be questioning the strength of our marriage. I looked up at his face and said, "Jamie, what's happening. Are you okay? Are *we* okay?"

Jamie sighed and said, "I'm not that *guy*, you know." I tried another attempt at humor and said, "So, if you're not Jamie Grayson, then who are you? Are you adopted or something?" He said, "No, I'm James Thadeous Grayson, but I'm not the guy you *think* I am. I'm not that guy you wrote about, in those pages of your diary."

At the risk of arousing him again, I rolled over on top of him yet again, and looked into his eyes. My brows furrowed as I said, "Jamie, what are you trying to say?" His voice was soft and low as he murmured, "When you look at me, you see this larger than life character, from some movie or something. I'm not a superhero…I'm not the man of steel. I'm just an ordinary guy, who loves you more than words could ever express. And let me tell you, I am starting to get tired of trying to live up to that image you have of me. It's hard work doing that!"

I laughed and said, "Jamie, are you kidding me? I know exactly who you are!" He shook his head, "No, you don't!" I put my finger to his lips and said, "Sandman, I know you're not bullet-proof. You have the scars on your chest to prove it. And I know exactly who you are. You're the same guy whose picture I fell in love with, when I was ten years old." His head moved from side to side, but I continued.

"You think I can't see the real you? *Seriously?* Your eyes are a dead give away! I always know what you're feeling. It's one of the things I love *most* about you! Because, I know that you'll always be honest with me. You *can't* lie to me. And you're the easiest prey for my practical jokes! You're my dream lover; you're the most wonderful man I've ever met. You're a fantastic father to our kids and an even better husband than I deserve. I know you're only human. But you're still my hero. You've rescued me more times than I can count - sometimes even from myself. When the plane crashes happened, you never gave up on me. You went to the crash site, searched through a pile of ashes and dead body parts, looking for me. And when Fairbanks kidnapped me, you found me. You took your life in your hands and fought against that monster. And then, you picked me up in your arms and took me home." I saw his eyes flash and his arms tightened around me.

"And no matter what life throws at us and our marriage, you're always there for me, with your undying love, waiting with open arms no matter what. And you forgive me and keep on loving me, no matter how badly I screw up. You're my best friend in the whole world…but don't tell Joey I said that, because for some reason he thinks *he's* my best friend." And I winked at him.

Jamie tried to stifle a laugh but was unsuccessful. His lips formed a huge grin and his head sank back into the pillow, as he laughed out loud. He said, "I love you, Raven!" I said, "I love you too, Sandman!"

From that point on, we lived our lives as though each second was the last. We spent more time with the kids and did all the things we loved together, making sure there was never a moment wasted. After everything that had happened to us, everything that we'd been through, we both knew that anything could happen at any moment; so we made every extra effort to enjoy life while we still could.

****

Three weeks later, we got a call from Daniel. Jamie was in the kitchen preparing dinner on one of our last nights before going back to Crystal Pines. I picked it up on the second ring. "Hello?" Daniel's voice was cordial, and we exchanged pleasantries before he revealed the reason for his phone call. "I think you might want to put me on speaker, so Jamie can listen in."

My brows slid together as I said, "Why? Is something wrong?" I pressed the speaker button and set the phone on the table. Daniel cleared his throat and said, "No, not wrong. It's just…" He sighed and I could hear the sound of shuffling papers in the background.

Jamie turned down the burner on the stove, where the vegetables were simmering and wiped his hands on the dish cloth. He pulled one of the kitchen chairs back, motioning for me to sit down, while he pulled out another one for himself. When we were both seated, Jamie said, "Daniel? Is everything okay?"

Daniel sighed again, "This is kind of unusual. And I'm not sure how you're going to take this." Jamie and I exchanged glances and then he said, "Daniel? What's wrong?" Daniel's voice was quiet as he stammered, "I just got a call from Ian Fairbanks'…er Arthur Craven's attorney…well, acting attorney, since Mr. Aubry is now up on charges for aiding and abetting…"

My heart started hammering in my chest. I swallowed hard and asked, "Daniel? What is it? What's happening?"

Daniel cleared his throat again before he said, "It appears that Arthur Craven slash Ian Fairbanks has left you his entire fortune, Amanda."

Part 2:

The Extended Family

I opened one eye and I saw that it was 3:12am on the display of my alarm clock, on the nightstand. I almost rolled over and resumed my slumber, thinking I still had just under three hours before the kids would be getting up, when I heard the sound of little footsteps out in the hallway. I groaned, reached for my robe and dragged myself out of the bed. I slid my feet into my slippers and shrugged into the robe, tying it loosely on the way out my bedroom door.

I glanced in through Chelsea's bedroom door and saw her bed was empty. I took several steps down the hall and glanced in at Nina's tiny sleeping figure on her bed. I kept walking and saw that Eric's bed was also empty. I turned my head and looked across the hall, toward the kids' and my bathroom and saw the door was closed and the light was on. I checked the doorknob and found it locked. I could hear the familiar splash of Eric's usual late-night bladder emptying session and rolled my eyes, as I imagined myself having to wipe the seat again, before using it myself in the morning.

I was still kind of fuzzy, so it took a moment for my eyes to adjust to the darkness, illuminated only by a tiny, plug-in night-light. I looked down the hallway and spotted Chelsea's tiny figure, just in front of Amanda and Jamie's bathroom. I figured she needed to pee as well, so I just waited in the hallway to make sure the kids didn't wander around, when they were finished. My heart jumped into my throat, as I heard the familiar muffled sounds of Amanda calling out Jamie's name and realized the shower was running. I saw Chelsea's right hand reach up towards the doorknob and I knew I only had a split second to rescue her from a sight that would probably traumatize her, for life. I flung myself down the hall and grasped her hand, just before it touched the knob. Chelsea looked up at me in surprise and I knew that she was about to say something, so I put my other hand across her mouth and said, "Shhhh!"

I could hear other sounds coming from the shower, which was much-used for my employers' lovemaking sessions. I pulled my hand away from Chelsea's mouth and used both hands to cover her ears, just in time, as I heard Amanda say words I knew Jamie would *never* approve of, under normal circumstances!

In the glow of the night light, I could see Chelsea bite her lower lip the way Amanda sometimes did, when she was about to get emotional. I saw a hint of a tear glistening in each of her eyes, which were round as saucers. My heart tightened in my chest. *Had I been too rough when I grasped her hand away from the door knob?* I checked the door to make sure it was locked, breathing a sigh of relief when it was.

I noticed the little one in front of me starting to dance on the spot and knew she was really in desperate need to relieve her bladder; so I snatched her up, flung her under one arm, in a football type hold and dashed as quickly as I could, towards the kitchen. When I slid across the floor, I almost crashed into the basement door, as I reached up my free hand to unfasten the hook from its eye. This temporary safety measure was added, when Alexander started showing signs of learning to crawl a couple of weeks back and would suffice until Matty had time to install a proper lock. I was grateful that hadn't been done yet, or I might have been too late getting Chelsea down those treacherous stairs, to the basement. Ditching my slippers at the top of the steps, I ran down with Chelsea still under my arm and managed to reach the lower bath and set her in front of the toilet just in time.

She pulled her pajama pants down and sat on the seat. I heard the familiar 'whooshhh' sound, which prompted huge praises out of her parents' mouths, when she'd finally started using the toilet on a regular basis. This was a big milestone for her, as I thought back – maybe only a couple of years. She sighed and said, *"Whew! That was close!"* I bent down, reached my hand out to her pajama pants, felt they were dry and did my own mental, *whew!*

I crossed myself, said a silent 'Hail Mary' and a little prayer, thanking God that Jamie was so kind as to let the staff use his little exercise room down here, when he wasn't working out himself, until our new staff residence was finished being built. I used the tread mill and rowing machine on a regular basis, to keep myself strong and able to keep up with the ever–growing family here. He really was a great boss. He promised us he would make sure there was a similar room in the staff residence, with the same equipment in it that he had down here.

Chelsea interrupted my thoughts, when she asked, "What were Mommy and Daddy doing upstairs in the bathroom?" My heart skipped a beat, as I thought about what my answer to that question would be. I supposed that subject would come up sooner or later, but at her tender age of six, never! I stammered, "Ummm, just what grown-ups that are in love sometimes do."

Chelsea's little brows slid together, as she said, "What?" *Oh, boy!* I took a deep breath and searched my brain, frantically, for something to say. I didn't need to answer just yet, because she interrupted my thoughts again with, "Are you and Uncle Steve in love?" My heart stuttered and my jaw dropped so low, I almost got a cramp! I knelt down on the floor in front of her, as I handed her the wad of toilet paper I'd been holding, so she could wipe. I moved away to give her some room to pull up her pants, flush the toilet and walk over to the sink, to wash her hands. I leaned back against the toilet and crossed my legs in front of me on the floor, as I absent mindedly reached for the towel on the rack, handing it to her, to dry her hands.

I was stunned! *Are the walls really that paper thin?* It only happened that one time, before we left for California, and I was careful to hold a pillow over my face; and surely the small groan that had come out of Steve's mouth wouldn't carry *that* far! We'd been so careful over the last couple of years, to make sure we never showed our affections in front of anyone in the household.

We'd had clandestine meetings off the property, when we were off duty, but it was only that one time, in the house – in my room. It was the middle of the night and Steve and I just wanted to have some alone time, before I went away for three weeks with the family, for their vacation. Maggie had been sitting in the kitchen watching for wandering kids, just in case...

Chelsea said, "Were you jumping on the bed?" I looked up, confused, as I'd been lost in thought. It took a moment, before what she said had sunk in. I mimicked her, "Jumping on the bed..." She said, "It sounded like that, like when Nina and Eric and me do that." I thought about explaining it away like that, but I couldn't lie to her. I shook my head and said, "No, I wasn't jumping on the bed." Chelsea said, "But I heard Uncle Steve laughing...after I heard the bed squeaking..." I thought back to that night. Steve was wearing those sexy leather pants and was doing a strip tease for me. But I couldn't wait that long, so I pulled him onto the bed. It really *did* creak and that's what made him laugh. I smiled for a beat at the memory and then let it fade…because I knew we might be in a lot of hot water now.

Chelsea turned around to face me after she'd neatly hung up the towel back in its place. She knelt down in front of me, with concern in her eyes. She said, "Auntie Bridget, are you okay?" My throat tightened, as I saw her reach her little hands up to wipe away the tears I didn't even know I was crying. I said, "Well, I guess the secret's out, *now!*"

"What's a secret?" Chelsea asked. I sighed and said, "It's something that only maybe a few people know, that they don't tell anyone else, no matter what." I then thought long and hard about what I was going to say next. I knew that Steve and I were likely in big doo-doo and might be fired for this, since there was a no fraternization clause in our contracts.

Chelsea repeated her earlier question, "Are you and Uncle Steve in love? Is that the secret?" I nodded and a sob caught in my throat, as more tears spilled out of my eyes. Chelsea said, "Why are you sad, Auntie Bridget?" I sniffed loudly, and said, "Because I love you and your brothers and sister more than anything…and I don't want to leave you!" Chelsea gasped, looked up at me with those saucer eyes again, and she said, "*Nooo!* You aren't really going to leave, are you?"

I tried, unsuccessfully, to regain my composure. Chelsea climbed into my lap and did her cute little thing that she did with her Daddy's scars and started giving me butterfly kisses all over my face. I laughed through my tears and said, "Thank you, my little princess!" She said, "I won't tell your secret, I promise! But why do you have to leave?" I said, "Because I work for your Mommy and Daddy and I'm breaking the rules." Chelsea asked, "What's rules?" I sighed and said, "Rules are rules, ummm – it's like…you have to wash your hands after you use the toilet and especially before you eat. And like, Daddy's rule of saying grace before dinner." Chelsea asked me, "So what's the rule you are breaking?"

I said, "Uncle Steve and I aren't supposed to…er…be in love." Chelsea furrowed her little brows again and said, "So it's *bad* to be in love?" I knew she was *really* confused now! I said, "No, it's not bad to be in love! Your Mommy and Daddy are in love and it's a very wonderful thing. But because Uncle Steve and I work together, it's, um, one of Daddy's rules. We're not supposed to be friendly like that." Chelsea shook her head and said, "But Daddy said it's okay to have friends!"

I said, "I know sweetheart, it's just that I signed a contract, agreeing to the rules, and I'm breaking one of them. So, if your Mommy and Daddy find out, I might have to leave." Chelsea said, "And Uncle Steve, too?" I nodded. Chelsea's eyes welled up and the tears spilled out over *her* cheeks now, as she said, "But I *love* you and Uncle

Steve! I don't *want* you to leave!" And her chin started to quiver, as she sobbed. It broke my heart that this was happening! She continued with, "Why does Daddy have to be so mean! He's *never* mean to us!" *Oh, boy!* I said, "Sweetheart, Daddy's not mean, *ever!* He's a great boss. It's just that..." I sighed and said, "We broke the rules." *How am I ever going to explain this?*

Chelsea's eyes flashed and she said, "It's a *stupid* rule! How can it be a rule that you can't be in love – that's really dumb!" I laughed through my tears and said, "I think it's just because we're here to protect you. And if we get distracted, because we're in love, it might put you, your sister and brothers in danger. Like what happened after Imagination Dreamland – to your Mommy."

Chelsea's eyes were like saucers again. "When that bad man took her away?" I nodded. Chelsea started to defend me, "But you were in the car with us, protecting us, like you're supposed to! How can that be bad! You're not here to protect *Mommy!* And Uncle Steve wasn't there. He was here, so how could he protect Mommy, when he was here?" I sighed and said, "But we're still breaking the rules, honey!"

Chelsea said, "I won't tell the secret. I won't ever tell, I promise! Don't leave!" And she was sobbing again. I pulled her close and said, "Baby, if I make you keep this secret, it would be like lying to your parents - and that would be bad." Chelsea shook her head and said, "I don't care! I would rather be bad than have to make you leave!" I thought about that. Steve and I leaving might put the kids' parents in a bad light. It would trigger resentment within this beautiful family they had. It was one of those catch twenty-two situations. The last thing I wanted was to be instrumental in tearing the family apart. I sighed and figured the best way to resolve this at this time was to just let it be.

There was no point in waking everyone up and disrupting the whole household. And anyway, Jamie told us there was going to be a staff meeting, in the morning. Maybe the jig was up already anyway. I mean, why had he been asking all those questions about my personal life, back in California the day before the abduction happened? Maybe he was trying to get me to confess to him, back then. Maybe he already knew. On the night before we left for our vacation trip, Maggie told me Amanda couldn't sleep that night and came downstairs to make herself Chamomile tea. She swore up and down that Amanda didn't say anything, but that didn't mean she didn't figure it out. Maybe I should just let this thing play out. Don't get the kids involved. Let it happen the way it's supposed to...

I held Chelsea close for awhile and dried her tears. I said, "Okay, let's keep our little secret for now, until I can figure this out with Uncle Steve. But I want you to promise me that if Mommy or Daddy asks you about it, you won't lie to them, okay? They won't like it if you lie. Let *me* be the one to take the heat, okay?" Chelsea frowned,

"What's the heat?" I said, "Let *me* be the one to get in trouble. I don't want you to get into trouble for lying for me and Uncle Steve, okay?" Chelsea nodded and said, "Okay. I promise. And I won't tell if they don't ask." I smiled and we shook on it.

I looked at the clock. It said it was four–fifteen a.m. Amanda and I had just finished another round - first in the shower and now in our bed. We were just enjoying the afterglow of our lovemaking. She was still on top of me and I was still inside her. Amanda was purring softly, having just reached her final climax. Normally we would fall asleep afterwards but for some reason I had to open my big mouth and ruin it...

I buried myself in her hair, which was falling all around me like a curtain. I drank in her intoxicating scent and said, "I love being inside of you." Amanda murmured, "Me too...I mean I love having you there." I thought that would be the end of a wonderful night, but then she said, "What's the difference?" My brows slammed together and I said, "What do you mean?" She said, "Why is it better than when I...you know?"

I knew she was referring to the occasional times I let her give me oral sex. I replied, "Nothing...er...well, not really." She rose up and looked at me with *her* brows crunched, "So why don't you let me finish you that way so much anymore?" I did a mental growl and thought, *why can't we just go to sleep?* I said, "Babe, I love you and it doesn't really matter." She said, "Yes it does! I want to know."

I sighed and said, "It's just different." "Different how?" *Oh, boy!* I rolled us both over onto our sides, so we could at least try to assume the position of maybe going to sleep. I said, "Different sensation and well it makes the whole thing different...er...more complete." Amanda propped herself on one elbow, so she could look into my eyes, while I was lying on my back. "But you said there's no difference. And now you're saying it *is* different? That doesn't make any sense!" I sucked in a deep breath, because I knew this wasn't going to end any time soon. I loved her more than anything, but this making her talk more about her feelings had really backfired now, when I just wanted to go to sleep.

I said, "Okay, it's like after you've had several...climaxes, you feel...um...different inside. And when I slip myself inside you, especially when I reach that part of you on the first stroke..." I had to search for the right words so I wouldn't hurt her feelings, "Angel, I really love what you do down there, but..." I saw her frown again, "But what?"

I groaned and said, "This is one of those situations where no matter what I say, I'm going to be the *bad* guy here!" Amanda giggled and said, "You'll *never* be the bad guy with me and you know it!" I shook my head and said, "You know what I mean! I love how you do the things you do, but, okay the end result is the same, but while it's happening, it's different." Amanda's eyes flickered and she looked perplexed. *Now, I've really confused her.*

I racked my brain for the right words to explain myself. But she interrupted my thoughts with, "You remember when we were on our honeymoon, that last night, when you explained to me about how you were trying to make up for Terry, but when we ended that night, you said you wanted to see my face?" I nodded, "Yeah, I remember." She said, "Is *that* why? I mean you once mumbled something to me about an addiction, but I never really understood what that meant." I sighed and said, "Honey, do you remember the first time you let me inside you?" She nodded and said, "Yeah, right before we broke up the first time." My heart nearly stopped beating in my chest.

"Raven, we didn't break up. I did *not* break up with you. I just put our sex life on hold, after you told me that you and Terry were still married." She said, "That's not how it felt to *me*!" I blew out a sigh and said, "Raven, I don't want to fight with you. Can we just go to sleep, please?" Amanda winced and gasped and I knew I had blown it. I put my hand on the back of her head and brought her closer so I could kiss her softly. I said, "That wasn't meant to hurt your feelings. I'm sorry." Her eyes softened and she said, "Go on..."

I said, "Remember how I showed you what's supposed to happen, when you're with the right person, why it's not supposed to hurt?" She nodded, "When you put that stuff on my stomach from inside me…" I smiled and nodded. I saw the light flicker in her eyes and she said, "Ooooohhhh!" She said, "Okay, so that makes it feel *better* for you too then?" I said, "Especially after the hundred^th time!" She giggled and said, "Well, I think if you tried a hundred times it would probably kill me!" And we both laughed till we cried.

I thought we were finished and finally could go to sleep, but of course she had to continue, "So what's the addiction part?" I knew I was in for it now. I said, "It's complicated." Amanda said, "Hey! You're not getting off *that* easy!" I growled and said, "Okay, there's two parts to the addiction. One is, the more you, er, climax the better it is in the end, for both of us, with the sensation, and the more times you climax the better the anticipation is…for Mr. Happy…"

Amanda interrupted me with, "But sometimes it hurts for you – and Mr. Happy, to hold off so long. That can't be good!" I said, "Baby, when it finally happens, and sometimes I have to stop on the first stroke to take a breather, but…" Amanda said, "Exactly! Why do you do that! Don't you think you've given me enough then? Why do you have to torture yourself?" I cleared my throat and said, "Because the best part of when you come, when I'm inside of you is the way your, it…you know…it contracts, around Mr. Happy, and that sends him right over the edge."

She said, "Oh." There was about thirty seconds pause, and I breathed a sigh of relief thinking we were finally going to sleep, but then, "So why did you lie?" I felt like I'd been kicked in the teeth. *"Lie? When have I ever lied to you?"* She said, "That last night on our honeymoon. You said it was because of *Terry!" Oh, boy!* I took a long, hard breath and said, "I wasn't lying. At first, it *was* because of Terry. When we first started making love, without the intercourse part, your pleasure was my addiction. I wanted to make up, for the way he treated you. But when it finally happened, *that part* became my addiction, you know? And I didn't tell you there was an ulterior motive, because it would have made me look selfish." Amanda snorted and then laughed so loud I thought she was going to wake up the entire household. I said, "Shhhh! You'll wake up the kids and then we'll *never* get any sleep! And why is that funny, anyway?"

She said, "I love you, Sandman! You actually think that giving me multiple orgasms makes you selfish?" *Okay, she has a point!* I said, "Now, at the risk of making you mad at me forever, can we go to sleep now? *Please?"*

Without missing a beat she said, "I could *never* be mad at you!" It was right there on the tip of my tongue, so I couldn't stop myself, *"Really?* Remember what you did after that charity benefit in Crystal Pines?" I knew I was a goner now! I'd made it through all these years, without bringing up that subject, but I was tired. *Dang!* Amanda's eyes flashed, "That wasn't my *fault!* I thought you *slept*

with her! And you said you forgave me!" *Oh, boy!*
Then she went on…

"I thought that subject was closed." It *was…and I have a big mouth.* Amanda's eyes welled and I pulled her close. I stroked her hair and said, "I'm sorry, darlin! That was really insensitive of me to say that." *But you did break Jeremy's taillight and rear windshield with those rocks - over a misunderstanding.* She said, "You didn't tell them about it, did you?" I said, "No, I didn't, but the insurance company did." And of course she wasn't done yet. "But I told them I was paying for it anonymously! They promised they wouldn't say anything!" I continued to sooth her and prayed for the end of the conversation. But of course, she wasn't done.

"What did Jeremy say?" I sighed and said, "He said he got a letter confirming that the claim had been withdrawn and that his insurance rates would not go up because of it. It was supposed to be billed to my house insurance, through his policy, since the car was in my driveway, when it happened. Then Jeremy asked me if it was me who told the insurance company to withdraw the claim. He asked me if I'd paid it out of my own pocket. I said I didn't *talk* to my insurance company, after that night. And I hadn't called *his*. So he called them and after a bunch of rigmarole and being transferred to this one and that one, they found a check from Terry Jackson, taking care of all the damages. Jeremy kind of put two and two together and figured out that it was you who'd caused the damage."

Amanda's face blanched. "So what did Jeremy say *then*?" I said, "Raven, that was, what...like maybe ten years ago now? Does it even matter?" She said, "It does to *me!*" I told her that Jeremy had just rolled his eyes at me, but the subject was closed, because the damages were paid, no harm no foul. It's a good thing it was dark and the moonlight wasn't on my face anymore because she would have seen that I was lying. That was the first time I'd ever been dishonest with her. Not because I wanted to go to sleep, but because I didn't want her to know that Jeremy and I had a huge argument over whether or not I should continue seeing Amanda. It was all water under the bridge ,and we were together and happy. Why she insisted on bringing up the past was beyond me. *Because you brought it up, stupid!*

Finally, she fell silent and relaxed in my arms and we went to sleep...

Shortly after we got home from California, I got the security team and Matty to do another sweep of the grounds and the houses. The construction of the house meant for the staff was well under way and I made sure there was a thorough background check done on any and all workers entering the gates each day. I managed to get Daniel to get a friend of his from the D.A.'s office who had connections to the Feds, ironically to Tina, (the technical guru who helped locate Amanda during her abduction), to use their resources, to make sure our home and families were safe from anyone who might be wishing us harm.

Tina referred me to a friend of hers that was, by her recommendation, as good as *she* was and as luck would have it, Tina's friend happened to be looking for a new job. After interviewing her and following up with her references, I hired her on to oversee the technical end of things on site. Her name was Sandra, and on her advice, I upgraded the surveillance equipment to a more hightech system. I wanted to make sure Amanda and the kids would be well looked after, whenever I was away in Crystal Pines.

It was also decided that since we were installing a new surveillance system, that we might as well do some upgrades to our home as well. Our attic room and some other rooms were going to be sound proofed. When we first purchased our home and had it upgraded in 1995, we were only thinking of a very small family. Since Amanda had so many fertility issues, we originally thought that Chelsea would be an only child. But in the past year, our family had grown quite a bit, so we figured the extra sound proofing was worth it. To make it easier, in addition to the sound proofing, we added an intercom system, since calling out to the opposite side of the house would no longer be possible, with the soundproofing.

Before starting the upgrades, I called a staff meeting while Matty and his assistant, Aaron, looked at the security camera feeds, to make sure nothing would happen during our meeting. In addition to announcing the upgrades to the house and introducing Sandra as the newest member of our staff, I discussed their contract renewals and let them know everyone would be getting a raise, for all their hard work. I also discussed the amendments I was making to their contracts, including the removal of the 'no fraternization' clause.

They all looked at each other with wide eyes when I mentioned this. In explanation to the changes, I said, "The reason I'm doing this is because, let's face it, you all spend ninety-nine per cent of your lives here on this property and, some of you travel with us, so many of you don't have lives outside of your jobs. It's unfair of me to ask you not to have personal lives; and although you guys usually take turns at vacationing occasionally, for the most part you are here doing your jobs.

Your contracts include three weeks paid vacation time annually, but most of you take no more than a week – if any at all. I want all of you to be happy here, and I think you are, because we don't usually have much turnover in staff. The house we're building, as your new residence, is going to be your home and, well, I want you all to feel like you can be comfortable there. And whatever you guys do between shifts is your personal business, so you have time to do whatever you need to do to chill out. This job is tough and we're always under the public eye, so it can't be easy for any of you here."

I made sure I didn't look at Bridget or Steve, while I was talking, so they wouldn't feel put on the spot. But Adam stifled a laugh and I could see him glance at Steve. Bridget and Maggie looked at each other and smiled, so I could tell that they'd all probably known about Steve and Bridget's relationship for some time.

"However, that being said, you need to keep in mind that while you're on duty, your focus remains on the tasks at hand. I know my wife and I are sometimes not very discreet about showing our affections for each other in front of you, but, this is our home after all; and we *do* appreciate you giving us the space we need, in order that we can have a good marriage."

I explained to them that in view of recent events, they would all be undergoing new background checks, which brought murmurings and whispers amongst them. "I apologize for any inconvenience this may cause and hope you understand the need for it. I don't want you to feel uncomfortable about this. No one's job is as risk here, unless of course something turns up with the investigation that doesn't look right. If anyone here wishes to come forward, with any concerns or should there be anything in your backgrounds that might be considered questionable, you can approach me to discuss it privately. With everything that's happened to us over the last few years, I just want to make sure that my family is safe from harm. This is going to be to your benefit as well. I'm sure you'll feel better knowing that you and your loved ones are safe too."

I ended the meeting, after thanking them for being so loyal to us over the years and setting a good example for any new staff hired on recently. Maggie approached me after the meeting and said, "Did Amanda say something to you about what happened, before you and the kids left to go on vacation?" She looked worried that she might be in trouble for 'covering' for Steve and Bridget on the night that Amanda told me about.

I looked at Maggie and sighed. "Maggie, you don't need to worry about anything. We made this decision because it's not fair to any of you for us to expect no fraternization between each other, since you live here most of the time. Just to be clear about what I said during our meeting. When you're on duty, you need to be focused on your job, okay?"

Maggie smiled and thanked me. "You're a wonderful boss, you know that? And I promise, I'll never let anything that happens outside of working hours affect my job or my focus on the kids." She pursed her lips and kind of glanced at Adam when she turned away. *Oh, boy!*

I went back to the kitchen after the meeting and found Amanda cleaning up the lunch dishes. Bridget and Maggie took the kids outside to play in the yard, and all the other staff were attending to their duties.

Amanda asked me, "How'd the meeting go?" I smiled and said, "Okay."

"Anything interesting happen?" I explained to her about Maggie approaching me after the meeting and, "...she kind of glanced at Adam as she was leaving... and well, there were kind of a lot of glances from one to another, after I made the announcement about the no fraternization clause. So it looks as though there's been a lot more going on here than we originally *thought* there was." Amanda smiled and said, "Yeah, I kind of figured that one out already." I tilted my head to one side and said, "You *knew* about Adam and Maggie?" She shrugged and said, "Not officially, but, you know, when you're gone, I spend so much time here without you. I don't really care much for watching TV, when you're not here. And other than spending time with the kids, I have to keep myself amused *somehow!*" And she gave me that Cheshire cat smile of hers.

I snorted and said, "Okay, spill it! Who else?" Amanda laughed and said, "I thought you said it's none of our business?" I groaned and said, "Okay, never mind!"

I helped Amanda finish cleaning up the kitchen. I took over washing and she picked up the dish towel to dry. Between putting away each dish, we kept talking small talk and she hinted at who else might be seeing each other. I gave her a sideways glance after she revealed each of her 'secrets,' and, as she was waiting for me to scrub the last pot, she put the dish towel down on the counter and laced her arms around me from behind. She kissed my back and started stroking my belly and chest, which of course was driving Mr. Happy insane! She said, "Baby, don't you think it's nice that everyone else around here is as happy as we are?" I said, "I guess I can't argue with that!" *She has a point.*

After the kitchen was clean, I expected Amanda to ask me if I wanted to go for a ride, since it was such a nice day outside, and that was how she'd ended her flirtations at the beach house, the day before all the crazy stuff happened. But instead, she wrapped her arms around my neck, looked up at me and said, "Wanna go upstairs?" *Thank you, God!*

After a couple of hours of 'afternoon fun', Amanda was laying on her stomach with her right arm tucked under her pillow, her right cheek resting on it and her left hand was stroking my beard as I lay on my side, our gaze on each other, enjoying the afterglow. I placed my fingers, moving down her spine with my forefinger and came to a stop at her unicorn tattoo. I traced around the lines of the tattoo, admiring it. I normally didn't find tattoos, especially on a woman, appealing, but this was my beautiful wife. She was a package deal, so even her tattoo was beautiful to me. She moaned softly and said, "Mmmmmnnnn, that feels good." I kept tracing the tattoo and glanced down at it. When I looked back up into her eyes, she looked kind of sad, as she said, "If you hate it that much, maybe we can find out if I can get it removed."

I looked back at her in surprise and said, "Darlin', why do you think I hate it?" She said, "Come on, Jamie! I saw the way you looked at me in 1994, after the Mega Awards. You were too nice to criticize, but I knew you hated the blond hair the moment you saw it, and later, when I asked you about the tattoo, all you could come up with was, *'it's your body!'*" Her eyes welled up with tears, a sob caught in her throat and she said, "The last thing I ever want to do is disappoint you!" A single tear escaped her left eye and rolled over the bridge of her nose. My heart tightened in my chest. She *actually thinks I could be disappointed in her.* I pulled my hand away from the tattoo, brought it up to her left cheek and tucked her hair behind her ear. I said, "Raven, I love you more than anything in this world, and that *includes* the tattoo! I don't want you to change anything, okay? And I don't care if you dye your hair purple and green! I'll love you no matter what!"

She pulled herself up on the bed and looked down at me. I sat up on the bed as well so that we were facing each other. Then she said, "You mean that? You don't hate that I have a tattoo?" I gave her a crooked smile, "It kind of grew on me, okay?" She smiled and gave me butterfly kisses all over my face. Then, I said, "If I got a tattoo, what do you think it should be?"

Her eyes widened into saucers and she said, "No way! You'd *never* get a tattoo, would you?" I said, "Maybe, if you think it's sexy or something. I mean, Terry had a bazillion tattoos, so you must have been attracted to them." Amanda sighed and looked down at my chest. She said, "I didn't really like Terry's tattoos." She wrinkled up her nose and said, "They were all skulls and snakes and stuff that's gross!" I said, "So, if it wasn't the tattoos, then what was it about him that attracted you?"

She said, "It was always about the music. I was in awe of him when he played the guitar. It was like it was part of him. Just like you and Joey." I cleared my throat and said sarcastically, "So you thought he was just *dreamy,* when he played guitar?"

Amanda snorted and said, "It wasn't ever like that. I mean, dreamy?" She shook her head and said, "The moment I saw that first picture of you, when I was ten...*that* was *dreamy!*" I chuckled and said, "You know, it's okay to admit you were in love with him, at some point. I mean, you *did* marry him after all." Amanda said, "I was never in love with Terry. Yes, I had feelings for him, but I didn't really know what love was, when I met him. He was just so, persuasive. He and Lana both kept talking about making me a star and how special I was and how magical our chemistry was, when we played together. I just got so caught up in the idea of being in love with my guitar player that I actually believed it at the time. But within five minutes after we got married, I knew it was a mistake. I just didn't know how to get out of it. And because I was such a strict Catholic, I didn't believe in divorce. That was a dirty word, you know? My mom stayed with Tristan Landers because she didn't believe in divorce either, so I didn't *know* anything else!" When I met you...*that* was dreamy!"

I smiled and said, "I know, I felt it too. The attraction was very strong. I guess it was like love at first sight." Amanda nodded, "Except that wasn't the first time I ever saw you. I was already in love at age ten. And every time I saw you on TV, and at that concert Jenny and I went to." She shook her head and said, "I guess I was just a love-sick teeny-bopper! And then when Jenny showed me the newspaper article, with the picture of you in your tux and Melinda in her wedding dress...it broke my heart…" Her eyes welled again. She continued with, "I cried for weeks and weeks after that. I was inconsolable by Jenny or her mom. Geraldine put her arms around me, while I cried and Jenny held my hand. I think it was just because I had all these dreams of you coming to rescue me on your white horse and taking me away from all of that…" She shook her head and said, "I was so silly!"

I said, "No you weren't. You've had a really hard life and I guess all that dreaming of me, well…that was your way of coping." She smiled and asked, "How did *you* cope, you know, after losing Melinda?" I shook my head and said, "Not very well, I'm afraid. I was a mess. Grew my hair and beard out, gained a bunch of weight…ate a lot of burgers, pizza and ice cream. I was so angry at myself, for not being there for her, when she needed me. It was like I was punishing myself for it. My family tried to help, but I guess eventually I just sort of figured out that my binge eating, lazing around the house and not taking care of myself - or my hygiene, it was killing me – literally. I ended up in the hospital once. The doctors told me to shape up, or I'd be dead before I hit the age of thirty." Amanda gasped. "Joey and Justin told me about all of that, but they never said you were in the *hospital* because of it!"

I nodded and said, "After a few years, my family talked me into selling the house. I started eating better and going to the gym. That's when I started taking the nutrition and cooking classes. I was still depressed for many years after that, I just learned to deal with it better. I took my aggression out on the bar bells instead. And of course my music helped too. It wasn't until after I met *you* that I finally let all of that anger inside me dissolve."

Amanda brought her hand to my chest and used her forefinger to draw a circle around my heart. She said, "Right there!" I furrowed my brows and said, "What?" She said, "I'd put it right there – if you got a tattoo, that is." I tilted my head to one side, smiled and said, "And what would it be?" She shrugged and said, "I don't know - something that means a lot to you, maybe to us. Like the kids, or something. Or maybe a drawing of our wedding rings linked together." I said, "How about a rose?" She gave me a curious look, "You're not really *serious*, are you?" I said, "You don't think I should get a rose tattoo?" She shook her head and said, "No, I mean about getting a tattoo. You're just teasing me!"

I brought my hands to her cheeks and drew her towards me, kissing her, deeply. When I pulled away, I said, "I'm serious!" Amanda looked at me with wide eyes again and said, "Your family would have a *cow!*" I smiled and said, "So, what? They'd never have to see it." She said, "But what if you go swimming with them or something, they would see it and I'm telling you, they'd go ballistic - especially your *mother!*" I shook my head and said, "Raven, my family's not as prudish as you think they are. Yes, we're religious and strict about that, but look how they reacted about us not getting married in the church. They were fine with it. And they never once said anything about us having sexual relations, before we got married. Not once. After they saw that interview with you and Olivia Harper, I figured they'd be judgmental about it, but they weren't. All they could talk about was me being happy – with you!"

She said, "I overheard you and Joey talking that time at the beach house and the argument you two had. But when Joey figured out that we were sleeping together, he got really quiet. How did he react then?" I took her hands in mine and kissed her fingers and said, "I explained to Joey about your sexual issues. He understood. He knew about the abuse, he just didn't know the extent of it. I mean, he was there when you and Terry split up and heard a lot more than he probably should have, about your marriage. So it wasn't hard to explain it to him. He knew you needed time to figure things out in the bedroom with me. I promise you, there was never any judgment there. And you know he loves you."

Amanda sighed and said, "So you really want to get a tattoo?" I nodded and said, "Maybe we should both get one?" Her eyes were round as saucers again. "Really?" Her voice must have gone up two octaves, when she said it. She was excited about it. I said, "Does it hurt?" Her smile faded and she bobbed her head up and down, "Oh, yeah! It hurts like crazy! It feels like a bazillion bee stings, for as long as they're doing it." She scrunched her nose up again, "Maybe it's a bad idea." I sighed and said, "My Dad always said, "No pain, no gain." Amanda snorted, "Your Dad would roll over in his grave, if he knew I was trying to talk you into this!" And she giggled. I shook my head. "He's up there watching us right now and smiling." Amanda looked at me like I was from Mars and said, "Really? You think he would approve?" I shrugged and said, "He'd probably say, 'You're a grown man, who can make his own decisions.'"

Amanda smiled again and said, "Can I draw it?" I frowned and said, "You want to draw it?" She said, "I drew the original sketch for the unicorn." I nodded and remembered the pages from the diary and all the sketches in her keepsake box of all my family, the several drawings of me and the sketches in the diary of her wedding dress. And all the flowers and other wedding outfits. They were good. She had a talent – for a lot of things. "Okay, what will it be? And do you want a matching one?"

She nodded and said, "We could do a sterling silver rose and have it linked to our wedding bands. And maybe have the kids' names somehow in there." I said, "What about a drawing of the kids' faces?" Amanda shook her head and said, "That's too much detail. In order for them to get it right, it would have to be really big. Mine and Jenny's each took four hours to do. With the kids' faces, it might mean going back and forth over several sessions of four hours each. That would be *way* too painful." I said, "Okay, but I want mine to stretch out over my scars to cover them up."

Her brows slid together and she said, "Baby, you want to cover them up? That's a big tattoo and would take a long time. And why do you want to cover them up?" I said, "Because they're ugly..." Amanda looked at me like I had two heads. "Sandman, they are not! Those scars represent how much we could've lost! Remember how Chelsea used to trace them with her little fingers every day and give you butterfly kisses all over them? That's one of the nicest memories I have of her with you!" I shook my head and said, "That was a very traumatic time for all of us, especially Chelsea...and that was just our way of coping."

Amanda said, "Okay, how about just getting Chelsea's name in a nice font just above this one..." and she traced a line across the one closest to my heart, "And then maybe Eric and Nina's names on top and Alexander's on the bottom of this one." She traced a line on the one on my shoulder. This was the biggest scar because they had to do the surgery there, to remove the bullet. She said, "I don't want them to cover up the scars. I want to see them, forever. We could just put the names above and below, like they're close to your heart."

I thought about it and liked the idea. "But you don't want an exact match, do you? I mean, I'm not sure I want this guy, whoever he is to be seeing all of you exposed, you know?" Amanda shook her head and said, "Mine would be close, but not quite the same. I would still have the rose right here," and she pointed to the spot where her cleavage was.

"And the rings would be just above it. And I would get the kids' names inside the leaves, or something. I don't want to mess with anything too intimate, in case it might mess up something, where you usually do your thing with me. I don't want to damage any nerve endings 'cause I love everything you do there!" And she smiled.

"Oh, and maybe we should put our names inside of the rings," she said. I thought about it. "But the rings should be, you know, to scale with the rose. If they're that small, you wouldn't be able to read them and it might look messy." Amanda nodded, "You're right. How about this?" She traced a line across where the rings would be and said, "You could have my name going across the linked rings just inside the first one spreading across to the second one. And I could have your name inside the rings on mine." I nodded and said, "Let's do it!"

Amanda set about doing the sketches that evening and by morning she had two pages, each of them depicting what each of our tattoos would look like. It turned out that the rings would actually be big enough that we could use the font from the engraving on her ring exactly how it was, with the 'Forever, Jamie' on the inside, at the bottom of her ring and her name on the bottom of mine so that it said, "Forever Jamie & Amanda" with the two rings linked together. We kept our plans a secret and we made the appointment to have our tattoos done at the same time. She said, "We could hold hands, while they do it and encourage each other."

She told me about when she and Jenny had gotten the first tattoos together, and it took all their strength to keep going, throughout the process. We booked a flight to L.A. to have the tattoos done, as Amanda said she would prefer to go back to the same artists that had done hers and Jenny's tattoos. It turned out to be a lot more painful for me than it was for her, because they had to do one additional step for me, before starting the actual tattoo. *I now have a newfound respect for what Amanda does to groom herself.* They had to wax my chest to remove all the hairs, where the tattoo was going to be. *Ouch!*

It was about six hours later when we left the tattoo parlor and headed back to the airport with our chests bandaged up and a bag full of some sort of petroleum jelly type of ointment, to put on the tattoos every day while they healed. They told us to try not to get them wet for at least two weeks. I said, "Does this mean we have to have sponge baths for those two weeks?" Amanda laughed and said, "No, we can have a regular bath, just keep the tattoos bandaged up with waterproof bandages – just no showers. And we can't immerse them in water." I did a fake frown, stuck out my lower lip and said, "But I *like* our 'together showers'." She smiled and kissed my pouty lip and said, "I promise, I'll make it up to you in bed, okay?"

Our wounds were very sore, for awhile and the staff looked at us kind of funny, when they saw the bandages. I walked in on a conversation between Bridget, Maggie and Amanda the next day, while the kids were outside playing with Big Matty, Crystal and Little Matty. The girls were laughing and had gasped when Amanda told them we'd gotten tattoos together. Bridget said, "*No way! Jamie* got a tattoo??? What did his family say?" Amanda replied, "They don't know yet." Maggie rolled her eyes and said, "They're going to have a *conniption* fit!" Amanda giggled and said, "We'll see! He seems to think they'll be okay with it."

The girls asked if they could see Amanda's, but she said, "Not for awhile, until we can take the bandages off. But I can show you the sketches I made." She pulled them out of her purse and Bridget and Maggie both cooed at the pictures when they saw them. *I guess they approve.* When they noticed me standing there, the nannies both blushed and got up to go outside, to resume their duties. I put my hand up and said, "Relax, ladies. I don't mind you having a chat with Amanda now and then. She doesn't get to have much girl time these days." I saw the flash of pain in Amanda's eyes. She knew I was talking about Jenny – which made me want to kick myself for mentioning it. I knew how much she missed her.

The ladies resumed their conversation, while I went outside, to spend some time with the kids, before I had to go back to Crystal Pines. The kids nearly pounced on me when Chelsea stopped dead in her tracks. They were all overjoyed to see me, after our short trip to L.A. But I'd been careful to keep my shirt done up to the top button. I'd forgotten about it that day and left a few buttons undone, leaving the bandages visible. Nina and Eric were still running towards me, when Chelsea reached her hands out to her sides and pulled them back, grabbing their hands tightly.

I could see the shock and pain in her eyes, as she looked up at my chest. Nina and Eric both looked at Chelsea confused as they saw tears welling up in her eyes. I bent down on one knee and opened my arms to welcome them, but Chelsea held them back. I saw her trembling, as the tears flowed freely, down her cheeks. I looked down at the bandage and realized how much of an effect this was having on my daughter. *She remembers.*

I swallowed hard and said, "Baby, come here! It's okay!" Chelsea slowly released her grip on Nina and Eric's hands and gingerly stepped towards me. Big Matty and Crystal were looking at me and the bandage, with confusion in their eyes. I guessed that Amanda had only told Bridget and Maggie so far. I looked up at them and mouthed the word, "Tattoo."

Big Matty frowned and said, "*You??!*" And he stifled a laugh, seeing the effect the bandage was having on Chelsea. My little girl stepped closer but refused to accept my hug. She put her fingers up to my chest and traced a square around the bandage the way she'd done after our London scare. She was breathing heavily and still had tears streaming down her face. Finally, she said, "Daddy! You have a boo boo??" Her little chin was quivering and my heart broke in two. *Dang!* I should have warned them!

I sighed and said, "Just a little one! Baby, I'm sorry! I didn't mean to scare you! Mommy and I, when we went away, we..." I didn't know what to say. How could I have been so stupid! I struggled with my own emotions as I tried to figure out what to say to my poor little frightened child. Finally, I said, "Baby, it's okay. It's not like before. This is different. This is a good thing, I promise!" I pursed my lips and closed my eyes, as I desperately tried to figure out how to tell her that this wound was self inflicted. How could I make her understand? *I* didn't even understand why I'd done this. It was such an impulsive thing to do!

I waited a few beats, while Chelsea continued to trace around the bandage and Nina and Eric looked on, with worry in their eyes. I heard footsteps behind me and heard Maggie and Bridget's voices. I could hear them, but I didn't understand them. My heart was beating so loudly in my chest; all I could hear was the drumming in my ears. Finally, my breathing and heart rate slowed down enough, so that I could hear what Bridget was saying. Maggie didn't understand the way Bridget did. *She wasn't here back then.* I could hear Bridget calling to Amanda to get her purse. Amanda must have been standing behind me, as I heard the sound of her sandals shuffling around on the patio, as she ran back into the house. When she returned, she had the pictures in her hand and she knelt down beside us, showing them to Chelsea.

She said, "Mommy and Daddy wanted to show you all how much we love you and each other, so we got something done, when we went away."

She pointed to each of the pictures and said, "You know how Uncle Steve has those pictures on his arms and shoulders, right?" Chelsea took a breath and said, "And Uncle Adam and Uncle Matty, too?" Amanda nodded. She pulled her t-shirt down to show the kids her bandage. Chelsea dried her tears and said, "So it looks like this?" She pointed to the pictures. Amanda and I both nodded. Amanda pointed at the one with their names on the rose leaves and said, "This is Mommy's." And then pointed to the other one, "And this is Daddy's."

Nina and Eric stepped towards us and looked at the pictures, which were now in Chelsea's hands. Eric's eyes widened into saucers and said, *Hey! That's our names!"* Nina looked closer and Chelsea looked from the pictures to our faces and back again. Then she spoke, "And these are your rings!"

We both nodded and I asked, "Is that okay? Do you like the pictures?" All the kids looked at the sketches in wonder and then all nodded their approval. Chelsea said, "Daddy, does it hurt like before?" I breathed out a sigh of relief and said, "Not that much. But we can't touch it too much, for a few days, okay? That's how long we need to keep the bandages on.   After that, you can see the pictures, but they won't look very good for awhile, until the swelling goes down. And you can do what you did before and kiss them better if you like." Chelsea smiled, showing those pearly white teeth of hers as she said, "Okay!" Her bright blue eyes twinkled and her smile melted my heart. Amanda stroked my back and said, "I guess we should have included them in on our plans. I'm sorry, babe. I can see how much this has rattled you."

The kids went back to their playing on the swings and I got up, shakily, taking a few deep breaths. Amanda rose, slid her arms around my waist and I said, "You should have seen her face! It was just like…" Amanda said, "I know. That must have been awful for you to see!   But they understand now. They're okay! *See,* they're smiling and laughing again!" I put my arms around her and kissed the top of her head. We watched the kids while they played.

****

The next time I went to Crystal Pines, my tattoo had healed enough to show it to my family, without Melissa or Mom fainting. I could tell they were very surprised by it. Mom looked kind of annoyed, but she didn't scold me. She said, "It's nice," but I could tell she didn't approve. Melissa admired it and said, "So Amanda got one too?" I said yes. I also told them this was not her first time. The guys all teased me, then Joey said, "*Man,* you're – what do they call it? Pussy whipped?"

The rest of the guys all laughed and nodded their heads in agreement with Joey. And Mom chastised Joey for using the 'pussy' word. Melissa asked what and where Amanda's first tattoo was, since I was the only one who'd ever seen it. I told them and Melissa said, "I *love* unicorns and so do the kids! How long has she had that one?"

I said, "Since 1993, I think. She showed me for the first time after the 1994 Mega Awards. You know, when she dyed her hair blond." The guys snickered again and Justin said, "Yeah, I remember when we saw her. I knew you hated that! You *hate* bleach blondes!" I said, "Yeah, well I guess she didn't know that back then. But she told me she dyed it back right after that, even though we were still broken up at the time."

I felt shards of emotional fragments piercing my heart like tiny daggers, when I thought about how it was, during that time. Amanda was in a dark place back then and was trying to make herself feel better by getting a makeover, with the change in hair style, color and getting the unicorn tattoo. And I had likely slashed what little self esteem she had in those days, with my negative reaction to it. She'd come a long way since then regarding her happiness and self confidence, but I knew I still had to treat her with kid gloves at times.

She did a great job of hiding it, deep in the crevices of her heart. But every now and then, when I looked deep into those beautiful blue eyes of hers, I could still see traces of that battered, frightened child she'd once been. And I knew I had to be careful with what I said to her or how I reacted to anything she said or did. Because, although she'd become so much stronger with my attempts to build her up all these years. In the wake of everything that happened between us and to us, I realized that our life, our love and our happiness could be blown apart at any moment. Our marriage was strong, and we were deliriously happy, but we both knew how fragile that bubble we were living in could be...

I told my family that Amanda had done the original drawings of all the tattoos and Joey said, "Well, we always knew she could draw." Melissa and Mom both said they loved the sentiment behind the body art, but Mom said, "You shouldn't mess with Mother Nature's canvas." What she *really* meant was that God never intended for our bodies to be altered from their natural form. I supposed I got off easy. If I had done this when I was younger, I might have been spanked and grounded for life!

I leaned on the door, snapping it shut. My eyes scanned the room as I raised my hand to flip back the hood, shrugged out of my jacket and hung it on one of the hangers in the closet. It was the usual small motel room, but it would serve its purpose. The only sound to be heard was the pouring rain that drenched the streets of Chelsea tonight. I watched her as she drew the curtains closed, before shedding the brown curly wig, wagging her head from side to side, shaking her blond ponytail free. She tossed the wig on the well-aged dresser and turned to face me, with mischief in her eyes.

My heart raced in anticipation, though we'd done this countless times in the last couple of years. It felt as though we were teenagers, slipping out into the night, away from Mommy and Daddy's watchful eyes...Mommy and Daddy, in this case, being our bosses, Jamie and Amanda. But this time, the need for disguises wasn't necessary. For whatever reason, Jamie had removed the no-fraternization clause from our contracts.

But Bridget was still uneasy about revealing our relationship. And of course, there was the ever-watchful eye of the Paparazzi, permanently camped out in front of the Grayson's front gates since their return from Malibu. We'd done the usual – Bridget pretending to retire for the night and then slipping out the back French doors, while Maggie locked up. She'd run across the terrace, past Matty and Crystal's place through the dense brush. Trevor being the culprit tonight, shutting down the security cameras at the exit point, where Bridget escaped, wearing her usual disguise, and meeting me on Oliver Rd.

****

Our lips locked in a deep, hungry kiss, while I pulled the elastic band from her hair. Her golden locks feathered all around her shoulders, as we groped and tore at each others' clothing. She yanked my t-shirt from the waistband of my jeans, slipping it over my head and tossing it on the floor. I felt her shudder as my thumbs raked across her nipples through her shirt, making them harden like bullets. She put her hands up to my chest, nudging me backward toward the bed. We tumbled onto the mattress and bounced as we continued with our quest for release.

The world seemed to melt away around us, while pieces of clothing flew across the room. She straddled me as I lay on my back, while her fingers fumbled with my belt buckle. I dared not help her, as she liked to be in control during our love-making sessions…much to my delight! When the buckle finally complied, she yanked hard and I heard a whipping sound, as she pulled the belt free and flung it to the side. She was already working on the button and zipper of my fly. I lifted my hips as she hooked her fingers over the waistband of the denim, pulling it down, just enough to get the job done. *She's always in such a hurry.*

Before I could even blink, her lips were on my shaft, planting urgent kisses from the head to my balls. It was all I could do to maintain control. I felt her fingers wrap around me, lifting it up and into her hot, wet mouth swallowing swiftly, as my hardness sunk deeply inside. My sex-crazed brain felt the high that could only be compared to the effects of a double-shot of my favorite Scotch. I let her play for as long as I could hold out, and then, laced my fingers through her hair and eased her away.

Her eyes shot up toward my face with a look that could kill me faster than a speeding bullet.

But tonight, I wanted more than a quick fix.

Her lips curled into a snarl, her disapproval apparent, as I murmured softly, "B - we have time. We both have the night off. Slow down, honey!" Before she could protest further, I reached down and pulled her up by the arm pits, rolling us both around, so that I was on top of her. She was an Amazon, standing six feet tall in heels, but she was no match for my muscle-bound strength.

I leaned in for a hard, smoldering kiss and she relaxed, letting me take the lead, for once. I pulled away and whispered into her ear, "My turn!"

My lips grazed her neck, briefly, and then made their way downward. I suckled her breasts, one at a time, caressing her arms and legs with my fingers. She writhed beneath me and a deep moan gurgled up inside her throat. As I switched sides with my mouth, I brought my hands up and stroked the swell of her ample bosom, while I nibbled on the perfect rosebuds, making her gasp.

My mouth moved downward. She opened herself up to me and I saw her glistening, neatly trimmed, sweet-smelling haven of pleasure, ready for me to feast on her. My tongue delved deep and she shivered. "I love you, Stevie!" A chuckle escaped from deep inside my chest. She swatted my arm and hissed, "And just what is so *funny?*" Risking her wrath at the rude interruption, I lifted my head and glanced up at her beautiful face as I said, "You know, you're the only one who can get away with calling me that? Anyone else would get his block knocked off, from here to kingdom come!"

Bridget's lips curved up, revealing gleaming white teeth as she said, "Your queen awaits her pleasure!" I chuckled again and said, "As you wish, Your Highness!" I began devouring her most sensitive spot and proceeded to make her scream.

****

I rolled off the love of my life and laced my fingers through hers, while we gasped for air. We'd just finished another round of the most mind-blowing sex, ever. I was just starting to drift off when my cell phone buzzed. Bridget groaned and said, "Let it go to voice mail, pleeeease!!!" In the wake of all that had happened in the past two years, I knew I couldn't do that. I squeezed Bridget's hand and gave her a quick kiss before reaching over her, snatching the phone from the nightstand. It was a text. "It's Jamie."

I heard Bridget groan again, as she said, "So much for the night off!" I glanced at the clock on the nightstand. It was just after two a.m. She rolled off the bed and started to gather up our clothes, which were strewn across the motel room floor.

Jamie: *You awake?*

Me: *Yup. Everything okay?*

Jamie: *So-so*

Me: *Family okay?*

Jamie: *Kids and Amanda just fell asleep.*

Me: *More nightmares?*

Jamie: *Yup*

Me: *You need me to come home?*

Jamie: *You're off duty*

Me: *But you need me*

Jamie: *Could use a spotter*

Me: *Be there soon*

Jamie: *No…you deserve your night off*

Me: *And you shouldn't work out alone*

Jamie: *How did you know?*

Me: *How long have I worked for you?*

Jamie: *Good point*

Me: *Be there in twenty*

****

I watched as Jamie exhaled, sharply, through his mouth. We were downstairs in his workout room in the Grayson's home, in Chelsea. I was still technically off duty, but we'd agreed to spot each other, while we lifted weights. It was Jamie's turn with the bar bells. He was only at fifty of his usual hundred reps; but I could see beads of sweat forming at his brow, his bare chest glistening and he seemed to be pushing himself too hard. His gaze was fierce, and I saw deep, worry lines etched into his face, as he forged ahead.

Jamie often worked off his aggression with the weights when life gave him some pretty steep mountains to climb. In the wake of what that monster, Ian Fairbanks had put this family through, recently in California, and two years ago in London, England, I worried for my employer and friend.

After surviving being abducted, Amanda was rescued by the Feds and brought home, virtually unharmed…at least physically. But emotionally, it was a different story. Amanda, Chelsea and the twins were having terrible nightmares, which kept Jamie awake at night…like tonight.

Amanda's chronic anxiety was a huge issue and it affected the kids…and Jamie…more than he cared to admit. Amanda saw him as a super-hero. Invincible. But I knew better. He kept a lot inside. *Like me.*

I knew he was stressing, big-time, over the new security hires and technical upgrades. He'd spent endless hours interviewing and doing background checks – on everyone. Sandra was one of those new hires, a technical wizard, who came highly recommended by the Feds. Jamie was doing what he always did…looking after his family - protecting them at all costs.

My heart tightened in my chest at the thought of what could have happened. Things could have turned out much worse. *What if Bridget and the kids were inside the house when that psycho showed up?* I did a mental shudder at the thought of Bridget getting hurt…or worse. *And I wasn't there to protect her…them.*

I wasn't sure if Jamie knew about us...our relationship. He never brought the subject up. If he *did* know, *that* was most likely the reason he'd removed the no fraternization clause from our contracts. Bridget mentioned the conversation she'd had with him, just before the shit hit the fan in California. She was worried about our jobs. But I knew if it came to that...if I had to choose between Bridget and my job...Bridget would win, hands down. I loved her more than anything. But then, Jamie called the staff meeting and talked about the contract changes. He was a good man. A good husband, a wonderful father to his kids...a great boss...and fantastic friend.

Before coming to work for The Grayson Family, I'd taken a few security jobs...short contracts for other celebrities - to get away from all the death – the horrors of war. Serving my country had been important to me. But I'd done my time, gotten an honorable discharge, and I promised my son, Logan, that I'd stay safe...after being wounded during the last tour. And I never regretted that decision – especially after coming to work for Jamie. It was a dream job that paid well. And I'd made some lasting friendships - including the one I now had with Jamie. And this job brought me Bridget. I thought back to the first time Jamie introduced us. The chemistry was strong, even then. But we'd waited, knowing how dangerous a relationship could be.

I remembered the first time we'd met in the stables. It was after the 9/11 attacks and the twins had just been adopted by the Graysons. I'd just hired Darryl and Brad. They were brothers, who'd worked as Amanda's security team, while touring with The Bar Riders. They'd taken off the last month of that final tour, to spend time with their mother, who'd been ailing with Alzheimer's disease and finally succumbed and perished. They were just laying her to rest when the plane crashes happened.

Maggie had also just been hired, to help with the fast-growing family. It was a blessing for Bridget and I to have a much-needed break, after everything that had happened. I could hear the horses snorting, softly and the wind had picked up outside. There was a groan of an old elm tree's branches swaying just outside and scraping against the back of the stable. We were in Silver's stall – away from the security cameras' prying eyes. The conversation between us was as follows:

Bridget: "Hi."

Me: "Hi, yourself."

Bridget: "We shouldn't be here – like this."

Me: "Then, why *are* we here?"

Bridget: "I don't know."

Me: "Yes, you do."

Bridget: "I do?"

Me: "Come on, B! We've been dancing
             around this for far too long."

Bridget: "I know."

Me: "So what're we going to do about it?"

We'd stood there, staring at each other for a few beats, waiting for the other to make the first move. Her gaze was intense, and the sexual tension was fierce, for as long as I could remember. The stolen glances when the rest of the household wasn't looking. I'd wanted to kiss her for three agonizing years, but never took the chance. We both knew we could lose our jobs if we ever acted on our feelings. I was good at my job and took it very seriously. We both did.

And then, it was as though lightning struck, and she was in my arms, my lips on hers. The air was cool, but the heat between us was scorching. She'd been the one to make the first move…and the rest was a blur. My hands slipped under her sweater, groping her heaving breasts. I felt her hands move swiftly, undoing my fly with expertise, as she reached for my ever-growing erection. She stroked me up and down, while I kneaded and shaped her soft mounds of flesh. My mouth sunk into hers as I felt her shudder when my fingers brushed against her nipples through her bra. I heard a moan erupt from deep inside her, while she continued to caress my shaft. I moved one of my hands down and slipped it inside her leggings, my fingers reaching between her legs. Her lace thong was already damp with her desire.

I stifled her gasps with my kisses, as I found the spot she wanted me to touch. I hooked my forefinger over the side of the lace, moving it to the side and touched her there. Using my middle finger, I stroked her with circular motions, causing her to cry out as she rolled her head backward. "Don't stop!" she murmured. I watched her face fill with joy in the moonlight, creeping its way through the small window of the stables. Her climax was strong, as she bit down on her lower lip, stifling a scream. I kept up the gentle strokes, making sure her orgasm was complete, before pulling away...but not before inserting a finger, deep inside of her. She was hot and dripping wet.

I hooked my fingers over her waistband, yanking the leggings down to her ankles. "Shit!" She was cursing herself, trying unsuccessfully to free herself from the tight spandex. I kneeled down in front of her as she lifted one foot slightly, so I could pull off her sneaker and ease the pant leg over her foot, the sock coming off with it. I straightened and slipped my hand into my jeans pocket, pulling out the condom. She tore it from my fingers impatiently. I watched in awe, as she unwrapped it expertly, using her teeth, spit the plastic out the side of her mouth and sheathed me in one fell swoop.

She lifted her bare leg as I grasped her behind, pulling her close. Both legs were wrapping themselves around my waist, as we came together at long last. Our eyes locked in a smoldering gaze as we rocked together in perfect rhythm. The storm that had been brewing outside finally broke loose and the thunder rolled in the sky, echoing our own dramatic crash into oblivion.

Our passion was as strong and explosive as I'd been imagining...

****

I was brought back to the present by a groan. I gave myself a mental head slap that I'd let my mind wander so far. *You're supposed to be spotting him, you dope!* Jamie's breathing was labored, and I saw his arms start to shake. "Whoa! Okay, that's enough. You're pushing it too far, buddy!" I reached down and grabbed the barbell from his grasp, just before his strength gave out. Several moments passed before Jamie could speak, while his breathing slowed. He shook his head as he said, "I don't understand...I usually make it to a hundred!"

"Give yourself a break, Jamie. Life hasn't exactly been easy for you in the past several weeks." I set the weights on the stand, circled around and sat down on the stool near the bench, while Jamie pushed himself to a sitting position. I leaned over towards the little bar fridge, reached inside and took out two bottles of icy water, handing one to

Jamie. He took it and we both chilled for a bit. I stared at my friend, wondering if he was okay. Heart disease ran in his family, after all. And Jamie had turned forty-nine in the spring. His breathing, though still labored, began to even out. "You okay, Jamie?" He nodded and murmured, "Just tired. Not much sleep…too much stress…you know, the usual!" He reached for the towel that was lying on the floor next to the bench and wrapped it around his neck.

I chuckled and said, "I thought *Amanda* was the manic-depressive insomniac!" Jamie lifted one side of his mouth in a half smile that didn't reach his eyes. He shrugged and said, "My kids are supposed to be having the time of their lives…in Animation Dreamland. Not being afraid of some boogeyman who might take their mother away!" I watched his Adam's apple bob up and down as he blinked back the tears that threatened to fall. He turned his head away, taking a moment to regain control.

I reached over and gave his shoulder a reassuring squeeze. "Jamie, you know it's *my* job to protect you – and *them*, from the boogeyman, right? That's why you pay me the big bucks." And I winked at him. He huffed out a wet chuckle. Then I said, "From now on, whenever you go on the road, for whatever reason, I'll be there, okay? This last time was…I should've –"

Jamie's hand went up to silence me as he said, "It wasn't your fault, Steve. No one could have known that crazy son-of-a…" He caught himself before uttering the curse words. But I knew he was thinking them in his head. We both were. We stared at each other with knowing eyes. "That crazy son-of-a-bitch is dead. He can't hurt Amanda…or the kids anymore." I knew as soon as the words left my lips, I regretted uttering them. That monster would probably haunt this family from his grave for a long time…in their nightmares.

"Want to know a secret?" Amanda was feeding Alexander and Bridget was giving Chelsea and Nina a bath, while I was in Eric's room picking out his pajamas from the dresser. Apparently Eric had a secret. I grabbed his fireman PJs, slid the drawer closed and turned around to look at my son, who was sitting on his bed with his towel wrapped around him. His eyes sparkled with mischief. I walked over and sat down beside him, while he looked up at me with those saucer blue eyes he'd inherited from Jenny. I pulled the towel away, began helping him put his on pajamas and said, "Well, if you tell, it won't be a *secret,* then, will it?"

Eric looked pensive for a moment and then said, "But Nina and Chelsea know it!" My brows furrowed and I said, "Is it an important secret?" Eric shrugged and said, "Well, Chelsea says that Auntie Bridget and Uncle Steve are breaking the rules." I tilted my head to one side and said, "They are, are they?" Eric nodded, "Uh–huh!" I stifled a laugh and said, "And just what rule are they breaking?" Eric curled his lips around his teeth and then said, "Promise you won't tell?" I cocked my jaw to one side and asked, "And who am I not supposed to tell?" Eric said, *"Chelsea,* you silly!" And he giggled. I smiled and said, "Okay, I won't tell Chelsea, if you won't!" Eric nodded his head, shook my hand, and said, "Deal!"

I waited patiently for him to continue with his 'secret', which I had a feeling I already knew about. But I wanted to make sure that this secret wasn't affecting the way my staff was doing their jobs. Eric looked up at me and pulled himself up on his knees. He leaned over towards my ear and covered his mouth as he whispered into it, as if Chelsea and Nina might hear him over their shrieks in the bathtub. "Auntie Bridget and Uncle Steve are in love!" I couldn't help myself, I started to chuckle. But my smile faded because I was kind of concerned at how my kids knew. And that made me wonder if I hadn't been hasty about removing the no fraternization clause in their contracts. Eric started to giggle again. I cleared my throat and said, "Okay, so how did your *sister* know about this secret?" Eric shrugged and said, "I don't know, I just know it's supposed to be a secret because it's a rule."

I raised an eyebrow and said, "A rule?" Eric nodded, "I mean they're breaking a rule." I said, "And whose rule are they breaking?" Eric said, "I don't know. It's just a rule and Chelsea said if I told the secret, that Auntie Bridget and Uncle Steve might have to leave." I sighed, "So, you only know this because Chelsea told you?" Eric nodded. I smiled and said, "Okay, your secret is safe with me. I won't tell Chelsea you told me." Eric looked proud that he'd gotten away with telling Chelsea's secret. He held his hands up over his mouth and did a little, "Teehee!" as he bounced his shoulders up and down.

****

I waited for Amanda to come out into the hallway with A.J. and for Bridget to be done getting the girls ready for bed. Then, we all piled into Chelsea's room for our nightly ritual of telling three stories and singing three songs. The kids were tuckered out from a day of playing outside and were asleep by the time we finished the third song. Bridget and Amanda each picked up one of the twins and took them to their rooms, while I carried A.J. to his room and placed him into his crib.

I sighed and braced myself for a long night. I knew I had to confront Bridget with this. I was hoping there was some sort of good explanation, that she and Steve hadn't disobeyed me and snuck a kiss – or anything else, in front of the kids, while they were both on duty. Bridget and Amanda were just coming out of each of the girls' rooms, when I entered the hallway. I glanced at Bridget, who said, "I'm going to turn in early and read my book, if that's okay." Amanda smiled and nodded, but I put up my hand and said, "I need to talk to you, Bridget."

Amanda looked up at me and saw the seriousness in my eyes. She opened her mouth to speak, but I held up my hand again and she snapped her mouth shut, stifling her thoughts. Instead, she touched my out-stretched hand and said softly, "Do you need me to make myself scarce?"

I sighed and said, "Maybe you should be in on this conversation, since it concerns the kids." Bridget's face blanched as I glanced over at her. I gestured towards the living room and we all walked quietly towards it. I closed the hallway door carefully behind me, as the ladies both sat on the couch and I shuffled towards them, choosing my spot on the love seat.

Bridget looked apprehensive as she fidgeted on the couch, while she waited for me to speak. I was fighting with myself because I'd promised Eric that I wouldn't tell about the secret. But technically, I wasn't breaking that promise, because it wasn't Chelsea I was telling. I cleared my throat and said, "I'd like to think I'm a fair man – er - employer here." Bridget's eyes went wide as she looked across at me and said, "Are you going to *fire* me?" Bridget's whole body took on a deer in the headlights look and it was as if she'd stopped breathing. I said, "Easy, this is just a conversation for now." When I was confident that Bridget was more at ease, I continued with, "The kids seem to know your secret somehow."

Bridget said, "Secret?" I slid my jaw to one side and said, "Bridget, I think you know to what I'm referring." Amanda said, "Baby, shouldn't Steve be here for this conversation?" I nodded and said, "You're right. Maybe he should." I pulled my cell phone out of my pocket and dialed Steve's cell number. He answered on the first ring, "Can you come up to the house for a minute, please?" Steve said, "Is something wrong? I don't see anything happening on the monitors." I said, "This isn't about that. Please, just come in. We're in the living room."

We sat in silence, until we heard the front door open and Steve disarmed and rearmed the security system, before joining us in the living room. When Steve saw Bridget sitting there with us, there was a flash in his eyes. I gestured for him to sit and he did so, on the armchair. Steve cleared his throat and said, "Everything okay, here?" I held up my hand and said, "We're physically safe, as long as Adam and Trevor are at their posts."

I sighed and said, "You two have been here from the beginning and I wanted to say that you've been valued employees thus far. Steve's face was stone cold, unreadable, but his lips twitched, a tell-tale sign that he was concerned. His body was rigid, but his eyes flitted over to Bridget, who was still fidgeting in her seat. Amanda reached over and put her hand over Bridget's and squeezed it. She repeated my earlier statement, "This is just a conversation for now, Bridget, right Jamie?" She looked at me for confirmation and I nodded. I cleared my throat. The last thing I wanted to do tonight was fire anyone, but I needed to know that these team members were doing their jobs, the way they always had, without distractions.

I took in a deep breath and said, "I just had an interesting conversation with Eric, while the girls were having their bath." Bridget raised her eyebrows, glanced at Steve and then turned her gaze back towards me and said, "*Eric?*" It was as though she'd been expecting this conversation, but not because of *Eric* telling me anything. So it was true. Chelsea must have found out about their relationship, somehow. I sighed and asked them both if they remembered our meeting earlier in the week. I brought up the subject of the no fraternization clauses being removed from their contracts. I'd made the amendment effective immediately, so all the new paperwork had already been signed.

I said, "I *did* stress that while I was okay with whatever happened amongst employees here, while they're off duty, that if there are any relationships happening, that it should not affect your work." Bridget and Steve both nodded and waited for me to finish. "Well, it appears as though it's affecting my kids in some way." Bridget raised her hand above her head like a school child, waiting for me to give her permission to speak. I said, "Like I *said*, this is just a conversation, so feel free to say anything you want."

Bridget lowered her hand and asked, "Was Eric upset about something?" I shook my head and said, "No, he was giggling about a secret that Chelsea told him and he asked that I not tell her what he told me." Bridget and Steve exchanged glances and I saw their cheeks heat, realizing their relationship had been revealed. I continued with, "I don't think that Eric is really aware of what a secret is, but he whispered it in my ear as though it was serious. I almost laughed out loud because I kind of already knew. But what I would like to know is how my children *know* about your secret. I just want to know that my kids are safe."

Steve spoke up, "Jamie, you know that I would...*we*...would never let anything happen to you, Amanda or the kids, no matter what! Your family is safe. Bridget hasn't done anything wrong. I promise you. Your kids...I have no idea what they're saying, but..."

I held up my hand again and he fell silent. I said, "You know that I want my staff to be happy, I just..." I sighed and waited a few beats before continuing. "Eric said that Chelsea told him and Nina that you two are in love. He doesn't seem to know anything beyond that. But I would just like to know how *Chelsea* knows about it."

Bridget's eyes welled up with tears. *Dang! Please don't make me have to fire them!* Her voice wavered as she spoke, "It was the other night, the night before the staff meeting. I woke up when I heard footsteps in the hallway. It was after three a.m. Eric had locked himself in our bathroom to pee and Chelsea also had to go." She sighed and then, "You two were in the shower, er, together and Chelsea was just about to reach for the bathroom doorknob, but I stopped her. I could hear, well, you two were kind of busy in there and..."

I put up my hand again and said, "Okay, I get the point." She said, "I could see she had to really go, so I picked her up and brought her down to the basement bathroom." She continued the story of how they just made it in time and how Chelsea was curious about what Amanda and I were doing in the bathroom shower together.

"I just said that you were doing what grown–ups that are in love do sometimes, and she…well, didn't understand. I thought I was going to have a sex talk with a six-year-old, which I wasn't ready for, but then she just blurted it out. She asked if Steve and I were in love too." My heart tightened in my chest. *Here we go…*

Bridget said, "It was only that one time and we were very quiet. I don't know what to say. It was the night before we all went to California. And Steve and I were just trying to have a moment alone together. My heart nearly stopped when she said it. But then, she asked me if we were jumping on the bed, because she heard the bed creak and then she heard Steve laugh. I didn't want to lie to her and say that we were jumping on the bed, but I promise you, I didn't say anything inappropriate. I *swear!*"

Bridget looked down at her hands and curled her fingers into fists before she continued, "I sat down on the floor and I guess I got kind of upset because, well, the no fraternization clause was still in effect. I didn't even realize I was crying, until after Chelsea finished washing and drying her hands. She knelt down on the floor and asked me what was wrong. So I said, 'I guess the secret's out' and she asked me what a secret was. I tried to explain it to her, but I would *never* get her to lie for us. Please *believe* me! I even told her that if you ever asked her about it that I didn't *want* her to lie. I just didn't know how to console her, because when I told her that Steve and I were breaking a rule and that we might have to leave because of it, she was crying. And then I thought about breaking up this beautiful family of yours…" Bridget was sobbing now and there were tears rolling down her cheeks like a waterfall.

Amanda shifted in her seat and I saw her eyes well up as well. I had to do a mental double take at what Bridget just said. "*Whoa!* Who said anything about breaking anyone *up*?" Bridget murmured through her tears, "I thought that if you knew about me and Steve, the kids might resent you for firing us. It was stupid. I know I should have come to you right away. I should have told you. I'm sorry, Jamie! I just love those kids so much and I don't want to leave, but please don't fire us both. I will resign so Steve can stay. Please don't fire him, too!"

I took a deep breath and said, "Okay, so they never actually *saw* you two doing anything, right?" Bridget shook her head vehemently, and Steve said, "I promise, we never, *ever* showed our affections in front of your kids. We usually meet off site when we're off duty. That night was the only time there was any contact between us in the house. I'd just gotten off shift and Bridget was technically off duty too. And we locked the door. Jamie you *gotta* believe us, we would never do anything to hurt those kids!"

Bridget nodded in agreement and said, "Chelsea was crying so hard she was shaking, when I told her that you might let us go. I made up my mind that night that I was going to tell you after the meeting. But then you told us we were okay, that you were removing the no fraternization clause, so I thought we were safe. But I promise you, I told her the secret was only going to be a secret, just until I could figure out how to approach you with this. I didn't want her to get into trouble for lying to you, so I said she should let me handle it. I never meant for her to get involved in all of this. It just sort of happened. I'm sorry, Jamie! I'll pack my things and leave in the morning...or tonight if you want me to."

I buried my face in my hands and Amanda said, "Baby, this isn't their fault. You don't have to do this! *Please!*" I waited a few beats, before I raised my head and said, "Okay, nobody's getting fired tonight. What happened...happened. Chelsea just heard a laugh and a bed creaking. Amanda and I aren't exactly discreet about showing our affections towards each other, wherever we are in the house. And you guys have been good about getting the kids out of the room, when that happens." I felt heat rising to my face. "I guess I've made a really good decision in having the walls sound–proofed."

Steve said, "So we're *not* fired?" Amanda put her hand on her chest and it looked like she was holding her breath, so I said, "No. Nobody's getting fired here. You guys are still good at your jobs and I know the kids would be really upset if one or both of you left. So...no, you guys are okay. Your jobs are safe. Just, no more meeting in Bridget's room...er, at least until after the sound-proofing is done."

Steve, Bridget and Amanda both blew out sighs of relief. Steve said, "We won't be doing anything in the house, ever again. I promise. When the staff residence is built, we'll meet there, okay?"

Amanda sighed and said, "Ok, so what do we do about the kids now? I mean, they're going around telling each other secrets and asking people not to tell. That really isn't a good thing. It sets a bad example. They think that the members of the staff aren't allowed to be in love, but we *are?* That's gotta be really confusing for them." I said, "I agree. But how do we approach them about this? I mean," I looked at Bridget and Steve and said, "I don't want to put you guys on the spot, here, but we have to tell the kids that it's not a bad thing for you two to be together."

Bridget nodded and looked at Steve, who said, "It's okay for you guys to tell them about us. I mean they got it right, we *are* in love. That's not a lie." Bridget said, "Well, I kind of told Chelsea that night when she asked me about it. She was really upset. She thought her Daddy was so mean that he wouldn't let us be together. I told her it was a rule, for the people who work here, not to be friendly like that and she kept saying it was a stupid rule. But I set her straight and said that her Daddy was only trying to protect his family. I told her you're *not* mean and that you're a good boss."

She dried her tears, smiled and said, "You know your daughter's one smart cookie too. I tried to use what happened in California, with Amanda, as an example of what could happen, if we weren't doing our jobs properly. And she said that I *was* doing my job and that it wasn't my job to protect her Mommy. I was in the car with the kids and Steve wasn't there. She made a big deal out of how Steve couldn't possibly protect her Mommy from that man, if he wasn't there at the time."

I threw my head back and laughed out loud. "She has a point!" The mood in the room suddenly shifted to a different light and I was very happy that I didn't have to fire anyone.

We told the kids about it the next day - and I used the example of what happened in California, but I told Chelsea she was right. It *was* a stupid rule and I told her that I'd changed the rules, so Bridget and Steve could be together, as long as they could do their jobs at the same time. All the kids were happy that I'd changed the rules.

This set off a waterfall of news around the household, because, of course, there'd been a few more relationships blossoming amongst the rest of the staff, for awhile now. But all was well in the

Grayson household and our staff seemed to continue to do their jobs well, despite cupid's arrows in free flow...

I punched in the four-digit code to silence the high pitched whine of the alarm and then re-entered the code to set it to the 'Armed/Stay' setting. I shrugged out of my leather jacket, hung it in the closet, slipped off my cowboy boots, placed them on the floor below the jacket and shut the mirrored sliding door. I juggled my luggage and made my way up to the master bedroom.

The house was quiet short of the sound of music coming from the dance studio. I wondered where everyone was as I made my way up the attic stairs that led to our bedroom. I set the luggage down in front of the bedroom closet and placed the laptop case on top of my dresser. I glanced at my watch and saw it was a quarter to three. Alexander must have been still napping while Amanda danced in the studio. I pulled my cell phone out of my back pocket, set it on the nightstand and then grabbed some fresh clothes. I padded my way back down the attic steps, crossed the hallway and entered our private bath to grab a quick shower before greeting my family before dinner.

I dried myself off, slipped on some fresh clothes and tossed the dirty ones into the hamper. I made my way down the hallway towards the back of the house. When I reached the den, I spotted Bridget heading out the back French doors to the patio with the daily paper in hand. She smiled and said, "Hi, Jamie! Welcome home!" I smiled and nodded, asked her where everyone was and she responded, "Alexander's napping, Amanda's dancing in the studio and the twins and Chelsea are over visiting with Crystal and Little Matty."

My heart skipped a beat and I felt the corners of my mouth go up in hopes that I could spend a few moments alone with Amanda, before dinner. Bridget asked me, "Are you hungry? Would you like me to fix you something to eat?" She raised her eyebrows, as she looked up at me with baited breath, waiting for my response. I shook my head and said, "No, I grabbed a bite to eat on the plane. I'm good till dinner. Go ahead. Take a break and read the paper."

Bridget smiled, nodded and went through the French doors to sit at the patio table to read. I noticed Big Matty coming out of the stables carrying his toolbox, so I figured he must have been repairing something in there. He waved at me and I waved back at him, before turning on my heel and heading back towards the front of the house. I made my way through the kitchen and glanced at the basement door, making sure the lock was secure in case by some chance, Alexander got out of his crib.

I hurried down the hallway toward the dance studio and opened the door, walked through it and locked the door behind me. Amanda was pirouetting around the room as I stood there mesmerized by her graceful movements. She took a run and jumped up; separating her legs in a forward split, sailed through the air and made a perfect landing. Her right knee went down on the floor, followed by her left, twirling around on them and then rose on her feet again, in the blink of an eye. Her right leg crossed over her left as she kicked it high in a circular motion across to the right and then she jumped up once more, landing on the right leg again. She then rose on point and flitted across the floor as my eyes followed her path. My heart swelled with pride as I watched my wife engrossed in her dancing.

More spinning pirouettes followed as I noticed the clip in her hair was hanging on loosely by a small strand. It suddenly broke free, skidded across the floor and her raven mane flowed like feathers, falling all around her shoulders. Mr. Happy sprung up to immediate attention as I continued to watch her. *Dang! Why does that always happen?* I'd missed her, while I was working in Crystal Pines at the night club, with my brothers and sister.

Her arms waved up and down like the wings of a butterfly and then she lunged down on her left knee, kicking her right leg backward above her head. Her right arm folded at the elbow, as her hand bent downward at the wrist, as though she was waving at her imaginary audience, while her left arm rose behind her. It was like a graceful bow as the music came to a crescendo. The familiar piece was reaching the end, which meant that her routine was also finished.

I realized that I'd been so drawn to the dance that I'd moved towards her. I reached up with my left hand and traced a line down her raised arm. Her hair was now completely covering her face. I could see her breathing heavily from her exercise, and the strands of hair that were directly in front of her mouth moved forward, each time she exhaled. She slowly brought her leg back down. I reached up with the index fingers of both hands and tucked her hair behind her ears, revealing her beautiful face.

She was damp with perspiration, but her wildflower scent was what filled my nostrils. Her eyes sparkled like diamonds and her face was literally glowing, either from the joy she felt at the dance she'd just completed, or she was just that happy to see me. I decided it was the latter as she rose on her toes, laced her arms around my neck and brushed my lips with hers. I cupped her behind with my palms, raising her up so I could kiss her deeply. She wrapped her legs around me, while I moved us across the room. I opened one eye to make sure we were heading some place safe. I decided to veer towards the piano bench and set her down gently.

I got down on one knee as she laced her fingers through my hair, leaning in closer for another deep kiss. Our unspoken greeting continued, as I reached up with both hands and pulled her leotard downwards, exposing her bra. We were both breathless now as I fumbled with the clasp and her ample breasts broke free. She was still breastfeeding Alexander, so they were quite large to accommodate the milk, *much to my delight!* I started caressing the swell of her soft mounds and tracing lines up to the nipples.

She shivered beneath my touch. as we continued to kiss loudly and hungrily. I brushed my thumbs across the tips of her nipples and felt how engorged her breasts were. I knew it was almost time for her to feed our son, so I said a silent prayer that we could finish our lovemaking, before he woke up from his nap. I felt her fumbling with the buttons on my shirt, making her way down to undo the button on my jeans. My heart was thundering in my chest, as she unzipped my fly, releasing Mr. Happy from the agonizing grip of my now very tight jeans. I brought her hands up to my face and kissed each of her palms and wrists and placed them at her sides on the piano bench.

I began a trail of kisses from her neck to her breasts, sucking each nipple until they were both standing at attention. She whimpered and cooed her appreciation, as I lingered there a while longer, before moving downward to please her orally just past the damp curls at the apex of her legs.

Her orgasm was strong, as she cried out my name. I rose up, straddled the bench and was ready to insert myself into her hot, warm insides, when I heard the familiar whimpering sounds coming from the baby monitor remote, which was sitting on the piano next to a piece of sheet music.

We both glanced at the monitor as the whimpering turned to a full-blown cry. *Dang it!* My heart sank as I leaned back, missing the end of the bench to land on my butt on the cold, hard floor. I winced and groaned. I felt Amanda's hands touching my face and she stroked my beard to soothe me as she said, "Oh, Jamie, I'm soooo sorry!" I shook my head and murmured, "It's okay. Go feed Alexander." Amanda bent down and kissed me softly on the lips. When she pulled away, she said, "I promise, I'll make it up to you later, okay?" I shrugged and nodded, knowing full well, it might not happen. With four kids in the house to keep us both occupied, it was unlikely. With the heavenly smells that were wafting their way to the dance studio from the kitchen, I figured Bridget must be almost done cooking supper.

I sat cross-legged on the floor as I watched Amanda put herself back together and race across the room toward the studio door. I bent my head down and sent a mental apology to Mr. Happy, who was extremely swollen and unsatisfied. I pushed myself up off the floor and zipped up my fly. I noticed Amanda had left her leg warmers lying on the floor, so I snatched them up before trudging my way back down the hallway towards the kitchen.

I passed Bridget, who was cutting up vegetables. She glanced up and smiled at me as I waved to her and forced myself to smile and nod at her. I was glad that I'd left my shirt tails hanging outside of my jeans, avoiding the embarrassment of what would have been quite an obvious bulge between my legs. I made my way down the hallway toward the bedrooms, stopping at the doorway to the attic steps.

I glanced down the hallway and saw Amanda sitting in the rocking chair of the nursery, with Alexander suckling her breast. A pang of jealousy crept its way into my heart, but I pushed it away. The sight of her looking down at him with such love in her eyes made mine sting. She was singing the mockingbird song to him, while she rocked in the chair. The only other sound I heard was a slight creaking noise from the chair. I made a mental note to myself to ask Matty if there was some sort of lubricating oil he could apply, to silence the creaking sound. *Just another thing to add to the never-ending list of things for my brother-in-law to do.*

I made my way up the steps to our bedroom and flopped myself, face down on the bed. I rolled over and sat up, chastising myself for the self pity. I reached down to open the drawer of my nightstand and pulled out the book I'd started reading, before I left for Crystal Pines. After reading a few chapters, I glanced at the clock on my nightstand and realized at least thirty minutes had passed. I heard the sound of the door closing at the bottom of the stairs and then soft footsteps coming up. My heart skipped a beat as I said a silent prayer that

Alexander had fallen asleep again and Amanda was coming up to finish our reunion sex. I held my breath and saw my beautiful wife appear in the doorway…alone.

My heart soared! She smiled at me as she peeled away her leotard, her leg warmers, her bra and panties and dropped them into the laundry basket. Mr. Happy stood at attention under my jeans again and I felt the corners of my mouth go up. But then my heart sank, as I saw Amanda reach for her fluffy velour robe and pull it on. She tied the sash around her waist and turned to walk back down the steps. She was going to take a shower before dinner. I sighed, bowed my head down and apologized to Mr. Happy yet again.

Then…I heard my name being called from somewhere on the steps, "Jamie? Are you coming?" *Yes!* I bounced off the bed, did a hop, skip and a jump towards the doorway and raced down the steps. When I caught up to Amanda in the hallway, I laced my arms around her from behind. I reached up and pulled her hair back and nibbled at her ear as I said in a half whisper, "Is Alexander sleeping again?" She giggled and murmured softly, "I asked Bridget to take him outside, to enjoy the sunshine for a bit before dinner." *Thank Heaven for Bridget!* But then I frowned, "Who's looking after dinner then?" She tugged at my hand when she spun around, inching us into the bathroom. She said, "Maggie came on shift early, so she's going to finish making dinner, while Bridget spends her last half hour outside with the baby!" I made another mental note to myself to give Maggie and Bridget a raise, *again*.

I closed and locked the door behind me as we started giving each other loud, sloppy kisses, making our way to the shower. I heard the shower door slide open and the water start up. Amanda dropped her robe on the floor and pulled me toward the hot steamy shower. She fumbled clumsily with the buttons on my shirt, gave up and popped open the button on my jeans. She attempted to work free the shirt buttons again, but she got impatient and pulled me into the shower...*with my clothes still on*! I chuckled softly as she pulled my zipper down.

****

About another thirty minutes later, we were dried off and dressed in dry clothes. I took my wet clothes and the damp towels and made a beeline for the laundry room, while Amanda made her way to the back of the house. I put the wet clothes and towels into the washer, added soap and started it before joining her. Just as I reached the den, I saw her holding Alexander in her arms. I heard the the older kids laughing as they raced across the patio towards the French doors, with Big Matty escorting them safely home.

Alexander started wriggling around in Amanda's arms and he started to squeal when he saw me. His pudgy little arms reached towards me as he said, "Da...da!" He was only about six-and-a-half months old, but he could already say Da-da. I remembered the first time I'd heard that word, when Chelsea was just a little wee one. Amanda handed my son over to me. I swept him up into my arms and bounced him above me, while he screeched with delight.

The French doors burst open and I heard all three of the older kids saying, "Daddy!" in unison as they rushed towards me. All three of them wrapped their arms around me in a group hug. I brought the baby down to my chest and he reached up to tug on my beard. Then, my youngest son planted a wet kiss on the tip of my nose. I held onto him with my left arm as I brushed the fingers of my free hand through each of the older kids' hair, one at a time. My heart swelled with joy as I looked at my beautiful wife gazing at me with such love in her eyes at the sight of the children, showering their love on me. Whether it was Da-da or Daddy, it didn't make any difference. I loved all my children to the moon and back and adored hearing their voices saying that word to me.

After everything that happened to us over the years, we were all safe, together and happy. And all was well in the Grayson family household. The only thing missing was Amanda's music. In the aftermath of the 9/11 attacks, she'd given up on her career. Short of teaching the older kids to sing and play the piano and singing lullabies to Alexander, she hadn't done anything with her music, since losing her other family, The Bar Riders. *Well…we'll see about that!*

The Graysons were still working at their night club and Jamie often flew to Crystal Pines for performances. They decided to have a family reunion and booked a special anniversary concert celebration, which was to be held the weekend of August 23, 24, and 25, 2002. The Graysons had been performing since 1967, in some way or another, so it was to be a grand thirty-fifth anniversary celebration event.

Two Ocean Records contacted me a couple of months back, asking if I would consider returning to work with another band, but I made it clear to them that in no uncertain terms would I ever want to work with another band. I told them I was retired for good.

Jamie and Joey asked me if I wanted to appear as a surprise guest for one or all the concert nights and I said no. I couldn't bring myself to even *think* about performing without the Bar Riders. I told them I was just going to be a stay at home mom now and was content to just teach the kids to sing for fun. I also started teaching them to play the piano. Joey shook his head and said, "*Man!* You have such a God-given talent and you're just wasting it!" I said, "I've done my time on stage and now it's time for me to just be with my family." I could tell Jamie and Joey didn't agree, but Jamie just gave Joey a hard look and said, "Just leave her be, she's not ready yet."

Jamie decided to sell his two-bedroom condo in Crystal Pines and bought a four-bedroom one. It was a tight fit, but we squeezed ourselves in when we could, so we could be with Jamie, as the event date was getting closer. Jamie was practicing a new song that he'd been writing for weeks before the event. He was getting frustrated on how it was coming along. I told him I loved the song and that it was just fine the way it was. He kept saying it wasn't the sound he was going for.

It was the day before the opening anniversary concert and the guys were at the nightclub in their part of the old theatre, practicing for the event. I left the kids with Bridget and Maggie at the new condo and went to the night club, to surprise them with a lunch that Bridget prepared. When I got there, they were just finishing playing the song that Jamie had written. I could hear them having a discussion about it and as I got closer, Jamie's voice was getting aggravated.

I could tell he was tired. I walked up towards the stage and they were still discussing whether or not they were going to include the song in the concert the next night. Jamie kept insisting it wasn't ready yet and Justin and Jordie kept saying it was fine the way it was. Jamie said he wasn't going for a country song feel and didn't like the rhythm of it. "The whole thing just sounds corny. I don't like it at all. This isn't what I imagined when I first started writing it."

The guys kept discussing it and it was decided to scrap the idea of even using the song. They looked out into the seating area, where I was standing and Joey said, "Hey, Sunshine! What have you got there?" I held up the bag and said, "I think you guys need to take a break for lunch." The brothers agreed they were getting very hungry. It was two-thirty in the afternoon and they still hadn't covered everything they wanted to cover. But they decided to take a quick break to have some of the food I'd brought.

After we finished our lunch, Jamie kissed me to say goodbye, but I said, "Wait. I want to talk to you." Jamie said, "Can't this wait? We have a lot of ground to cover before tomorrow's concert." I said, "This *is* about tomorrow's concert." Jamie's brows furrowed, "What about it?" I said, "I think you should do your song." Jamie said, "It's already been decided we're going to scrap it." I said, "Babe, can you just hear me out?" Jamie shrugged and said, "We're running out of time, Raven…" I said, "Just listen to my idea, okay?" I got up onto the stage and walked over to the keyboard where Joey was sitting, ready to start rehearsing again. I said, "May I?" Joey got up and made room for me. I sat down at the keyboard and started to play Jamie's song, but with a more soulful, slower feel to it.

I showed Joey what I wanted and told him to play it like that. Joey sat down and started to mimic what I'd just played. Then I urged the rest of the guys to join in. I told them how they should play it and they looked at Jamie for approval. He lifted one shoulder and then nodded. I grabbed the mic and started to sing the song more slowly, with a bluesy and soulful feel to it. When I finished singing, I handed the mic to Jamie and said, "There! What do you think?" Jamie and the rest of the guys stared at me like I had two heads. Then, Joey said, "That was *fantastic!*" I said, "Okay, Jamie, now *you* try it!"

Jamie laughed and said, "I am not a singer like that!" I said, "What do you mean, you are *so!*" He shook his head and said, "I like what you did there. Joey's right, it *was* fantastic. But...it's not my song anymore." I looked up at him and asked, "What's that supposed to mean?" He said, "This is how I imagined it from the beginning, but it's *your* song now." I shook my head, "Baby, this is your song. *You* should be the one singing it!"

Jamie said, "Raven, you know this song is about *you*, right?" I looked at him and shook my head, but I knew he was right. The song made me feel exactly the way I had my whole life. It really *was* about me. Jamie pulled me into his arms and said, "Please, babe. Will you sing it with us tomorrow?" I couldn't believe it! *Is this some sort of set up?* I said, "Jamie, you know how I feel about going back to work. I'm never going to sing professionally again. Not without *them!*" My throat thickened and my eyes stung. Jamie kissed me on the top of my head and said, "Raven, you shouldn't give up on your music just because of the past. What happened was a tragedy, but that doesn't mean God was telling you to stop!" I blinked and forced the tears back down inside me.

I looked at Joey, Justin, Jordie and Jeremy and asked, "Do you guys all feel the same way about that song?" Justin said, "I knew it the minute you took the mic and started to sing it. It's *your* song and you should sing it tomorrow night. Your fans are waiting for you to come back and I think this song is the way to do it!" I stood there dumbfounded. Jamie put his hand on my cheek and stroked it with his thumb and Joey said, "I think that if Jenny were here, she'd tell you to go for it!"

Jamie said, "Remember what Sonia said at our wedding?" I shook my head and said, "She said a *lot* of things. It's all a blur now." Jamie said, "She told us our music was going to change. I used to think it was about that tour we did together. But now, I think she was talking about this. Your music with the Bar Riders changed a bit, but the old die-hard fans mostly came to see you play your old stuff. It was the *new* fans that wanted us to sing together. But I think that there's a whole world of new fans out there, waiting for something *else* from you. And this song could be just the beginning, you know?"

Joey said, "Just make some lemonade!" I remembered that being Mom Sylvia's favorite saying, when things went wrong in the Grayson family household. 'When life hands you lemons, make lemonade.' Joey told me that back when I was in school and I'd fallen and hurt my knee, when the doctors told me not to dance professionally.

That night, I tossed and turned all night. *Could I really do this?*

The Grayson family was starting their thirty-fifth anniversary three-night concert celebration. I looked out into the theater and saw that the room was packed. The tickets had virtually sold out as soon as they'd gone up for sale. I was dressed in a navy blue, shimmering chiffon gown that I managed to find in one of the shops in Crystal Pines that day. I was so nervous; I was literally shaking. There was a warmup band going on in a few minutes. The Graysons were out on the floor, checking things out to make sure everything was ready. I said a little prayer asking God to help me get through this song and hoped the Bar Riders were somewhere out there, giving me their blessing.

An hour later, The Graysons were introduced. Melissa was going to sing a few of her songs that night as well. Before I knew it, it was my turn to walk out onto the stage. I almost missed my cue because I was so scared. Jamie walked over to me, took my hand, and led me out onto the stage. He could see it in my eyes. I was petrified. The stage fright had come back with a vengeance!

Jamie and Joey looked at me and smiled. Jamie grabbed one of the mics and said, "You all remember my wife?" and the crowd cheered loudly.

He continued with, "Just in case you forgot…" More cheering. "This is Celina Jackson." And then, something happened that never happened before, when I'd been on stage. There were little flames flickering in the air throughout the audience. They were all holding their lit lighters and candles from the tables up in salute to the memory of The Bar Riders. My throat thickened. Joey and Jamie stood beside me and held my hands on either side of me. Joey said softly into my ear, "Make lemonade, Sunshine!"

Joey then sat at the keyboard and started to play. I took the mic Jamie was holding out for me and spoke into it, before I started to sing, "This song is dedicated to the Bar Riders." The crowd cheered again, but then a hush crept throughout the theater. I closed my eyes and started to sing:

I wake up in the morning
Draggin' myself through a brand new day
Pain I feel is a warning
But I keep on walking any way
I push through all the anger
Hoping against hope I'll find some peace
I think, "What does it matter?"
No matter how hard I beg him please!

Why won't you just love me, Daddy?
What did I ever do so wrong?
Is there nothing I can do, Daddy?
Won't you just listen to my song?

Years go by and here I am
Wond'rin' just now I got myself here
Knowing his love's just a sham
And she's not the only one, I fear
Scratching my way through this storm
Tryin' just to get some tenderness
So cold now, just need some warmth
Wasting my love, but nevertheless

Why don't you just love me, baby?
Why are my choices always so wrong?
Is there nothing I can do, baby?
Why must I always sing this sad song?

There was a musical interlude and then:

Flash forward to you, lover! (spoken as I pointed to Jamie which brought more cheering)

The music we just made together
Has me running for cover
Will this magic last forever?
Will my love songs be wasted?
On another wolf in sheep's clothing
Because my friend, let's face it
Not going to give it away for nothing, nothing, again!!!!

Do you really love me, darlin'?
Will this be another broken song?
Is your love for real, my darlin'?
How can I know if you are the one?

When I was finished, I heard thunderous applause. I opened my eyes, took a small bow and tried to turn around and leave the stage; but Jamie and Joey were holding my hands on either side of me again. The rest of The Graysons joined hands all in a line across the stage. We all took a long bow.   Then we heard the crowd tapping their glasses on the tables, indicating they wanted more. I wanted to run off stage and let the Graysons have their moment, but Joey spoke into the mic, "Who wants to hear more Celina Jackson?" And the crowd cheered again.   I looked at Jamie for support. I didn't have anything else prepared. He put his arm around me and whispered in my ear, "Let's do one of our duets, okay?" I looked up into his eyes to see if he was serious. He was smiling at me and nodding. Holding up the mic to my lips, I spoke into it.

"But first, I want to say something. "I want to thank you all for your love and support. It means a lot to me. Jamie and I have been through so much over the last several years. Sometimes, I never thought we'd see it through. I want to thank you all, from the bottom of my heart for your continued support and I love you all!"   There was more cheering. I then said, "Now I want to ask you a little favor. I'm not sure where this night will lead; but I now want to be known as Amanda Grayson. Celina was just a made-up name. My real name is Amanda Landers-Grayson. That's what I want you all to call me now. Until now, only a small handful of family and friends knew me by my real name. And I would like to think that you...are all my friends!" The crowd cheered and I heard some of them say, "We love you, Amanda!" I was suddenly filled with elation and could feel static electricity in the air, all around me.

Jamie then took the mic from Joey and said, "This is one of the songs from our duets album." I froze. I didn't know which one he would pick. He spoke to the guys for a moment. Joey sat down at the keyboard and started to play our wedding vow song. I prayed that I could remember the words and get through it. It had been almost a year since the last time I'd sung in front of an audience. The rest of the guys started playing their instruments. Jamie held my hand and started to sing with me.

We finished the wedding song. Then he sang the song that he sang, while I'd been walking down that interlocking stone path, in our back yard in Chelsea, at our wedding. I brought the mic towards my lips and sang in harmony to the chorus. Then he let me sing the second verse by myself. We sang the second chorus together. The song ended to thunderous applause, again. I turned to walk away to give The Graysons the next song.

Jamie pulled me back and kissed me deeply in front of the audience…and they went wild. I took a look around the theater and saw there were people of all ages there. They all had smiles on their faces and were cheering. I whispered into Jamie's ear, "Come on now, this is your concert. Do another Grayson tune for them." And I walked off the stage. The Graysons did two of their most popular songs and then, they asked me to join them on stage again.

Melissa came up behind me and said, "Go! You need to go now!" She pushed me gently and I walked out on stage. Jamie was holding the electric guitar and he started playing the intro to one of our up-tempo rock duets. It was one that I would dance to in the beginning and during the guitar solos. I started dancing, praying that I wouldn't trip in my stiletto heels. Jamie started the first verse and I joined in on the chorus. We finished the song and took a long, deep bow. I felt an energy from the crowd like none other…

****

The next morning, Bridget went out to the front stoop of our new condo to pick up the newspaper. Jamie and I were inside feeding the kids. I saw Bridget's eyes nearly pop out of her head, when she read the article on the front page. Jamie looked at her and asked, "Well, are you going to share it with us, or are you going to spontaneously combust right here in the kitchen?"

Bridget read the headline:

"**Celina Jackson Changes Her Name To Amanda Grayson In Sold Out Opening Night of Graysons' 35th Anniversary Concert.**"

Jamie took the newspaper from her hands and read it out loud:

"**Singer, songwriter and dancer, Amanda Grayson (formerly known as Celina Jackson) returned to the stage with a splash in a surprise guest appearance at the Grayson Family's opening night of their sold out thirty-fifth anniversary celebration, at their night club in Crystal Pines, Virginia. After telling the world that she was retiring from show business, following the 9/11 terrorist attacks, where the rest of her former band mates from The Bar Riders, their manager Trip Daniels and Two Ocean Records, agent Alex Tremain, all lost their lives in the tragic two-plane crash in New York, it was believed that she was too heartbroken at the loss of her friends to ever work again.**

"**However, last night, Ms. Grayson practically stole the show, when she sang a song written by her husband, Jamie Grayson. It was a very soulful account of her life story. During the song, she pointed at her spouse, when using spoken words of the first line of the last verse of the song, referring to him as her lover. After finishing the song and receiving thunderous applause, they asked her to sing with her husband, a couple of numbers from** their duets album. Just before they began the next song, she announced that she wanted to give up her stage name in favor of her real name, Amanda Landers-Grayson. At the end of the show, Ms. Grayson was asked again to come back to the stage for an encore number, which finished the opening night concert with an up tempo rock tune, also from their duets album. When Ms. Grayson was asked if she was formally returning to show business, and possibly recording and going out on tour with The Graysons, she replied, 'No Comment'."

The article went on to talk about the Grayson Family's successful thirty-five-year career, singing together and at times doing solo projects. It also said that tickets for all three nights' performances were sold out almost immediately after going on sale.

Joey stopped by earlier, and was in the kitchen, listening to the whole thing. He laughed and said, "Well *that's* a hard act to follow!" I shook my head and said, "There won't be any touring or recording going on, at least not for me." Jamie looked at me and said, "So you really think your fans are going to let you off that easily?" I shrugged and he said, "And by the way, nice touch you had changing some of those words to the song. It really made it pop!" I looked at Jamie and said, "You don't mind that I did that? And of course I added that extra chorus at the end. It just felt right, you know?" Jamie squeezed my hand and said, "It's your song, babe! You can do what you want with it!"

I said, "Can I sing about Chimpanzees and Orangutans, too?" Joey and Bridget looked at the two of us like we were from Mars, as we laughed at the memory of that joke…

A note from the author:

I hope you've enjoyed reading '**Jewels From The Ashes**', the third installment of the Jewel series. To elaborate on the ending, the joke refers to a telephone conversation between Jamie and Amanda in first book, '**Jewel From The Shadows**,' when Jamie and Amanda are planning their wedding. They cannot marry in the church as Amanda is not a member. But despite their differences in religious beliefs, they make it work.

Jamie: "I don't care if we have to get married naked in the forest, I love you! This is going to work, I promise you."

Amanda: "Naked, huh? Can we get married by a chimpanzee, too?"

Jamie: "A chimpanzee and two orangutans!"

In case you're wondering what happens after this, the Graysons' anniversary shows turn out to be very successful. They continue to play sold out shows at their nightclub for a few years.

Sylvia Grayson passes away from complications due to heart issues on January 14, 2003, with all of her children at her bedside. Jeremy Grayson is later diagnosed with Parkinson's disease, forcing the Graysons to sell their nightclub. Jamie's brothers decide to move in different directions, and, with the exception of Joey, they retire from the music business.

Joey continues to manage different bands around the globe, occasionally recording and touring with Amanda and Jamie. They record more albums together, featuring songs written by all three of them, with continued success. They start a tour called, 'Friends and Lovers,' taking the kids with them.

Amanda remains close with her family and is delighted to hear that her brother, Daniel and his partner adopt two children. Matty and Crystal have another child, a boy this time and call him Patrick, giving him the nick name of Paddy, as Amanda's natural father was known. Molly marries a man named Marcus, with whom she dances in New York and they have twins together. Diana and Mitch are still happily married. Zoey later marries a man named David and is very happy.

Joey and Angela have another child, Sylvia Louise Grayson, later in 2003. Jamie sells his four-bedroom condo to Joey and Angela, to accommodate their growing family. Jamie and Amanda purchase a ranch-style home in Crystal Pines, where the Grayson family celebrates Christmas each subsequent year.

They end up selling the beach house in Malibu because, when staying there, Amanda and the kids have terrible nightmares, remembering that fateful day. They purchase another beach house further down the beach that is much larger, to accommodate the family and anyone traveling with them. They continue to celebrate Chelsea's birthday each year, with an Animation Dreamland vacation.

Steve and Adam accompany Jamie and Amanda whenever they travel, being the most qualified to keep them safe, with their Special Forces backgrounds.

Bridget and Steve eventually marry, with a beautiful garden wedding - in Jamie and Amanda's backyard, of course. Maggie and Adam continue seeing each other, but no wedding plans are in the works.

Chelsea follows her mother around, imitating her dancing, sings like a bird and has mastered the piano. She is also quite advanced for her age, with respect to education – overcoming her special needs.

Nina and Eric both learn to play the piano quite well. Alexander follows his Mom and Dad around and tries to join in, whenever they're singing, pretending his hairbrush is a microphone – and, he has perfect pitch. Sonya's predictions all came true…

Turn the page to read an excerpt from the next sequence of the Jewel Series:

GRAYSON FAMILY SECRETS

Anita Post

January 14, 1996

"Mom, please! I need this money to start fresh," I pleaded. My mother looked up from her latest knitting project, peered over her glasses and said, "Likely story. You're just going to spend it on drugs or give it to Tommy to spend on drugs." I closed my eyes to tamp back the tears, "Mom, I haven't used since…" *since I found out about the baby.* "Mia needs this money too," I murmured. "*Don't bring that poor child into this!*" she spat. "This has nothing to do with Mia and you *know* it! You're just going to go straight to that dealer boyfriend of yours and give it to him for a hit! No means no! I am *not* giving you a dime towards your nasty habit!"

I let the dam burst and Mom sighed. "Please, Mom! I'm begging you! I gotta leave town. I need to start fresh with Mia and…" I tried to stop the sobbing and bit my tongue to prevent myself from telling her there was a new baby coming. But I knew it was the only way I could convince her. "Please, Mom, I'm pregnant!" I whimpered. Mom slowly set down her knitting needles and said softly, "I know. Who do you think this blanket is for?"

My heart nearly stopped dead in my chest, "You *knew?*" Mom nodded, "I'm not stupid, you know!" I looked at her with pleading eyes and said, "Then you know I need this money to get Mia and I out of this God-forsaken town and start fresh...*without* Tommy. I swear to you, Mom. I won't tell him where I'm going. And if you want you can come with me. We'll start fresh in another place. We can be a real family this time. I promise, I'm not using any more. As soon as I got the results back from the pregnancy test, I quit cold turkey. Honest to God, I did!" I was four months along, but not showing yet. Tommy would skin me alive if he knew.

Mom resumed her knitting. The needles clicked together at the speed of light. I could have sworn there was smoke coming from them, she was knitting so fast. The air was thick between us. So thick with tension, you could have sliced it with a knife. Finally, after what seemed like eons, she spoke, "I'm not leaving Amber Birch. It's my home and where would we go, anyway?" I cleared my throat and said, "I've thought a lot about this. We could go to New York or L.A." Mom's needles clicked even faster, "And why would you want to go *there*?"

"Mom, you know I've always wanted to go into the business. New York and L.A. are good places to start. I'm really good, thanks to the music and dance lessons you sent me to, when I was a kid..." Mom interjected with, "And that's *exactly* what got you into this mess to begin with! Tommy and his merry band of Hippie Hoppie Rippers, dancing in the street! And then you started coming home drunk and stoned, after partying with them, till all hours of the night. You flunked out of high school, because you got hooked! And then you came crawling home pregnant, just like you are now. What makes you think I'll fall for this crap again?"

I swallowed hard, "Mom, it's Hip Hop and Rap. But I won't be doing that. There are other styles of music that are popular nowadays too. And I won't go near Tommy again. I promise you. This baby…and Mia, are the reason I want to go away. And when I make it big, I'll pay you back.   I promise!"

Mom rolled her eyes because she'd heard that same line out of me before. But then, she blew out a sigh and set her knitting aside. She got up from her rocking chair and walked into the spare bedroom, where she kept all her important papers.   She returned a moment later, with her checkbook and pen in hand. She sat at the kitchen table and began writing. When she was finished, she started to hand me the check, but when I reached for it, she pulled it away and said, "This is the *last* time I'll give you anything. If you go back to your old ways, I will take Mia and that baby away from you. And you will never see them again, is that clear?"

Behind me, I heard the shuffling of little feet. I turned to see Mia was coming out of the spare bedroom, where she and I would sleep, when we came to visit. We must have roused her from her nap, with our arguing. I could see Mom's face light up when she saw her, "*Mia!* My little Sugarplumb! You're awake!" Mia ran into her waiting arms and they embraced. My heart squeezed as I saw how much my little girl loved her Granny. *Could I do this? Could I take Mia away and start over?*

Two hours later, I was at the bank, cashing Mom's check for a thousand bucks. *Would it be enough for a fresh start?*

****

June 5, 1996

It was almost that time. I'd found a place to stay, just outside of New York City. It wasn't paradise, but I was working at a part time waitressing job, to help pay for the tiny apartment. I called my mom as often as I could, from the payphone just down the street from the diner, where I worked. I left Mia in Amber Birch until I'd gotten settled. We managed to elude Tommy. I hadn't heard from him and Mom said he stopped calling her and pestering her about me.

Mia cried a lot and said she missed her Granny. It was one week till I was due to deliver and my boss told me to take the week off, because my ankles were so swollen from carrying all the extra weight. Doing my job was becoming almost unbearable. I decided I would chance a visit to Amber Birch, to let Mia see Mom, before the baby was born. On the last phone call, Mom said she might come back to New York with us, for a visit and to help with the new baby.

It was late and I was just singing the mockingbird song to Mia and the baby. *I think she's asleep.* The baby stirred inside of me when I got up to go next door. My friend Callie was also a waitress at the diner. She sometimes let me use her phone, when I gave her some of my tip money, to call home. I knew she just spent it on stuff for Mia and the baby. I tip toed my way to the apartment next door and quickly made my call. Everything was all set for the morning. Mom had sent me two plane tickets and we were supposed to be at the airport by six a.m.

"I miss you sweetheart and I'm looking forward to seeing you tomorrow!" I hung up the phone and went back to the one-bedroom apartment I shared with Mia. I made sure I had the bags packed and sitting by the door before I lay down on the couch to catch a few hours sleep.

June 9th, 1996

Mom and I were getting ready to leave for the airport. Mia was playing outside in the backyard on the swings. The phone jangled, making me jump. "Hello?" Mom's face blanched. My brows slid together as I watched Mom move the receiver towards me. I didn't have time to say hello, as when I put the receiver to my ear, I heard the familiar male voice on the other end. "I have Mia. Get your mom to write you a check. You can have her back when you cash it and bring the money to me." My heart stopped beating as I glanced out the kitchen window and saw the empty swing.

I was on my knees pleading into the receiver, "Please, Tommy, please don't hurt her!" I was sobbing as I hung up the phone and watched, while Mom's trembling hands wrote the check. It was for five thousand. I knew that was a lot and would likely mess up our plans for Mom coming back to New York with me. But Mom would give up everything she owned to get Mia back.

An hour later, I stood in front of the door to Tommy's place, with the money in my pocket. The door opened before I could even knock. The place reeked of beer and pot. I called into the apartment, "Mia! Where are you, sweetheart? Mommy's here to bring you back home to Granny!" I felt Tommy's iron grip around my arm as he pulled me into the dingy, slummy apartment. He scanned me up and down, pointed to my swollen stomach and growled, "Whose is *that??!!*" I winced as I murmured, "Yours, Tommy." I saw his eyes turn dark and I thought he would throw a conniption fit, but instead he barked, "Where's my fucking money?"

I swallowed audibly, "First tell me where Mia is!" The back of Tommy's left hand came down hard on my right cheek, which sent me reeling. I landed on the wall and slid down to the floor as my knees buckled and everything went black. The last thing I remembered was a ringing in my ears and the sharp prick of the needle in my arm…

Chapter 1 • Chelsea

I'm in that dark tunnel again – trying to get to Mommy and Daddy. There's a black mist-like fog all around me. The only light I can see is when I look back towards Auntie Bridget, who's standing there reaching for me, with her arms wide open. But I need to find Mommy and Daddy. I reach the end of the tunnel and there's a big dark wall in front of me - too tall to climb it. I can go right or left, down another corridor. The same black fog lingers down both ways. I choose right this time. Maybe Mommy and Daddy will be down there.

It's like a maze in here. It seems to go on forever. All the hallways are dark, with that misty black fog all around. I can hear Mommy's cries. Sometimes I hear her crying out my name and sometimes it's Daddy's name. "Mommy, I'm here!" But she can't hear me. I can't even hear me. I scream for Mommy and Daddy, but my screams are silent. I have to get to them! I can hear Auntie Bridget calling me back, but I need to find Mommy and Daddy!

****

I woke up in a cold sweat. My lungs were on fire. *It's the same every time.* The nightmares were still coming in full force – but Mom and Daddy didn't know it. They thought it stopped years ago. My throat was always sore, as though I'd really been screaming like in my dream. No matter which path I chose in the dream, I was never able to find them. When I dreamed back then, Mom and Daddy would always be there, when I woke up, soothing me and stroking my hair, to calm me down and dry my tears. But I had to be strong now. I needed to stop making them worry about me so much. Mom had too many of her own demons to deal with.

My name is Chelsea Sarah Grayson. I live in a one and a half story refurbished century home, with a huge lot on Riker Road, in Chelsea, Ohio. And yes! I *was* named after the town I live in. I was born on June 10, 1996 somewhere near Crystal Pines, Virginia. My natural history was pretty sketchy at best. All I knew was that my Aunt Melissa (Daddy's sister) found me in an orphanage called Auburn Oaks Children's Center. She and my Uncle Tom were supposed to adopt me, but then my Aunt Melissa found out she was pregnant.

My parents told me that when *that* happened, it was the best thing that ever happened to *them*, because they've always referred to me as a gift from God. But then again, they said that about my siblings, too. I was adopted on Christmas Eve in 1998, which was when my Daddy brought me to my grandparents' place in Crystal Pines, as kind of a

Christmas gift to my Mom. My Mom said that was the best Christmas ever for her, because she couldn't have kids and it was the beginning of a beautiful family.

I always thought there was more to the story than that, but my parents didn't like talking about things that made them sad. Well, actually, it was my Mom. Daddy just didn't talk about those things, out of respect for my mother. There were a lot of secrets in my house and I always *hated* that! It's not that I had a bad life. It was just the opposite. I had the best family anyone could ever have. I loved my parents and siblings more than anything in this world.

But there was always stuff that nobody wanted to talk about – mostly because of my Mom. Every time I brought up any sort of subject that my Daddy knew would upset my Mom, he would change the subject. The only one I could get anything out of was my Uncle Joey; but even *he* sort of hemmed and hawed and beat around the bush about stuff – probably because he knew he'd be in deep doo-doo if my Daddy ever found out Uncle Joey told me stuff he wasn't supposed to.

Sometimes Uncle Joey let stuff slip, and then he would get really quiet and say, "But don't tell your parents I told you!" And he would wink at me like it was a joke; but I could always tell he was worried, because he would look over his shoulder, just to make sure nobody was listening. He always said, "Your Mom had a really hard life." That was usually where the conversation ended…

I have a sister and two brothers. Eric and Nina are fraternal twins and were born on December 25, 1995, which made me just over six months younger than they were. But they weren't adopted by my parents until October 2001. They were actually my Aunt Jenny and Uncle Bobby's kids, but they died in a plane crash on September 11, 2001.   Aunt Jenny and my Mom grew up together in Honeywood, Ohio. The plane crash was one of the things we weren't allowed to talk about around the house, because it made my Mom sad.

I guess I could understand that, being that Aunt Jenny was my Mom's best friend and she died. But we always included Aunt Jenny, Uncle Bobby and Aunt Jenny's mom (Eric and Nina's Granny), in our prayers at night. There were lots of pictures of them in Nina and Eric's bedrooms, because my parents didn't want them to ever forget about them.

I also have a younger brother named Alexander James, A.J. for short. He was born February 1, 2002. He was the biggest surprise *ever* because my Mom actually gave birth to him. My Mom was supposed to be on the same airplane that crashed in New York that day. But she didn't get on the plane because she was sick. Of course I didn't know that it was morning sickness, until I got older. I remembered when that happened, because my Daddy, Aunt Bridget and I were in Crystal Pines, where my Daddy's family lived. I was only five then and my parents didn't think I remembered much. But there were a lot of things they didn't know – because, like them, I didn't talk about the stuff that made anyone sad.

I remembered my Daddy getting really freaked out when the stuff about the plane crashes was on television on all the stations. He was trying to find something for me to watch after breakfast that day. But because of the plane crashes, I had to go into the den to watch something on DVD. I ended up staying with my Daddy's family for awhile. My Daddy, Uncle Joey and Uncle Justin went away for a few weeks. My Mom was away, singing on tour, before the plane crashes happened. My aunts and uncles kept telling me that she was still away on tour. When my Daddy and uncles came back, my Mom was with them. That's when suddenly, my family got a *lot* bigger! My Mom and Daddy were Nina and Eric's God parents. So, after Aunt Jenny's mom died of cancer, Mom and Daddy adopted the twins.

Oh, yeah, my parents are music stars. That's probably a big deal to other kids, but to me it was always normal. I didn't know anything else. My Daddy used to sing with his family. When they were younger, he and my uncles were in a boy band called 'The Grayson Brothers.' My Aunt Melissa also sang and sometimes went on tour. My Mom used to sing with a rock band called the Bar Riders, with Aunt Jenny and Uncle Bobby – till everybody died in the plane crash. It took a while for my Mom to go back to work because she was so sad from losing her friends.

That was one good thing about the Bar Riders being gone – not that them being dead was a good thing. But now, when my parents worked, they worked together. They would take us with them, when they went on tour. I liked that we could be together when my parents worked. It used to be that I sometimes went with my Mom and I would have to miss my Daddy a lot! But during the last Bar Riders tour, for some reason my parents decided it was better for me to stay in Crystal Pines, with my Daddy, for the second half of the tour. They didn't talk about it in front of us, but I overheard them say a couple of times, if I'd been with Mom for the last part of the tour, well – *you* do the math.

Most of my Mom's family lived in Honeywood, about twenty minutes from Chelsea. She had two brothers and two sisters. One of my Mom's brothers, Uncle Matty, lived in a second house on our property, with his wife, Aunt Crystal and their kids, Little Matty and Paddy. Uncle Matty was the caretaker of our property here in Chelsea. He took care of the horses, the land and most of the repairs in the three houses on the property.

The third house was for the staff to live in. The staff consisted of several security guards and our two nannies. We needed lots of protection. For the most part it was because of all the reporters outside our front gates, trying to get a story - and sometimes, from my parents' fans. Most of the time, the fans were pretty good, but occasionally, there were some pretty crazy fans.

Uncle Steve was hired as head of security when my parents got married. And Aunt Bridget was my nanny for as long as I'd been here. My parents also hired Aunt Maggie as a second nanny when Nina, Eric and A.J. came along. A few months after A.J. was born, my cousin Little Matty was born, so our two nannies went back and forth between Uncle Matty's house and our house, to help wherever they were needed.

Another one of the *'secrets'* us kids were not privy to, was the reason my Uncle Matty's last name was McDougall and the rest of my Mom's family's last name was Landers. Whenever one of us asked, the subject was always changed, without discussion. I've always known Mom had a lot of demons to deal with. *But seriously?* It's not that they lie. We've always been told it's bad to lie. But certain subjects were off limits because of my Mom and her 'issues.'

But recently, I started to find out about things on the fly. My Daddy sometimes let me use his laptop to do my homework, because I needed the internet to do research.

We were always home schooled with tutors. Daddy said that because we traveled so much, it would have been hard for us to go to regular schools. Sometimes Daddy left me alone in my parents' bedroom to finish up my homework and I found out that Bubble Search was a wonderful thing! I haven't had enough time yet to find out everything, but I *have* found out about 9/11. That was a big one. Because Mom got sick, before their flight was supposed to leave Boston, she didn't get on that plane. She ended up getting on a private jet, which also crashed. But somehow she survived that. There were a lot of conflicting stories on the internet about that, so I never really found out all there was to know. And I couldn't exactly ask my parents about it.

The only thing we knew about was that Nina and Eric's other parents died in a plane crash along with the rest of Mom's band and their agent and manager. Because of all the stories still circulating around on T.V. and the newspapers, we got bits and pieces of it from time to time.

We learned about 9/11, but Mrs. Wilson was very strict about what we could to know about, so she only talked about it in vague terms, not relating to us or our family members. When we asked questions about stuff my parents didn't want us to know about, Mrs. Wilson always said, "That is not part of your learning curriculum."

I probably would get grounded for life, if they knew I was searching for information about *them,* instead of doing my homework. But if I played my cards right, I might actually figure stuff out on my own.

The nightmares I've had for years still haunted me almost every night. My Mom's nightmares were less frequent, at least that I knew of. They usually happened at certain times of the year. Those were the times she would get really depressed. She would sometimes hide in her room, when that happened, because she didn't want us to worry about her. When I was younger, I asked my Daddy how we could help her. But he just shrugged and said, "Just let it be, my little Chelsea girl. It'll pass soon enough." And it usually did. But sometimes her mood swings lasted months.

That being said, my parents had the perfect marriage. My Daddy never, *ever* yelled at her, or us. Mom sometimes got upset, but if Daddy was home, he would go to her and hold her, until she calmed down enough, so we wouldn't be scared. She never really yelled at us, but we could tell when she was losing patience. Daddy was always good at calming Mom down when she was upset. I could always see the love in their eyes that they had for each other, and for us.

They never fought. Not that they didn't disagree. There were sometimes moments, when you could tell if they had some sort of altercation, they got very quiet. But there was never any anger shown in our house. Neither of my parents ever raised a hand to us in punishment. There was always a diplomatic solution to anything that we did to get in trouble. When Daddy was away, Aunt Bridget and Aunt Maggie would kind of steer us away from any negative situation. If Mom was having an episode, we were always shooed out of the room. Over the years, Mom got better at controlling her emotions around us, because I think she knew how it would affect us. When she felt better, she would always give us hugs and kisses and tell us how much she loved us and that whatever she was going through had nothing to do with us.

And she would always say she was sorry for being *that way*. But no real explanation was ever given. Uncle Joey told me once that my Mom was much worse before she married my Daddy. He said, "You guys have it really easy. Your Mom didn't fare so well before she met your Dad." Uncle Joey and my Mom were best friends since high school, where they met. I guessed she had *two* best friends. Uncle Joey told us that when they went to high school, Aunt Jenny, Mom and Uncle Joey were kind of joined at the hip, whatever *that* meant!

****

A lot happened to us over the years. When I was six, Mom was taken by a bad man. We were never really told what happened to her while this man had her. That was the first time I ever saw Daddy cry. There were policemen all over our beach house and on the property in California. We'd just spent a few weeks at Animation Dreamland and on the beach. We were almost ready to go back to Chelsea, when all of a sudden, my Mom went missing. We were all really scared and my brother A.J. was just a baby. I knew Mom was still breast feeding him back then, so her having gone missing was a really big deal. My Daddy took us into the one room and tried to talk to us.

I could tell he was really struggling to find the right words to make us feel better, but when he said, "I know you are scared. Daddy's scared too!" That's when he started to cry. My heart almost shattered into a million pieces when I saw the tears running down his cheeks, so I did what he always did, when *we* cried. I hugged him, gave him butterfly kisses all over his face and told him that Mommy was going to be okay. Daddy was always the strong one, but that day, I had to grow up *a lot*. Daddy was, and *still is,* my hero. It turned out that *he* brought Mom home. He never made a big deal about it. He kept saying it was the police who saved her. But Mom always said that Daddy found her and brought her home. They still never talked about it much. No details, but Mom always said that Daddy was *her* hero too.

It was shortly after that time our nightmares all started. And it was also when Mom got really scared of going into the basement. Well, I don't remember her ever going down there – *ever* – at either one of our houses in Chelsea and Crystal Pines. But after we all came back from California, after Mom's abduction, she would have these strange episodes. I remember one time, when A.J. was starting to crawl, he went near the basement door, and Mom freaked! Aunt Bridget had to pick A.J. up and get all of us out of the kitchen quickly.

I could hear Mom screaming and Daddy trying to calm her down. The basement was where Daddy's workout room was. She still never goes down there. It's like something bad must have happened to Mom in some basement.

There was another time, before that, maybe a couple of years, when something else happened. I was young, so I don't remember much, but I remembered being away. My Daddy was on tour with my Mom and her band. Then, something happened and my Daddy and Mom had to be in the hospital for awhile. I remembered visiting Mom and she had a bandage on her arm. I just remember being really scared.

When we finally made it home, my Daddy had to sleep in one of the bedrooms downstairs for awhile, because he was too weak to climb the steps up to their attic room. They didn't talk about that time at all. But when I saw the big bandages on his chest and shoulder, I was petrified!

I remember Mom telling me, "Daddy's got a booboo! Just like when you fall and skin your knees and Daddy kisses them better." So whenever I could, I would sit in his lap, trace a line around his bandages and kiss them better. After the bandages came off, there were these big, ugly and puffy scars for a long time. I would continue my daily ritual of kissing his booboos better. He couldn't pick me up or play with me the way he used to for awhile after that. The scars were still there, but they just looked

like deep lines on his chest. They're hardly
noticeable now.

I remembered back then was when my Mom's
mood swings began, or at least that's when I
remembered them start happening. I didn't
understand much about what was going on, but I
remembered her getting mad at Daddy a lot for
doing stuff he wasn't supposed to and she would get
really strange, when he tried to go outside. It was
like she would be frozen in one spot looking at him
at the doorway and she couldn't breathe. Daddy
would always have to come back inside and hold her
when that happened. Aunt Bridget would usually
shoo me out of the room during those 'episodes.' It
took a long time for things to get back to *normal*
after that.

****

It was June 1, 2008, my Mom and Daddy's
anniversary. It was quiet in the house, so I figured
either everyone was still sleeping, or my family and
the staff were getting the house ready for a party.
They always celebrated their anniversary in a
special way. I rolled out of bed and was pulling the
blanket and sheets up to make my bed when I saw
something red. I knew I was sweating when I woke
up from my nightmare, but I didn't know I
somehow hurt myself. The red stuff had to be
blood, but there was so much of it my heart started
racing. I kept thinking that I might have missed
one of my paint bags, when I was cleaning up my art
stuff the night before. It *had* to be that! My

fingernails were getting long, but they were never sharp enough to scratch myself in the middle of the night like that! I examined my arms and legs and when I looked down I saw the red was also all over my nightgown. I had to pinch myself to see if I was dreaming. Suddenly, my heart started racing!

What if it was quiet in the house because some bad man had gotten into the house and tried to hurt us? Like back in Malibu when that man took my Mom!

I turned on my heel and reached for my bedroom doorknob and twisted it carefully. Uncle Matty always greased the hinges on our bedroom doors so they wouldn't squeak, because my Mom and Daddy traveled so much that they never wanted anyone to get woken up in the middle of the night. I opened the door slowly and peeked down the hallway. I stepped out gingerly and saw that Aunt Bridget's bedroom door was open, so she must have been up already. I glanced into her room and saw that her bed was made and the book she was reading was sitting on her nightstand, like it always was. I padded further down the hall and saw that Nina was still in bed, sleeping soundly. No red stuff on *her* bed. I passed Nina's room, turned the corner and saw Eric was also still in bed, sleeping – also no red stuff. Beside Eric's room was A.J.'s room. He was in there sleeping too. No red stuff.

I looked across the hall from Eric's room and saw the bathroom door was closed and the shower was running, so Aunt Bridget must have been in there. I continued down that hallway towards Mom and Daddy's bathroom. The door was open and the bathroom was empty. I turned my head and looked across the hallway and saw that my parents' bedroom door was open, so I started to climb the steps up to their attic bedroom. I was careful not to make any noise as I held my breath. I made my way up the steps and felt pain down low in my belly. It was a dull ache, but it wasn't like I was going to be sick or anything. I looked back down the steps and saw a trail of blood all the way up to where I was standing. My heart started pounding so hard it was like a drum in my ears and I started to panic!

I ran the rest of the way up the steps and started to cry out, "Mom! Daddy! Help!" When I reached the top of the steps, I expected Mom and Daddy to have blood on their bed too, but they didn't. I was crying so hard by then, I couldn't breathe and started to choke. I heard Mom groan, with her head on Daddy's chest, the way she always slept. Daddy's eyes were open and he bolted upright in the bed, sending Mom flopping over onto her pillow. Mom said in a scratchy voice, "What the…?" Daddy was looking at me and his face was going white as a sheet, but he didn't say anything. He just let his jaw drop so low, I thought it was going to fall off!

I said, "Mommy, Daddy! I think I hurt myself!" My voice was muffled because I was sobbing so hard and my chest was heaving. I saw Daddy reach his hand out towards Mom and he started tapping her arm as if to wake her up, but she was already awake and staring at the red stuff on my nightgown. Daddy's chest was heaving and his eyes were purple, like he was scared. That was one of the things Mom said she loved about Daddy. The color of his eyes changed with his moods, so we always knew what he was thinking, all the time. Mom groaned again and said, "Oh, boy! I guess we forgot that our little girl is growing up." Daddy looked like he was trembling and Mom reached out and touched his arm and said, "It's okay, baby, it's just – you know!" She sat up in bed and rubbed his chest to calm him down, as though nothing was wrong. *Was she nuts?*

She kissed his shoulder and said, "I guess we have to go shopping for some supplies." Daddy's breathing started to slow and his eyes turned from purple to grey, which meant he was sad. *Are you guys kidding me? I'm dying here and you aren't freaking out?* My Mom saw my distress and she rolled out of bed, grabbing her robe off the chair beside the bed, pulling it on. Good thing she was wearing a nightgown. Sometimes, when I surprised them like this in the morning, neither one of them was dressed – at all. Mom said, "Come here, sweetheart. It's okay. We need to have a talk. I forgot that this happened when I was about your age. But at least *you* have a Mom to talk to about it." And then *her* eyes filled with tears. *Oh, boy!* Was she going to have another episode, now? When I needed her the most?

Daddy still looked sad. What was *he* sad about? *He* wasn't bleeding! Then he said, "Chelsea, honey! Don't be scared. Mommy's going to help you." I didn't understand. It was *Daddy* who always did that kind of stuff. Mommy was always a wimp when we kids hurt ourselves. She would cry and the tears would fall all over the booboos and get the bandages all wet. And why was he sad? I said, "Daddy, are *you* okay?" He smiled despite his grey eyes and said, "Yes, baby! I'm just sad because you're growing up so fast!" *Whatever that meant!* Mom mumbled something about borrowing stuff from Aunt Bridget for now, until we could go to the store and get stuff for me. Then she grabbed my hand and led me down the steps.

About four hours later, we returned from the store, after Aunt Bridget, Aunt Maggie, Mom and I had bought out the stores of new outfits, new underwear, a bra, new shoes, new night gowns and all these supplies that I had to wear inside my underwear, for a week every month. The whole thing was a blur and they were acting like my bleeding from somewhere between my legs was supposed to be something to celebrate. I felt like crap. My stomach hurt, I wanted lots and lots of chocolate and I had to pee almost every five minutes! What's to celebrate?

They kept saying that I was a woman now...*Oh boy!*

****

Mom and Daddy went out for a nice quiet dinner for their anniversary. I was still awake with, what Aunt Bridget called cramps, so I could hear their conversation in the kitchen, when they got back. I got up to go use the bathroom, but A.J. was in there doing his nightly pee, so I went down the hall to use Mom and Daddy's bathroom. I was just coming out, when I heard Daddy say, "With all this estrogen in the house now, I'm going to be surrounded by mood swings from more than just you and the nannies! I hope Nina doesn't get it soon, or I'll surely be a goner!"

Mom laughed and said, "It's not going to be *that* bad! You have Steve, Adam, Matty and the rest of the male staff to hang out with, when we get to that time of the month." I could hear Daddy chuckling as he said, "Well at least your time of the month doesn't happen anymore, since you had Alexander." *Except for her mood swings!*

Mom said, "Well at least we can be prepared for when Nina goes through the change, now that we know what to expect. It shouldn't be long now." Daddy groaned and said, "Oh, boy!" Mom said, "Well, I'm glad it didn't happen on Chelsea's birthday. The poor thing would have had to remember her first time every year after that!" She said, "Hmmmn, the twins are six months older, so we should maybe have a talk with them. Maybe you should talk to Eric about, you know…things?" Daddy groaned and said, "Why do they have to grow up?" And Mom said, "It's life, baby! Just, you know, talk about the birds and the bees or something." Daddy said, "Speaking of the birds and the bees…" There was a long pause and then I could hear them smooching loudly in the kitchen and giggling like school kids. I guessed that

Daddy's eyes were going bright blue. Aunt Bridget and Aunt Maggie always shooed us out of the room when that happened. I was kind of jealous that Daddy never looked at the rest of us with those color eyes. But I guessed that it was what happened when, as Aunt Bridget said, "…what grownups who are in love do sometimes…" as was her explanation when Mom and Daddy got amorous.

I wondered why the rest of the men in the household didn't have eyes that changed color like that, when *they* were looking at their other halves like that. Uncle Matty and Aunt Crystal lived in a different house, so we never saw any of that going on with them. But sometimes I saw Uncle Steve looking at Aunt Bridget that way.

They were married too, so I guess that was why, but they never smooched in front of us. I remembered when Daddy changed the rules in the staff's contracts because of Uncle Steve and Aunt Bridget. I thought he was going to send them away, because Aunt Bridget was really scared and sad, when she found out that I overheard Uncle Steve laughing in Aunt Bridget's room one night. I smiled despite my "cramps" at the thought of how Daddy was an 'old softy,' like Mom always accused him of being.

And I giggled when I thought about how Daddy was always trying to look at us so sternly, when we misbehaved, but we always knew we could almost get away with murder because his eyes

would always be either turquoise or baby blue,
when he was happy. He was only mad when his
eyes went dark navy blue and that *never* happened
with us. It only happened when he thought we were
in danger…